DESERT ECHOES

ABDI NAZEMIAN

HARPER
An Imprint of HarperCollinsPublishers

Library of Congress Control Number: 2023948488
ISBN 978-0-06-333963-7

Typography by Julia Feingold
24 25 26 27 28 LBC 5 4 3 2 1

First Edition

To Jeni, Mummy, Sue, Nitz,
so many names and memories,
one friendship

PART 1

JUNIOR YEAR

I'm always being watched. Sometimes, I close my eyes to escape the burden of their gaze. It rarely works. In the hallway. In the locker room. Even in public sometimes, when I'm recognized as *that* kid. Some call me the boy who lived. Some call me the boy who killed. Most call me nothing; they just whisper and stare.

Right now, two sophomores lock eyes on me walking through the bustling school doors. I can almost hear their accusations over the sound of the morning bell and the stomping feet. I hold on to Bodie to steady myself. He's on his phone, showing me some video he finds hilarious. It involves a frenzied French bulldog, a whole lot of bacon, and a sped-up version of a song I love when it doesn't sound like it's sung by Alvin and the Chipmunks. I don't laugh.

"You okay?" Bodie asks as he sends the video to Olivia Cole, who will undoubtedly love it.

"Yeah." He's my best friend, so he knows I haven't been okay for almost two years now. Olivia sends him a GIF of Nicki Minaj laughing. Bodie puts his phone away, satisfied.

We sit in the back of our homeroom. When we arrived as first-years, we were always early to class so we could claim the first row, and I know that if it weren't for me, Bodie would still sit front and center. He's remained an overachiever. I used to be one too. Top of my class. Perfect grades. All the extracurriculars I could cram into my day. My mission used to be making my mother proud with a perfect report card. Now my mission is finding Ash. Nothing else matters.

I pull out my phone to check for new posts on the online grief forum I've come to rely on. I usually check before school, after watching a few minutes of the countless hours of Ash videos I filmed back when he was still with me. But there was no time for my usual routine this morning because I snoozed my alarm too many times and my mom wasn't around to wake me up. She was already at some property she and Bodie's mom are trying to sell, staging it with rented art and furniture to make it look flawless for prospective buyers. My mom is an expert at making the chaotic seem perfect on the outside.

"What are you doing?" Bodie leans over for a glimpse of my screen.

I shift away from him. "Just some research to figure out which author I want to write my English paper about."

"You still haven't chosen your author? The paper is due

before Thanksgiving and we're well into November."

"We're three days into November, Bodie. I'll get it done."

"I mean, sure, but will you get it done *well*?" The old me would've been the first to complete the assignment. Bodie's paper is already written. He chose Anthony Bourdain, which was easy for him since he's already read all his books. Bodie didn't even know who Anthony Bourdain was until he died and our parents made us watch the episodes of his show where he travels through Iran sampling the food. But since then, the guy has become Bodie's hero. Bodie doesn't want to be *just* a chef. He wants to be a brand. "So who are you considering?" He moves a little closer, trying to see my screen. I quickly shut the phone down.

He knows I wasn't researching authors. We've been inseparable since kindergarten. He can tell when I'm lying through the kind of secret body language nobody else catches. "I'm taking you to the library after school to choose an author," he says firmly. "You're supposed to write about their entire body of work. If you don't pick someone soon, you'll never do a good job. Unless you choose someone who only wrote one book, I guess. Didn't Emily Brontë only write *Wuthering Heights*? Pick her. Your thesis can be that she was the OG one-hit wonder!"

"Well, it's not like she wouldn't have written more books if she hadn't died so young, right?" I feel the ache inside me grow, wondering if Ash is still alive, if he's out there somewhere, still writing poems and making art. I would give anything to read a new poem from him. See a new drawing.

Bodie is momentarily silent. He wants to talk about homework and stupid internet videos and our moms. Not Ash. Not untimely death. Finally, he says, "This is important, Kam."

"Not that important in the grand scheme of things," I say flatly.

"It's your junior year transcript," he argues. "It's the most important year for college applications. And colleges are going to be looking at your transcript really closely because we're taking a gap year."

"You always say that admissions departments love kids who take gap years. That it makes us look cool and sets us apart."

Bodie laughs. "We *are* cool. And we're already set apart because we're gay-ass Iranians and, like, how many of us are there in the world?"

"According to the former president of Iran, zero," I say with a shrug. "According to me, at least two confirmed cases."

"Confirmed cases!" He cackles. "That's genius."

"Possibly three if we're counting your dad's cousin who dresses up as Googoosh every Halloween."

Bodie's face brightens. This is the version of me he likes. "Amu Behzad! We'll definitely visit him during our gap year. He lives in Mexico City now. Imagine what I could learn there." Our gap year plans, which our parents don't know about yet, revolve entirely around Bodie's desire to study different cuisines before applying to culinary school, which his parents don't know about yet either.

I smile. "I very much look forward to eating your barbacoa." I can't imagine life without Bodie. I guess that's why I'm planning on following him on his culinary quest. It's not like cooking is my passion. It's not like I have a passion.

"I'll make it extra spicy just for you," he says.

He's waiting for me to keep the banter going, but I don't. My fingers twitch for my phone. I pull it out and get back to that forum. To see if someone left me a message about where Ash is. One day, I know I'll find him. Maybe that day is today.

"Give me your phone right now," he demands.

"What, no." I quickly lock the phone.

"Give it to me." The phone lights up when he snatches it. On screen is my wallpaper picture of Ash in bed, his long red hair flowing past the confines of the screen like a waterfall. The radiance of Ash's crooked smile, glowing through the screen, illuminates Bodie's face like an ethereal spotlight. Not that Bodie needs a spotlight. People look at him almost as much as they look at me. Not because they think he killed someone, but because they can't resist his beauty. He didn't always have the square jaw, the full lips, the height. Once upon a time, we were both awkwardly cute kindergartners, and then awkwardly pubescent tweens. No one at our high school saw Bodie when he had acne, when he tragically tried to grow his first mustache, when his voice would crack. Now he's the guy girls are describing when they say all the hottest guys are gay. Bodie taps my old password into the phone, but it doesn't work. "You changed your password?" he asks. I don't say anything as I grab my phone back. "Don't lock me out of your life, Kam." I want to cry because I don't want to shut him out. I need him more than ever. But I also know that he wants me to move on, and I don't know how.

Homeroom begins with one of Mr. Silver's morning speeches laying out the day's goals. I can't focus. I grab a bathroom pass from the teacher's desk and rush to the bathroom. I have exactly six minutes. The teachers who actually care about us, like Mr. Byrne and Ms. Robin, don't enforce the six-minute bathroom policy. They believe in giving us autonomy over our own time. But Mr. Silver is not one of those people.

I find an empty stall and lock it. The back of the stall door is etched with doodles and words, most of them pornographic or hateful, or both. These are the wall carvings that would tell future generations everything they need to know about who we are right now, in November of 2023. The hateful pornographic messages will disappear soon enough, cleaned up by the janitorial staff, and then they'll reappear in new variations. I take solace in this fact. If gross bathroom scrawls can reappear, then so can Ash.

I sit on the toilet and unlock my phone. I go straight to the grief forum and scroll. Two guys enter the bathroom. I don't recognize their voices but I feel disgust as I hear them talk about some girl they want to fuck. Sometimes I want to escape this school, this city, this whole world. It all feels so shallow.

I put my earbuds in and blast Lana so loud that it silences the guys talking about tits. When Lana sings, Ash is with me. If I listen to her enough, he'll come back. Maybe it's magical thinking, but these are the kinds of games my mind plays with itself.

I have a new forum message from someone who calls themselves Youdiditasshole. *You were the last person to see him.*

True.

You conveniently remember nothing.

True, except nothing about it feels convenient.

Did you bury him? Eat him? Burn him?

Why would I hurt the person who lit up my life? But then I remember that they're right. I can't say for sure that it wasn't me who killed him, and I have to know it wasn't me. I can't move on until I know I'm not the one who hurt the boy I loved.

Whatever you did to him, someone will do to you someday.

Deep breath. I steady the shake in my body. I could send this message to the police, but they're always cranks. No one has tried to kill or kidnap me . . . yet. Besides, if I've learned one thing in these years, it's that the police won't do anything to help.

Just wait. You'll be murdered, eaten, buried. Just wait, terrorist faggot. You'll see.

I feel my blood boil like lava. Maybe I should respond.

Thank them for making me feel alive with rage, which is better than feeling emotionless. I delete the message and close my eyes. Ash's face comes back to me in the darkness. His smell, a mix of tea tree oil shampoo and sweat. The residue of acrylics and watercolors always on his fingers. The taste of his thin lips, his slender fingers, his neck. His bright voice, always full of energy, always rolling like thunder, even when it was sharing secrets with me. He told me there was lava in Joshua Tree. He pointed to the volcanic rocks that rose high over the desolate desert landscape. He used words I had never heard before. Understood things I never could. Science. Nature. Cinder cones and magma and geology. He told me those cinder cones began erupting almost eight million years ago. The things Ash loved were timeless. Eternal. Just like he is. I'll find him, and when I do, he'll tell me I'm not responsible for his disappearance.

I open my eyes to another message, this one from Your-FriendEmily. We write each other at least once a month. Her daughter June disappeared twenty years ago, in a place called Devil's Den State Park. She sent me articles about it. Photos of them together through the years. At first, I wondered if it was really June's mother writing me, or some impostor pretending. But the things she's said to me about the specific grief of not knowing . . . no one else could write them. And even if she were catfishing me, would it matter? Her words help me. Make me feel less alone.

I had a horrible thought that fills me with shame, Kam. I asked myself, what would I prefer? That she be out there

somewhere, living a happy life, but that I never get any answers
or get to see her again. Or that they find her remains, and tell me
exactly how she died.

I get distracted by three quick knocks on the stall door, followed by two slow knocks. My and Bodie's secret knock. I take my earbuds out and hear Bodie's voice from the other side.

"Everything okay, Kam?" he asks.

"Just going to the bathroom," I say.

He makes a point of sighing loudly. "You're watching porn, aren't you?" I laugh. He knows I'm not watching porn. I never watch porn. All I need to get off are memories of Ash. "Nothing wrong with a little morning pornography."

I open the stall door. My six minutes are almost up, and there's no point in hiding from Bodie. "I'm sure our Persian mothers would disagree."

"Do you remember when I asked our parents what an X-rated movie was?" he asks, laughing at the memory.

"I must've blocked it out." I flinch at the scalding heat of the sink water as I wash my hands.

Bodie hands me a paper towel. "You better keep me around to remind you of all the hilarious shit that's happened in your life. I'm the only person you're not related to who remembers it all." He's right about that. We met as the only Iranian kids at our kindergarten in Toronto. Our friendship was so strong that it turned our mothers into best friends, and eventually, into business partners. Bodie's basically the sibling I never had. "How can you not remember

11

my mom telling us the *X* in X-rated stands for extra long, boring, and philosophical, which is why kids don't watch those movies?"

"I like things that are extra long, boring, and philosophical." We head into the empty hallway.

Bodie rolls his eyes. If he were willing to bring Ash up, he'd say that this is Ash's influence. Like the rest of the school and like my parents, Bodie thought Ash was weird and pretentious. Instead, Bodie tells me about an article he read about Pornhub's most popular searches, and how many of them are incest-y. But it's Emily's voice I hear in my head as we get back to class. I've never spoken to Emily, but I've always imagined she sounds like one of those TV moms from an old sitcom. Comforting and warm. The opposite of my tough-love mom.

I feel like I'm betraying my child by even considering that I would prefer knowing to unknowing, even if unknowing meant she was alive and happy. I'm sorry to burden you with this, Kam. Maybe the only way not to feel shame for these thoughts is to share them with each other. I'm holding you in my thoughts, always.

I wish I could actually talk to her face-to-face, but she lives in Arkansas and I live in Los Angeles. I've never even met her, this woman who understands me in a way my own mother and my best friend can't.

I still hear her voice in my head when the bell rings and we rush to our next class. Still hear her as we sit for math class and I remember I didn't do my homework. Her question swirls in my head. I pull out the trigonometry problems we were assigned and try to speed-solve them.

"Kam, listen. I wanted to talk to you about something before tomorrow's GSA meeting," Bodie says quietly.

"Later," I say. "I forgot to do my math homework."

"Yeah, but—" The disappointment in his voice tells me he has something important to share. He's probably going to tell me that he's finally dating someone. It must be someone from another school because no one here is good enough for him. Maybe the GSA already knows about it.

"You'll have my undivided attention after school." We both know that's a lie. I can barely get through reading the first trig problem I have to solve. Emily's question still haunts me. Would I rather have Ash living joyfully out there if the trade-off is me forever stuck in this cycle of unknowing? Or would I rather know, finally *know* that he's gone, and how he died, so that I can move on?

Move on.

I've been told to move on so many times, by so many people. My mother doesn't use those words, but it's what she wants.

My father used those exact words—"Move on already, you're destroying us"—before he left us, because one disappearance wasn't enough, I guess.

My therapist never used those exact words, but I knew it was our goal. A year and a half of therapy helped a lot, but it didn't get me to move on from anything but more therapy.

Bodie watches me curiously. "You're not doing any of the

math homework. You're just staring at it."

"I have to read the problems first, don't I?" I snap.

"You don't seem like yourself." He doesn't even try to conceal the worry in his voice.

"Maybe I'm not the same person you met in kindergarten. Maybe that innocent kid is gone." I hate the sharpness in my tone.

"I don't want you to be a five-year-old. I want you to be my friend."

"You want me to be joyful and light." I don't look at him. I can't right now. "You want me to joke around about our moms and our annoying classmates and porn hubs, but—"

He raises one of his thick eyebrows. "Not porn hubs, plural. One Pornhub, singular. It's . . . a website."

I shake my head. "Whatever, you know I'm not interested in watching random guys fuck their fictional stepbrothers."

"I guess I have to watch porn since I've never had a boyfriend and probably never will," he says bitterly, and I suddenly doubt that what he wants to tell me is that he's dating someone.

I hate seeing my beautiful friend, who could get any guy he wants, sounding so defeated. "Every gay or bi guy in school would go out with you," I say. The Persian parents like to say that Bodie looks like a young Marlon Brando, and they're right. If he hasn't had a boyfriend, it's because of his pickiness. Every guy he's ever gone out with or hooked up with is ruled out for some bizarre and specific reason. One guy used the word *like* too much. Another hated

Chinese food, which is Bodie's favorite. Then there was the guy who cracked his knuckles too often, and the one who thought Bodie painted Van Gogh's *Starry Night* himself. It's always something.

"Whatever, my sad love life isn't what we're talking about right now. I need you to know that I don't want you to pretend to be light and joyful for me. What I want is for you to be . . . here. It's like you're somewhere else all the time."

I know he's right. I don't deserve his loyalty or his friendship. All I've done since Ash disappeared is push him away. And I'm doing it again.

"Just listen—"

"I know what you're going to say. You think I don't hear my mom begging you to get me to move on every time she corners you in private?"

"That's your mom. That's not me."

"I can't move on, okay? I can't!" The high pitch of my voice startles me. Immediately, I can feel their eyes on me—the other students. And our teacher. I've learned to recognize all the different ways a person can look at you. The concern from my mom. The suspicion from my classmates. The curiosity from strangers. It really doesn't matter if they're looking at me because they think I'm a murderer, or because they want me to be who I was before Ash disappeared. What they don't understand is that there is no *before* for me. I can't turn back time. And I'm reminded of this every day.

When math class is over, we head back into the hallway

toward the music room. Even from the other end of the hall, I can hear Byrne tuning his guitar. He tunes the low E, adjusting the pitch up. I walk toward the sound. Close my eyes as he moves from string to string, note to note. I feel Ash by my side, telling me about the man who built a cupola structure just outside Joshua Tree called the Integratron. Ash used words I didn't understand. Electromagnetic frequencies and multiple wave oscillators and negative air ionization. The Integratron *could* turn back time, or at least that's what the guy who built it believed.

"Wait, Kam," Bodie begs when I start to walk. "I need to talk to you."

"I don't want to be late for choir." I barrel ahead. "It's the only part of school I love."

"Because it reminds you of him," Bodie says softly.

I take a breath and stop walking. He's my best friend. My honorary brother. I have to at least try to let him in. "Ash thought creativity could be a form of time travel," I say.

If we were still first-years, Bodie would tell me that Ash sounds weird and pretentious. But Bodie can't criticize Ash the way he used to, so he just says, "Okay."

"Think about it," I say. "If Ash drew some imaginary futuristic world, wasn't he time traveling? When we sing some old Irish song in choir, aren't we time traveling?" Once I start opening up, I can't stop. "I know we can't *really* travel through time. Not the way I wish I could. But maybe, someday, those tech bros our moms sell houses to will invent a way for me to go back to that night when I let Ash disappear. Maybe—"

"You didn't *let* him do anything. You and I both know that Ash did what he wanted, when he wanted, and didn't listen to anyone else."

"There it is," I say.

"What?" he asks, letting a hint of annoyance seep in.

"You've been waiting years to say I told you so. You told me he wasn't right for me. That he was hiding things from me. You told me he didn't know how to laugh at himself, and that was a huge red flag."

"That's not what I'm doing. This is not an I-told-you-so moment."

"Yes, it is," I argue. "But I'm sorry, Bodie. You break up with guys after one date because they don't like dumplings; you're not exactly the person I want to take relationship advice from."

He grits his teeth, trying to control his anger. "Just because you're sad doesn't mean you also get to be an asshole."

"I'm sorry," I say faintly.

"All I'm saying is that what happened to Ash is not your fault, and maybe if you just stop blaming yourself, you'll stop looking for a way to turn back time, because you can't." With a smile, he adds, "Just ask Cher."

I can't help but smile back. Bodie knows just how to defuse tension with a carefully timed joke. What Ash knew about stars, deserts, and patience, Bodie knows about pop divas, food, and persistence.

"Hey, Kam, I have a serious question for you," Bodie asks, deadpan. Before I can say anything, he sings in his best Cher voice, "*Do you believe in life after love?*"

I roll my eyes, then I smile, because it brings back a memory of me and Bodie on his bed, hunched over his iPad, covertly watching Shangela and Carmen Carrera lip-sync for their lives to that song.

"No, but seriously," he says. "You do, right? Because there is life after love."

The void inside me swirls. "Sure, yes, I believe in life after love." But it's a lie. I don't even feel alive anymore.

Ken Barry and his goon squad pass by us on their way to the soccer field. "Watch out when you go back to that desert, kids. I heard UFOs are abducting people there. If you see a huge orb with a reddish-orange flickering light, run for your lives, okay." They all laugh as they walk away. I feel my pulse race as I remember a message I got yesterday on the grief forum from someone who called themselves Xenomorphius.

I think I can help you. I was camping in Joshua Tree last weekend when I saw a reddish-orange light. Then a huge orb landed, a door opened, and robotic voices told me to come with them to their planet.

"Fuck them," I seethe.

Bodie puts a gentle hand on my forearm. "I know. I'm sorry they were the ones to tell you. I've been trying to tell you all morning, but you don't make it easy."

I asked the aliens how they spoke English. And then I heard a voice tell me that he taught them our language. I asked him his name and he told me it was Ash.

I always suspected that some of my classmates wrote the cruelest of the crank messages on the forum, but now I have confirmation. "I hate them."

"We don't have to go."

"What are you talking about?" I ask. "Go where?"

He squints at me, confused. "Wait, what are *you* talking about?"

"It's nothing." I feel my lips tense, and I try to relax. "It's just . . . I think those guys wrote me a message on the forum, about seeing Ash abducted by aliens."

Bodie's fingers ball into fists. "Uh, that's not nothing. That's fucking evil."

"It's my fault," I say. "I should never have told anyone but you about the forum."

"Don't blame yourself. You did nothing wrong. They did." His eyes light up from the fire inside him. The flames of his rage burn bright, especially for bullies of any kind, for racists and misogynists and homophobes and transphobes. I can feel how badly he wants to protect me right now. He spits out, "I'm going to kick the shit out of them."

"They're not worth getting suspended for," I argue.

"You're right. We need to be more creative about our revenge." His eyes sparkle with an idea. "We'll sneak into their gym lockers and rub jalapeño peppers onto their jock-straps!"

"That is truly deranged." I can't help but laugh.

"A chef always finds a way," he says devilishly.

"I'm not saying they don't deserve to feel their balls burn, but the best revenge is just to ignore them."

"No it's not," he insists. "That's not revenge at all."

With a hint of sarcasm, I add, "You have to let go and let God."

"Fuck Byrne's Al-Anon shit right now. They deserve some blowback." He pulls out his phone and quickly navigates to the Wikipedia page for Ken Barry's dad, a conservative businessman who ran for mayor of Los Angeles and thankfully lost. Bodie speaks aloud as he amends the Wikipedia page. "Byron Barry, in addition to having the name of a supervillain and too many prejudices to list here, also has an idiotic son who shares a birthday with Hitler. His only child, Ken, is a high school bully with the tiniest cock in the locker room. He shaves his pubes to make it look bigger, but all that does is give him razor burn."

"Bodie, don't," I say, but I'm laughing, and it feels good.

"Published. How long do you think it'll take them to notice?"

"You're unhinged," I say lovingly.

"Isn't that what you love most about me?" he asks. "My unique mélange of unpredictability and reliability?"

I don't answer. Instead, I ask, "Hey, what were you talking about? Where do we not have to go?"

He leans back against the wall. "To Joshua Tree. For this year's GSA trip in December."

"Sorry, what?" I feel my pulse race.

"That's what I've been trying to tell you," he explains. "That's why Ken told us to be careful in the desert. Because he assumes we're going. But obviously we're not." He lets me process what he's saying. Byrne is done tuning his guitar, and our fellow choir members stream past us into the music room.

"I mean, I don't know . . ." I feel my voice linger in the air, unsure.

"What don't you know?" He's unable to mask his annoyance. "It's where Ash disappeared. Why would you go back there and retraumatize yourself?"

"I didn't say I want to go." I look away from Bodie. There's too much certainty in his deep brown eyes. He always knows who he is, and what he wants, and who I should be, and what I should want.

"Well, you're not going," Bodie commands in the same tone my mom loves to use, the one that tells you the conversation is over.

"I just said I don't know," I mutter. "That's all I said. I just . . ."

Sensing the grief bubble up inside me, he softens. "Then let me help you. Trust me." I do trust him. Maybe Bodie never understood what I saw in Ash, but he's stuck by me through the anguish. He's gotten used to the way it comes in waves. He scooped me up and got me home when I broke down at the planetarium. He held me for hours after I first listened to *Did You Know That There's a Tunnel Under Ocean*

Blvd for the first time. I wept as Lana sang, "*Don't forget me*," like it was Ash singing those words, his distant voice an echo of hers.

"Look," he says gently. "I know I didn't . . . get to know him, and I wish I had. I wish he let me get to know him. Not that I'm blaming him. I know he's not here to defend himself."

"He has nothing to defend," I snap. "And if you're implying that he's dead . . . we don't know that."

He bites his lower lip. "All I'm saying is that I was *your* friend. And you were the one who would call me crying when he would disappear—"

"Don't use that word. Please."

"I'm sorry. Fuck, I'm sorry. I didn't mean it that way. I meant, when he wouldn't call you back."

"That was in the beginning," I explain. "Before I understood him."

"I know," he says. "But it's just . . . It was hard to like him when he would just ghost you like that."

"But he also made me happy," I insist. "I know you didn't see it. Because he didn't show the best parts of himself to you. And because you were my sounding board every time he . . . ghosted me. But he made me happy. You have to accept that the same person who can hurt you can also love you. People can't be perfect."

"Fine" is all he says.

"Fine," I echo.

He offers me a smile. "I *still* want you to be happy," he says.

I try to say thanks, but it comes out as more of a sob than a word.

"Come on." He takes my hand in his. "We're going to be late for choir."

When I sing in choir, my thoughts go beautifully silent. Everything disappears except for the music. As we rehearse "We Found Love" and "Molly Malone," I relax, forget, connect, rejuvenate, disconnect. I feel peace.

We found love in a hopeless place.

The rest of the kids prefer it when we sing the modern songs. Bodie begs Byrne to let us sing Taylor, Cardi, Dua. He gets a kick out of turning a pop hit into something haunted and a cappella. But I prefer the old songs, the ones that predate my life, the ones that Byrne told me his grandmother back in Belfast used to sing to him, before he left Ireland for a place where he could be free of the burdens of his father's Catholic guilt and his mother's drinking.

She died of a fever. And no one could save her. And that was the end of sweet Molly Malone.

Byrne is so many things to me. Choirmaster, English teacher, Alateen sponsor, and one of our two GSA faculty advisers. I barely knew him when Ash disappeared. He was just a new teacher to me then. Byrne never tells me to move on. He just reminds me that the goal is to get through each day, one at a time. It's the best advice I've been given since Ash disappeared.

"When we get to the burden, I want your voices to soar," Byrne yells over us.

Alive, alive, oh, alive, alive, oh.

"Think of your voices as ravens, flying together into the sky."

Alive, alive, oh, alive, alive, oh.

"You know what we call a flock of ravens. A conspiracy. Because they're always plotting something together. Let your voices be conspiratorial. Let them be unified."

Alive, alive, oh, alive, alive, oh.

When the song ends, one of our first-year singers asks, "What's the *burden* of the song?"

"It's the chorus," Byrne explains. "The refrain."

"Why is it called a burden?" the first-year asks.

Byrne moves across the room as he speaks. Past the music theory wall. Past the culture of the month wall, Turkish this month. Past the composer of the month wall, Satie this month.

Toward the word wall, covered in music words and definitions. Byrne taps his finger on the word *burden*. He looks right at me. "Kam, what can you tell us about why we call the chorus of a song the burden?"

"Well, a burden is something that is often repeated." Byrne's gaze tells me to keep going. "It's something on which we dwell, something we keep coming back to, because we just can't let go of it."

"That's right." Byrne seems to be speaking only to me as he adds, "Songs are like people. They dwell on certain words and melodies. That's why we call it a burden. Because songs, like stories, like us, *need* structure."

I offer Byrne a smile. I know what he's saying. Ash is my burden. The thing I return to in my head.

Alive, alive, oh, alive, alive, oh.

I officially met Ash in choir, or just after choir in the hallway. We sang together for two weeks before we finally spoke to each other. He was the youngest senior in school, a year ahead because he was that smart, and new to the school just like me. And Bodie and I were the oldest freshmen, held back because our moms both read the same article when we were toddlers about how letting your child be the oldest in kindergarten is good for their confidence and sets them up for a future as a leader.

Then, one day, Byrne asked us all to suggest one new song for the choir to sing that year. He had us write the titles down on a note card and place them in the paddy cap he almost never takes off. He read the names of the songs out loud, everything from "Uptown Funk" to "Bad Guy," "Despacito" to "Shake It Off." And then he read my card, "God Knows I Tried" by Lana Del Rey. Or at least I thought it was my card, because a few song titles later, he once again read, "God Knows I Tried" by Lana Del Rey. I looked around at the choir, wondering who else picked a relatively obscure Lana album track. I could see Ash doing the same thing. Our eyes found each other. Recognized something in each other. I knew instantly that, like me, he wanted life to feel like poetry. That he longed for romance.

When rehearsal is over, Byrne asks me and Bodie to linger behind. "Kam, there's something I wanted to talk to you about before tomorrow's—"

"I already know," I say. "You're going to Joshua Tree."

"I have to go as a chaperone, but you don't have to."

"You shouldn't," Bodie says. Then he quickly changes it to, "*We* shouldn't."

"I'm a senior. It's my last trip with the GSA," I say. Every year, on the weekend before the winter holidays, our GSA takes a school trip. It was Byrne and Ms. Robin's idea, to give the queer kids a chance to travel together and focus on learning about queer life and history. Last year, we did a trip to Washington, DC. We protested outside the Capitol building. Bodie carried a sign that read "Fuck Your Religion." Olivia's read, "Your God's Hate Isn't More Powerful Than My Love." The year before was New Mexico, where we learned about Native cultures and their openness to different genders and sexualities. Freshman year was San Francisco. Ms. Robin introduced us to the trans sisters who were the first members of her chosen family, and to the revival theater where she discovered her love for cinema. Our club motto is "We contain multitudes." We've screamed it into the open sky in Taos, at members of Congress, outside the spot that used to be Castro Camera.

"The budget was severely cut for our trip this year, which meant we were limited to campsites we could drive to. We have no money for airfare or hotel rooms." He gives me a moment to speak. When I don't, he says, "You don't have to go."

"You already said that," I mutter.

"Please don't go back there," Bodie begs. "You're finally doing a bit better."

"Am I?" I ask. "It doesn't feel that way."

Bodie won't stop. "We can make our own special weekend plans. I'll cook you whatever you want, and we can binge *The Great British Bake Off* until we pass out."

"But you love the GSA trips," I tell Bodie. "I don't want you to miss one because of me." I see Bodie struggle to contradict me. When Bodie finally joined me and Ash for a meal, he asked Ash why he wasn't a part of the GSA. The conversation they had still swirls in my mind, their rancor for each other still an unresolved thing inside me.

"Can I take some time to think about it?" I ask, ignoring Bodie.

"Of course," Byrne says. "We need a head count before Thanksgiving break."

I think about the things Byrne tells me all the time. Like, I have to face even the darkest moments with a grateful heart. Or, every crisis is an opportunity for growth in our relationship to our Higher Power. But I don't have a grateful heart or a Higher Power. I have a best friend who thinks God-loving people use religion to oppress us, and I was raised by two people who hate religion.

"I'll think about it," I say. "But I don't think I should go without talking to Ash's parents and his sister. I don't want . . . I don't know . . ."

"You don't want to hurt them," Byrne says. "That makes sense. And it's very thoughtful of you."

"I'm seeing them on Sunday. His sister has a tennis match. I guess I can ask them then."

"Maybe after the match," Byrne suggests. "Let them enjoy their daughter's moment, and let her focus on her game."

"Yeah, good call." I nod sadly. "Do you think it's a good idea, for me to go back to the desert?"

Byrne offers me his warmest gaze. He takes his paddy cap off to scratch his balding scalp, then puts it back on. "I can't answer that for you. It could be healing. Or it could be painful. Perhaps even both. But if you do decide to join the trip, you'll need one of your parents to sign the permission slip."

A throaty laugh emerges from my body. "Well, I don't even know where my dad is, and my mom . . . well . . . we all know what she's going to say. She was scared of me going back then. But now . . . Going back to Joshua Tree for me . . . It's like my mom going back to Iran. Which she'll never do, even if the regime falls. My mom looks forward, not back. But sometimes, we have to look back in order to move forward, right?"

After classes are done, Bodie forces me into our school library to choose an author for our English assignment. The most studious members of our school have already claimed their after-school study spots. Our library was redesigned two years ago to foster more community and less isolation. Gone are the old cubicles. They've been replaced with round tables and group study rooms.

"Okay, who are you considering?" Bodie asks as he leads me to the fiction section.

I glance at the student and teacher recommendation cards as I make my way across the alphabetically organized books. Olivia Cole recommends *The Black Flamingo* by Dean Atta. Ms. Robin recommends *Detransition, Baby* by Torrey Peters. Danny Lim recommends Bram Stoker's *Dracula*. Mr. Byrne has placed a handwritten card under *The Picture of Dorian Gray* by Oscar Wilde. In his cursive scroll, he scribbled, *My favorite work from my favorite fellow Irishman.*

"Okay, you just moved from *A* to *Z*. Any thoughts?" I can hear the impatience in Bodie's voice.

"I guess I'm considering Pablo Neruda," I say quietly. "And also Rilke. Or maybe William Blake. Or . . ." I don't say Paulo Coelho, because I don't want to remind Bodie of his argument with Ash about *The Alchemist*.

Bodie's eyes pierce me. "Ash's favorite writers." He's unsurprised. "You didn't include the writer of that everyone-has-a-personal-legend book."

Of course he was already thinking of his argument with Ash. I say nothing.

"I'm not discouraging you from picking one of them, but maybe it might be, I don't know . . . less emotionally taxing to choose an author that won't remind you of him. Maybe an author who writes happy, funny books."

I ignore Bodie and shuffle toward the poetry section.

I run my fingers along the well-worn spines of the books. Mr. Silver recommends T. S. Eliot. I turn to Bodie and smile when I see he wrote a recommendation card for Rumi. "Look at you, getting all poetic."

"I guess all the Rumi poems my parents have framed around the house made an impact," he says.

I pull out a Neruda book and flip the pages slowly. In the hours of video I took of Ash, there are so many moments of poetic magic. Ash, lying on the grass, reciting Neruda, telling me that poetry is meant to be experienced covertly but aloud, like a secret being passed on from soul to soul. He would write me poems that were accompanied by his own original artwork, the words swirling inside the imagery like a puzzle. He would hide them in strange places for me to find. For months after he disappeared, I found his hidden poems in my backpack, in the inside pocket of a blazer, underneath our living room rug.

"So . . . Neruda?" Bodie asks.

"Maybe." I'm not ready to commit, so I make my way to the William Blake section. I pick up a small book of poems. On the cover is an illustration by Blake of a very well-built angel seemingly abducting a child. I turn the book over. On the back is a devil figure lunging for the child. I read the name of the image aloud. "The Good and Evil Angels struggle for possession of a child." Something about the image chills me.

Bodie peeks over my shoulder to see the image. "They're still fighting for possession of our souls, aren't they? All the assholes who want to stop us from seeing drag shows and reading queer books are the evil angels—"

I laugh. "Except in their own minds, they're the good angels, saving us from the sinful influence of Alaska Thunderfuck and Aristotle and Dante."

"God forbid we discover the secrets of the universe," he says with a knowing smile.

I put the poetry book away and pick up a bigger Blake book full of poems and imagery.

Blake was Ash's biggest inspiration. He loved that Blake treated creativity as a form of spirituality.

I flip through the pages and a thick piece of paper flies out. I know the minute it hits the floor what it is, like I can still smell his scent on it.

My heart pounds as I lean down to pick up the paper.

Pounds even faster when I unfold it.

It's huge, at least three times as big as printer paper. On it is a pencil sketch of spectral figures floating in the sky. They look like clouds, but I can tell they're ghosts. Words are scrawled through the clouds, like God wrote the words in the sky. At the top is the title of the poem. "Burden."

Bodie reads the poem in a hush. "*Shh. Shh, listen. Listen, we are here. Here is everywhere. Here is where you transcend the senses. Here is—*"

"Stop. Please." I nervously fold the paper back up and put it in my pocket. I'm not ready to read it. Not now. Not with Bodie hovering over me.

"I thought you found them all," Bodie says.

"I thought so too." I look around the stacks, wondering if there are more covert gifts for me in other books. But I know that Bodie will judge me if I start throwing every book open. I also know that I need to be alone with this poem. Now. "I'm going to do my project on Blake. I'll go check these books out and go home to start my research."

I grab every Blake book on the shelf and rush to the counter, desperate to be alone so I can read what Ash wrote for me. But Bodie follows me. Maybe he knows it's the moments when I most want to be alone that I most need his friendship. "Pit stop at the dog park for a few rounds of Scooby-Doo?"

"Yeah, sure."

My bag heavier now, my mind weighed down by thoughts of Ash, I follow Bodie to the dog park to play the game that probably only makes sense to us.

"You pick the first dog," Bodie says.

I look around at our options, making eye contact with a huge Siberian husky and a miniature schnauzer before pointing to an excited mutt with a regal stature, long white hair, and the cutest underbite. "That one." I point to the mutt. "You ready?"

"Ready as I'll ever be."

On Bodie's count of three, we both say which celebrity we think the dog looks like. "Anya Taylor-Joy!" I yell out just as Bodie blurts out, "Sir Ian McKellen." We both laugh. The game never fails to cheer us up.

As Bodie scans the dog park for our next canine celebrity lookalike, I look out to the darkening sky. In it, I can almost see the spectral figures Ash drew for me. Like they're watching over me. Like I'm their burden.

FIRST YEAR

Mr. Byrne reads aloud from a small strip of paper. "Once again, we have 'God Knows I Tried' by Lana Del Rey." He pauses. "Interesting," he says. "Two of you suggested the same song, and I've never even heard it. I clearly have some musical homework to do."

I look around the music room, wondering who else picked the same song as me. My eyes land on two emo sopranos, seated six feet apart, but then we're all six feet apart from each other. And we're all wearing special singing masks that Byrne got for us last week. One of the emo girls braids her never-cut hair tight. The other clicks her jet-black nails against each other, filling the room with a grating clicking sound. It has to be one of them. They both look like extras from Lana's *Tropico* movie.

I feel my phone buzz in my pocket. It's a text from Bodie. Normally, he'd just whisper to me, but the six feet of distance and the fabric barrier make hushed conversations harder. *Guess you're not the only person here who loves bathing in a stew of maudlin music.*

I look his way and roll my eyes. I quickly text him back. *NOT maudlin. Cathartic. Wait, no. CATHARTIQUE.*

I watch his fingers peck at his phone. Soon enough, his next text appears on my screen.

Well done. The word cathartic *is maudlin. But CATHARTIQUE . . . shantay she stays.*

I laugh, but I want to argue that there's nothing maudlin about catharsis.

I give his text a quick *Ha ha* and put my phone back in my pocket while I keep scanning the room. My eyes reach the back corner. I land on our sole tenor. Ash Greene, recently transferred senior. He always sits alone, usually sketching something, rarely interacting with anyone else. I could pick out the pure timbre of his singing voice anywhere, but I have no idea what his speaking voice sounds like. Or what his face looks like, for that matter. I've seen a lot of the students maskless in the schoolyard or in our outdoor cafeteria these first two weeks of school. But not Ash. He pulls his long red hair back with a black hairband, revealing twinkling blue-green eyes I've never noticed before. When he looks my way, it feels like the sun is shining on me alone. He offers me a half nod, and that's when I'm certain it was him. He chose the exact same song as me, like he read my mind. Or maybe like I read his. It feels like everyone but us has evaporated into fog.

"I'll listen to all your suggestions this weekend, and think about which songs would work best for our purposes," Mr. Byrne says. "I can tell you now that if you chose a song with explicit lyrics, it will be disqualified. School rules. Now, before we leave, let's hear 'Paddy's Lamentation' one last time."

Following Mr. Byrne's lead, we all begin to sing the old Irish song about an immigrant who comes to America seeking a better life, only to end up fighting in the Civil War, losing his leg, and being denied pension. Bodie thinks the song is completely depressing. I think it's poignant. I close my eyes when we begin to sing, and think of my own immigrant parents, who left Iran for Canada before I was born, and then came to America when I was in middle school. Always seeking a better life. Or in Lana-speak, always inching their way out of the black and into the blue.

Oh, it's by the hush, me boys. I'm sure that's to hold your noise. And listen to poor Paddy's narration.

"Sing through those masks," Mr. Byrne urges us. "A little fabric can't keep your voices down, can it?"

I was by hunger pressed, and in poverty distressed. So I took a thought I'd leave the Irish nation.

"That's better, but don't scream the song. Let it soar naturally. Think of your voices as birds, flying effortlessly."

When we reach the last line of the song—*For I'm sure I've had enough of their hard fighting*—I do feel like my voice is a bird. An eagle, maybe. Or no, something less special. Just an everyday bird. A pigeon.

"That was beautiful. Keep practicing it. If you want to listen to the song at home, a reminder that my favorite version is by Sinéad O'Connor."

We push our metal chairs back in unison. They squeak against the vinyl floors, creating their own wall of sound. We throw our sheet music for "Paddy's Lamentation" into our backpacks. Zip them up. Pull out our phones and turn our ringers on. A chorus of different ringtones fills the space as we scurry into the hallway. "Did your mom text you about tonight?" Bodie asks.

I nod as I read a message from my mom. "Yeah, we're on our own. Again. Do you think our parents are the only people who chose their pandemic pod based on who they gamble with?"

"Persians and poker nights, an inseparable pair," Bodie says, laughing.

"Like salt and pepper," I say.

"Like you and maudlin . . . I mean, um, *cathartique* music," he offers.

"Like you and those jeans," I crack. "I think you've outgrown them."

"The tighter the jeans get, the better they make my butt look. Agree or disagree?"

"Abstain," I say, smiling. "Wait, I've got an amazing autocorrect disaster from my mom." Our parents' constant typos amuse us to no end. "She said that there's Legionella in our fridge for us to eat."

"Legionella?" Bodie echoes. "Sounds like the pork chop

queen of *RuPaul's Drag Race Italia,* season diecimila."

"I'm pretty sure she meant leftovers, because she made way too much gheymeh bademjoon last night—"

Bodie turns his phone my way. "Um, one would hope she meant leftovers, because *Legionella* is a killer bacteria."

"Oh, cool. Want to come study at my place and eat some deadly bacteria?" I ask.

Bodie cracks up as he says, "Let's die another day and order Chinese at my place."

Bodie and I are headed toward the exit when I hear a voice behind me call out, "Hey, Kam." I know exactly who it is before I turn around to see him, eyes shining. Turns out his speaking voice isn't so different from his singing voice. It soars through his mask, like a rare bird. A peacock, maybe. "I'm Ash."

"I know," I say. "I mean, we've been in choir together for a while now."

"Two weeks isn't that long," Bodie says.

Ash doesn't turn his gaze to Bodie. He keeps it pinned on me as he says, *"All time is eternally present."*

"All time is unredeemable," I respond with a knowing smile.

"What the fuck are you two talking about?" Bodie asks. He hates being left out.

Ash still doesn't look at Bodie. Instead, he keeps his focus on me. "Nice song choice," he says.

"Yeah, I mean, it's one of my favorite songs and I, um,

thought it would sound good in choir. I don't know . . ."

Ash lets me stammer out my ineloquent response before he says, "I think you do know. That's why you picked it."

Bodie, who pecks at his phone, taps my shoulder impatiently. "I did two orders of har gow since they insist on serving their dumplings in odd numbers, which is criminal, honestly. It divides people. Our biggest fight ever was over who was going to eat the last dumpling, remember?"

I turn to Ash, my face hot with embarrassment. I don't want him to think I'm petty enough to fight over a dumpling. "It wasn't our biggest fight."

"Of course it was," Bodie insists. "Which is a good thing, right? I mean, we never fight."

"Except about who eats the last dumpling," Ash replies jokingly, but Bodie doesn't laugh.

"Okay, we rarely fight," Bodie corrects himself. "Wait, should we put a proposition on the ballot to ban all restaurants from serving dumplings in odd numbers? It wouldn't even be close to the dumbest prop, and who would vote against that? Everyone would rather have six dumplings than five."

Ash looks confused at Bodie's rant. "California's propositions are sometimes laughable, but in general, they've allowed the state to be far more progressive than other states."

The subtle tension between them reminds me of the way my parents snipe at each other when they're trying not to fight in front of me. I quickly try to change the subject. "Whatever, it's not like Bodie and I can vote anyway. We're not American citizens. We're resident aliens."

Ash smiles when he says, "And also, you're fourteen, so there's that."

"Fifteen, actually," I say. "We're both the oldest in the class."

"I'm the youngest in my class," Ash says.

"Why did you come to this school?" Bodie asks.

"Same reason anyone goes to any school," Ash counters. "Because my parents made me."

"Right, sure," Bodie says. "But most people don't start a new high school their senior year is all I'm saying."

"It feels like maybe that's not all you're saying," Ash responds coolly.

Bodie turns his gaze toward me. He wants me to be as annoyed as he is, but I'm not. I'm fascinated by the mysterious new senior.

"I'm sure his number got chosen in the lottery just like ours did, and his parents transferred him 'cause this is one of the best charters in this city," I explain.

Ash nods and smiles, but doesn't say anything.

Bodie goes back to reciting the order. "Okay, so we've got sesame chicken and kung pao pork. You want fried rice or is that enough?" Before I can answer, Bodie glances up to Ash. "Sorry, I just want to put in our dinner order now. I'm starving."

Ash ignores Bodie, who isn't used to being ignored. His

gaze fixed on me, Ash says, "While he orders your dinner, let's talk Lana. Meet me outside so we can take these masks off?"

A huge, hidden smile grows on my face. I wonder if he's smiling too. "Yeah, sure. Give me, um, five seconds to get there?"

"It's a date." I wonder if Ash chose that word deliberately. *Date.* I've never been on one of those.

As Bodie puts in the order, Ash and I both head out through the exit doors into the fresh air. We stand across from each other at the top of the school steps. Neither of us takes our mask off yet.

"Okay," he says. "Show me yours and I'll show you mine."

I feel myself blush under the fabric. "On the count of three, okay?"

We both count out the numbers, and then unhook our masks to reveal our faces. Time feels like it stops when I see his whole face for the first time. He doesn't look anything like I was expecting. His face is rounder than I thought it would be, his cheeks redder, maybe because they're covered in a constellation of freckles. He has wisps of stubble on his face, and a hoop pierced into his septum. He looks both childlike and dangerous at the same time. Like a puzzle, the pieces of him don't feel like they should fit together, but they do.

"So, Lana," he says.

"I love her," I declare.

"Well, obviously. You wouldn't suggest we sing a random

song from her most unfairly ignored album—"

"My favorite album!" I hear the exclamation point in my voice.

"Mine too." He smiles. "And that's my favorite song on the album. But most people prefer nihilistic Lana, not spiritual Lana."

"I mean, they're the same person," I say.

Ash's face lights up. "Right. Exactly. The nihilist is the spiritual seeker. Two halves of the same coin. People are complex. She's a baddie and a spiritualist."

I want to listen to him forever, so I ask, "What else do you love about her?"

"I love that she hasn't turned herself into a brand," he explains. "She'll break my heart if she ever sticks her name on a flowery fragrance or a hydrating cleanser or something."

"Blue Jeans, the new denim collection by Lana Del Rey," I say in a movie trailer voice. He laughs, so I keep going. "Ultraviolence, Lana Del Rey's first fragrance, with hints of old money and white sunshine." I love his laugh. There's a freedom to it.

"I almost want that to happen now." He shakes off the laughter. "The thing is she runs counter to our culture, you know. She's not scared to create her own lane, whether that means standing up for a kind of vulnerability that doesn't jibe with the age of self-empowerment, or whether that means releasing nine-minute songs. She's a nonconformist, which I guess makes me feel seen, 'cause look at me." He finally takes a breath. "Your turn. Why is *Honeymoon* your favorite album?"

"Um . . . ." I look over and see Bodie next to us now, maskless and annoyed. I didn't even hear him come out. If Ash did hear him, he didn't care to acknowledge it. "I guess I like how slow the album is. It feels like taking a long, hot bath, you know. Comforting."

For a brief moment, I wonder if whatever's happening between me and Ash will end now that he's seen Bodie's face. His perfect movie star face, the strong superhero jawline, the dramatically long eyelashes. But Ash doesn't even seem to see Bodie, which only makes Bodie's obvious frustration grow. Maybe because he's not used to someone being more interested in me than in him. That makes two of us.

"Yes!" Ash exclaims, his eyes locked on me. "It's like the music is warning us to slow the fuck down before our fast-paced world careens over a precipice."

Bodie eyes me impatiently. "Food will be at my house in about fifty minutes. Should we go now?"

"God knows you're in a rush," Ash says slyly.

Bodie looks over at me. His eyes beg me to find Ash as grating as he clearly does.

"God knows we have a lot of homework to get through tonight," I say.

"Okay, enough God talk," Bodie snaps.

"Not a God stan?" Ash asks.

Bodie leans in. "Yeah, no, not a God stan. Religion's been used to oppress people like me for centuries."

"What does religion have to do with God?" Ash asks.

"Is that a joke?" Bodie's tone is sharp.

Ash shrugs. "No. I'm not good at jokes. My sister says I need to work on my sense of humor."

"Do you have one?" Bodie asks.

"Bodie, chill," I say. "Everyone has a sense of humor."

"I don't know . . ." Ash is thinking through what he's saying as he speaks. "A sense of humor is like good taste, isn't it? Everyone thinks they have it, but obviously not everybody does."

Bodie rolls his eyes. "Speaking of taste, I'm starving. Let's go, Kam. I hate cold food and I despise microwaves."

"You still have forty-five minutes until your food arrives," Ash says.

"You're gay, right?" Bodie asks Ash.

I suck in my breath.

"Yeah," Ash says. "Why?"

"Don't you have an issue with how religion is used against us? My and Kam's parents were born in Iran. You can be killed for being gay there. Religious assholes in this country want to ban queer books from our libraries. All over the world, religion is—"

"Take a breath," Ash suggests.

"Don't tell me what to do," Bodie barks.

Ash doesn't get mad. His voice stays calm when he says, "Then don't educate me about the atrocities of religion. Like I said, God has nothing to do with that. Religion is man's folly. Religions are just tax-free corporations. I'm talking about—"

Bodie's phone dings with a text from Olivia.

As Bodie watches whatever Olivia sent him, Ash takes the opportunity to turn his attention back to me. "Maybe we can hang out sometime," he suggests softly.

"Oh, yeah, I mean, sure, here, put your number in my phone." Quickly, I add, "I mean, if you feel okay touching my phone."

Ash smiles. "We're tested three times a week, and the virus is airborne. Give me that phone."

I hand him my cell. He creates a new contact with his phone number, then gives it back to me.

"Cool, I'll text you mine now so you have it."

"Oh, you can't text me," he explains. "That's my family's home number. I'm a landline-only kind of queer."

Bodie, who laughed his way through the video Olivia just sent him, looks at Ash with sympathy. "Your parents won't get you a phone?" Bodie asks him. "That blows."

"Oh, no, it's not—"

Bodie cuts Ash off. "Our parents got us phones for our eleventh birthdays, mostly so they'd have a way to track us, let's be real. Persian moms hate the CIA but love surveillance."

"We're not twins or anything," I explain to Ash. "We were just born a week apart—"

"In the same hospital in Toronto—"

"Delivered by the same doctor—"

"And we had the same birth weight too, although now Bodie's tall and lean and I'm—"

"Amazing," Bodie says. Then, turning to Ash, he quickly adds, "I mean, he can be infuriating too. But everyone can be. Especially when they've been your best friend since kindergarten."

"That's a long time," Ash observes. "Explains why you finish each other's sentences." Ash looks at Bodie, then at me. Like he's studying us. "But you're not the same astrological sign, are you?"

"Wait, how did you know that?" I ask.

"Your energies are different," Ash says, nonchalant.

"Yeah, Kam's a Leo and I'm a Virgo," Bodie declares proudly.

"That explains it," Ash says.

Bodie tenses up. "Explains what? What's wrong with Virgos? Beyoncé. Keanu. Zendaya. Virgos are iconic."

Ash seems amused. "There's nothing *wrong* with any astrological sign. It just explains why you two have different energies."

"Please ignore Bodie when he goes into defense lawyer mode," I say. "His dad's a criminal defense lawyer. Arguing is in his bloodline."

"Ha ha," Bodie says, feigning laughter. But Ash genuinely laughs.

"I'm not trying to win an argument here," Ash says to Bodie. "But just so you know, my parents would gladly get mc a phone if I wanted one."

"You don't . . . *want* a phone?"

"Shocking, I know." Ash smiles. "I just don't think constant distraction is good for artists."

"Then let's not distract you any longer." Bodie locks his arm through mine and tries to pull me away, but I let go of him and linger near Ash as Bodie begins his dramatic descent down the steps.

"I should go," I say.

Ash nods. "Yeah, your friend hates cold food and microwaves."

I laugh. "Bodie's really into food. He wants to be a chef someday."

"What do you want to be?" he asks.

I shrug. "I don't know." After a pause, I say, "Happy, I guess."

Just as I'm about to leave, Ash calls out to me. "One more question. What's your favorite color?"

I turn around. "I don't think I've been asked that question since I was five."

He smiles. "Then maybe it's time to reconnect with your inner five-year-old. Five is a great age. Nobody asks you about your life goals or your future like I just did when you're five. They just let you be yourself."

"You clearly don't have Persian parents. My mom was obsessed with my life goals before I was even born."

"Sounds rough." The simple empathy he offers me makes me feel empathy for my own younger self for the first time.

All my life, I just accepted my mom's intensity and pressure as the norm because it's all I knew. And because both Bodie's parents were like her. Having overbearing parents is one of the many things that bonds us.

"It's not that rough, in the grand scheme of things," I say, my voice small.

Ash's eyes stay on me with a suddenly discomfiting intimacy. "Someone always has it worse than you. It's still okay to acknowledge that parents putting that kind of burden on you sucks."

"It's mostly my mom," I say. "My dad is . . . fun." It's not entirely a lie. He used to be fun, and sometimes, when he has just enough alcohol, he still is. "What are *your* parents like?" I ask.

He smiles. "They want to be my best friends, which I don't mind most of the time. But sometimes—"

"KAM!" Bodie yells from the bottom of the steps.

"I should go." I turn to leave, then quickly turn back to him. "Oh, wait, my inner five-year-old's favorite color is pink," I say, surprising myself. Then I shock myself by opening up even more. "I could never say that out loud back then because my dad was really obsessed with keeping me away from anything girly. So I always said my favorite color was blue. It feels kind of absurd now that I'm confessing that out loud."

"I thought you said your dad was fun," he says.

"He is. He was. I mean, he could be. He can be." I feel myself stumble with my words, part of me desperate to confess everything about my dad, another part anxious to hide it all.

"Pink is a great color," Ash says with a smile. "It's the color of cherry blossoms and flamingos and cartoon panthers and Angelyne's car."

"Yeah, I agree. Why do you care about my favorite color?"

He shrugs. "No reason. Just curious to know more about you. Now I know that you're a Leo who loves pink and Lana. I hope to find out more next time we see each other."

"Yeah." I feel myself blush nervously. "Me too." I turn away from him, feeling like an idiot for not asking him more questions. I want to know his favorite color, his astrological sign, all the details that make him the person he is.

As Bodie and I walk toward his place, the sun begins to set and it's a magnificent one. The sky looks bathed in a pink glow. The floating clouds look like cotton candy. And the sun looks like a hot-pink heart dipping down into the earth. I feel like it's a sign about me and Ash, but I don't dare tell Bodie what I'm thinking. Not when he spends our entire walk home venting about Ash. "Can you believe that guy? He thinks he's better than us because he doesn't have a phone?"

I want to say that Ash never said he's better than us, but I don't dare interrupt.

"*Religion is man's folly,*" Bodie spits out, mocking Ash. "*All time is eternally present.* Who talks like that?"

"The time quote is from a Lana interlude," I explain. "It's T. S. Eliot actually."

"Right, well, most people don't go around talking in T. S. Eliot quotes. You know what he reminds me of? A cult member. The super long hair is a choice, right?"

"I like his hair," I say defensively. "It's cool."

"Wait, do you think he was raised in a cult?" Bodie asks, excited by the story he's building in his head. "LA is cult central. There's the one with the *Smallville* girl. Xenu, obviously. And the one that actor from *10 Things I Hate About You* started in Venice Beach."

"I haven't heard of that one, but I'm pretty sure the *Smallville* girl's cult was headquartered in Albany."

"Wait, really?" Ahead of us, Jack Spencer does some kind of hyperactive fitness workout on the front lawn with a bunch of other jocks. Jack waves to Bodie as he squats and leaps up into the air. Squat. Jump. Wave. Squat. Jump. Wave. Eventually, Jack calls out, "Bodie!" But Bodie's too wrapped up in his phone. He's looking up my facts. "Okay, you're technically correct. The NXIVM cult was in Albany, but it had super strong Hollywood connections."

"Just say I'm right and stop there," I say with a smile.

"Never!" he proclaims, still pecking away at his phone. "But seriously, if we expand out to all of California, the list of cults is epic. I mean, Manson. The Children of God. Heaven's Gate. Oh my God, Jim Jones and the Peoples Temple! They're the ones who drank the—"

Before Bodie can finish, Jack interrupts him by running

up to us, sweat dripping from his annoyingly chiseled body. "Bodie, hey, didn't you hear me calling you?"

Bodie barely glances up at Jack. "Sorry, I was doing some research. Jesus, over nine hundred people died at Jonestown." Bodie types something into his phone.

"What are you researching?" Jack asks with innocent curiosity.

Bodie keeps typing. "I'm adding something to the Wikipedia entry for Jonestown. It says it was a mass suicide, but I'm not sure that's a fair description. Those people were brainwashed by a cult leader. They were victims." When Bodie puts his phone away, he looks up at a confused Jack. "Sorry, but someone has to keep Wikipedia accurate."

Jack smiles, clearly amused. He does that thing jocks do where he stretches his arms so high that it exposes his ripped ab muscles. "Did you get my DM?" he asks Bodie.

Bodie shakes his head, then pulls his phone out again to check his messages. I'm not trying to read Bodie's messages, but I can't help it. Jack's message reads, *I think you're really kewt. Wanna go out sometime?* I can feel Bodie cringe at that spelling.

The grin on Jack's face tells me that he is expecting an easy yes. His endorphins are high, his body is perfect, and his confidence has never been damaged. That is, until Bodie says, "That's really nice, Jack. I'm just so busy with schoolwork and extracurriculars that I'm not looking to date right now."

Jack looks at me with the fresh glow of shame, surely

wishing no one had observed his rejection. Then he mutters, "Yeah, cool, I totally get it," before running back to his workout buddies.

Bodie and I don't say much to each other until we're far enough away from Jack to speak freely. "He's cute," I finally say to Bodie.

"Yeah, well, I'm looking for more than *kewt*." Then he adds, "Honestly, it's our first year of high school. We're just establishing ourselves as students. I think we should both commit to focusing on our studies and our activities and not, you know, getting distracted by boys."

I say nothing because I'm distracted by Ash, thinking about the depth in his eyes, the mystery in his words. When we get to Bodie's place, we don't talk about Ash or Jack or local cults. We focus on homework. When we take a food break, Bodie tries to explain why dumplings are the best food ever, and develops a theory about how every culture has their version of a dumpling. He makes me watch silly TikTok videos of dogs eating whole oranges, whole apples, one dog trying to eat a blow-dryer. We laugh and work and laugh and work. It feels good. But I still can't stop thinking about Ash.

Ash lingers in my mind when I get home. "Mom? Dad? You guys here?" I yell into the darkness. Ash fills my imagination as I brush my teeth and take a shower. He's soaping me up when I touch myself in the shower. He's in front of and behind me, above and below me—seemingly all at once—as I erupt into my hand and watch as our sad water pressure struggles to erase the evidence of my passion from my fingers. I pick up a bar of soap and wash my hand off with it.

"KAMRAN!" my dad bellows, and I flinch. I quickly rinse and dry myself off. "KAMRAN, COME DOWN-STAIRS NOW!" I fold and hang the towel back up symmetrically, because my mom is a stickler about every-thing in the house being perfect. She's always straightening the art on the walls, fluffing pillows, dusting the parts of the house no one sees. Our house is suddenly filled with music. Dean Martin. One of my dad's favorites. I can hear my dad sing along in a happy slur from below. *"When the rumba rhythm starts to play, dance with me."*

My mom gently corrects him. "You drank too much, and that's not even right. It's *marimba rhythm.*" She's right. She's always right.

"Maybe it can be both. Maybe we shouldn't limit our-selves." He's right too.

I throw some sweatpants and one of my dad's old T-shirts on. When I get to the kitchen, my dad pulls my mom onto the stained Mexican tiles of our kitchen, like he's trying to turn it into an imaginary strobe-lit dance floor.

"It's late," my mom says.

"Kamran is still awake and he's a kid. How late can it be?" My dad spins my mom around and, against her better judgment, she lets herself be led.

"I'm fifteen," I say. "That's not a kid."

My dad dips my mom and holds her there as he says,

"Someday, you'll understand we're all kids forever. Look at me. Young at heart no matter how much the world tries to beat me down."

"Pull me up, Bahman!" my mom demands, her face red. She doesn't look happy when she's standing straight up again. "Okay, enough of being young at heart. It's time to sleep."

But my dad stops her when she tries to shut the music off. He turns to me, his face manic and excited. "Let's make a video like old times. I'll pretend I'm Dean Martin in Vegas."

"Dad, come on, it's late," I say. "And we haven't made a video in years."

"I never said no to you when you asked me to be a pirate, an astronaut, and, what else . . . an angry Frenchman! Remember that?"

I laugh at the memory of my dad's terrible French accent. He's right. He always humored my need for playacting. And when I discovered how fun it was to record the playacting, he became my first muse.

My dad grabs my hand. "At least dance with me," he pleads as he pulls me onto the tiles. *"Make me sway,"* he belts in my ear in his truly terrible voice. I can't help but get swept up in his energy. I let him spin and dip me until I'm giddy and free.

"Dad, you should go on *So You Think You Can Dance*," I suggest.

"Maybe I will. Who knows what my next move will be if—"

My mom quickly cuts him off. "Bahman, it's bedtime!" She turns the music off and the dimmed lights up. I can tell how desperate my dad is to keep the party going. He grabs a bottle of his best whiskey and pours himself a tall glass. "Haven't you had enough?" my mom asks him.

"It's just a nightcap," he says.

"I guess I'll say good night, then," I say. I know what happens when my mom starts telling my dad what he can and can't drink, do, or say.

"Kamran, wait." My dad reaches into the inside pocket of his blazer and pulls out a shockingly thick wad of cash. "I had a very good game tonight. Here." He yanks out two hundred-dollar bills and holds them out to me.

"Bahman, stop, please," my mom begs.

"Why shouldn't I spoil my son?" he asks, a hint of anger bubbling out. "Why shouldn't I share my joy with my family?"

My mom shakes her head. Her eyes tell me I'm allowed to take the money, so I do. I kiss them both on each cheek and say good night. Then I head to my room. I'm not thinking of Ash anymore. How can I when my parents are arguing in what they think is a hushed whisper?

"Please stop drinking so much," my mom says icily.

"Drinking helps my game," my dad slurs. "I can't bluff when I'm sober."

"You had one good night," she says. "That doesn't make up for all the money you've lost gambling."

"I wish you would stop micromanaging every part of my life," he snaps.

"And I wish you wouldn't put me in the position of *need-ing* to micromanage every part of *our* lives," she snaps back. "What happens if things don't go your way next week?"

"I told you I don't want to talk about that." I can hear him grab the bottle and pour himself another.

"I'm just saying we should be careful with money until we get the news," she says. I hold my breath, wondering what *news* she's hinting at. Whatever it is, it sounds bad.

"But I won," he babbles sadly. He doesn't sound young at heart now. He just sounds like a child.

"I'm going to bed. Please don't drink any more. You need to be alert for work tomorrow."

My mom's heels click as she walks from kitchen to bedroom. My dad's breath huffs as he sings sadly to himself, still getting the lyrics wrong.

My stomach turns. Is one of them ill, or worse . . . dying? All my grandparents are gone. Cancer, execution, heart attack, cancer. What if one of my parents is next? What if the reason they need to be careful about money is that one of them is sick and they'll need more money for medical bills? The thought chills me. I didn't feel this level of fear when we all got COVID over the summer, a few months ago, but maybe that's because we'd all been vaccinated and none of us had underlying conditions or serious symptoms. But now, I can't help but wonder if the virus weakened their immune systems, made them more susceptible to infections. All the horrible moments I've had with my parents seem to evaporate when the thought of one of them no longer being here is real.

I put my earbuds in. Silently beg Lana to sing me to sleep, the kind of deep, numb slumber where you don't remember your nightmares. Her voice floats, and soon my worries float too. They're replaced by memories that I wasn't even aware I had. Little moments these past two weeks of observing Ash. A distracted woman's dog licking Ash's face as I walked to school one morning. Ash painting his sneakers sunshine yellow on the soccer field as jocks kicked and grunted in the distance. Ash drawing some kind of monster in his sketch pad in a dark corner of the cafeteria, tears in his eyes. All these little moments come back to me in my sleeplessness, like buried clues that lead me to an undeniable fact: Ash fascinates me.

The next morning, I'm awoken by my parents arguing downstairs.

"Stop worrying so much, Leila," my dad says. "I can't handle your constant anxiety."

I can hear liquid being poured. I assume it's coffee or tea until my mom says, "Really, Bahman? The sun is barely up."

"Hair of the dog," he says gruffly. "It'll help with the headache you're giving me."

She laughs. There's disdain in her voice when she says, "Sure, blame me for your headache. Not the ten drinks you had last night. Or maybe you had more after I went to sleep."

"What's it to you what I drink?" His voice is like a blade

now. "My body, my choice. Isn't that what you feminists believe?"

"I'm not even going to respond to that." The more rageful my dad gets, the calmer my mom remains. That's their dynamic. Her ability to remain cool in the heat of his fire makes him burn even hotter, which in turn makes her icier, and on and on. Hot and cold. No in-between.

"Fine, don't respond," he says. "Do what you always do. Worry. Control. Judge."

"I'm sorry for being anxious," my mom says quietly. "And I'm sorry for being a feminist who contributes a decent salary to our home. But let's face facts, if you lose your job, we won't be able to make ends meet."

So that's the *news* they're waiting for. I breathe a sigh of relief. Neither of them has cancer. No one is sick or dying. With all the death in the world this last year, losing a job feels small in comparison. I roll out of bed, feeling a little better already. Feeling downright joyful. I want to rush down and tell them that life is all about perspective. If they could see how lucky they are in the grand scheme of things, they'd stop fighting.

"I have a degree in finance," my dad argues. "They won't replace me with a robot."

"Your degree is from Iran. The robots were developed in Silicon Valley. Who do you think they'll trust more with their money?" my mom asks.

"I don't know, Leila," my dad says. "And neither do you. So can we move on?"

But my mom's not good at moving on. She's good at doubling down, bending the world to her will. "Okay, let's talk about what we do know," my mom says. "I know that if you had gone back to the office, *in person*, like everyone else—"

"Not everyone else. Only a fraction of us went back. It was *optional*."

"Well, you should've taken the *option*," my mom shoots back. "If they saw you as an actual person rather than some virtual thing, maybe they wouldn't be able to replace you with some other virtual thing so easily."

"I'M NOT FIRED YET SO STOP ACTING LIKE I AM!" he yells. It shocks me.

My mom still remains calm. "Maybe if you had been in an office all this time instead of home, working in the same sweatpants every day, playing poker on your computer—"

"Have you been spying on me?" he asks.

"I don't need to be James Bond to notice the money that's disappeared from our bank account and the alcohol that's disappeared from the pantry."

"You want me to apologize for allowing myself a little fun once in a while? I work so that I can enjoy life. Isn't that the whole point? And they're not firing me, they're firing hundreds of people. Is everyone else also getting fired because I play online poker and enjoy a glass of whiskey at the end of the day? Or maybe, just maybe, is it because a global pandemic and technology have changed the world?"

I hold my breath, hoping my mom doesn't fight back. I

want this to end. I want my dad not to lose his job. For the pandemic to end and everything to be fine forever.

Thankfully, my mom says, "You're right. I'm sorry. Let's not fight in front of Kamran, okay?"

As I get myself ready for school, I wonder if my parents really believe I can't hear them when they go at each other. They both have such clear, loud voices.

When I go down, my dad is, shockingly, dressed for work in a button-down shirt and slacks. The scent of his woodsy cologne is so overpowering that it takes away my appetite. But still, I take the crispy barbari bread my mom has toasted for me, and smear some cream cheese on it. I take a few bites, then reach into our COVID drawer, where we keep masks and hand sanitizer and home tests. In the back of the drawer are the disposable gloves and face shields we once thought we needed, gathering dust as we've learned more about how the virus is spread. I pull a rapid test from the drawer.

"You want me to do it?" my mom asks.

"It's easier to do it to myself." I remove the swab from the packaging and lean my head back. I swirl the swab around my left nostril fifteen times. Then my right nostril. When I'm done, I move it in circles in the liquid, then carefully place four drops onto the test. I've become an expert at testing myself. I guess the whole world has. At least those of us lucky enough to have access to easy rapid tests.

"Will you test me too?" my dad asks. "I'm going into the office today."

"You want *me* to test you?" I ask.

My dad nods. "You have the most experience. Which means you're the best at it. Experience has to count for something, don't you think?" My dad's gaze is fixed on my mom when he says this.

I pull out another test and tell my dad to lean his head back. It feels really weird to stick the swab up his nose. The power dynamic between us shifts. I could push the swab up to his brain if I wanted to. I could hurt him like he hurt me when I came out to him, and he told me it was a phase and suggested we find a doctor to help me get over it. Like being gay is some curable virus you can test for. But the thing is, I don't want to hurt him. All I want is to be loved and accepted by him. My mom's love is steadier, more reliable. But my dad's love, when it chooses to express itself, makes me feel like a shooting star.

When I'm done swabbing him, the two of us stare at the tests, waiting for the lucky red line, or the unlucky double red lines, to appear. "You know how much experience I have as a financial adviser?" my dad asks my mom. "Almost two decades."

My mom puts a hand on my dad's shoulder. He flinches a little, but he relaxes when she squeezes him. And I realize that maybe he wants the same thing I want, love and acceptance. "You're a brilliant man," my mom says. "I knew it when I married you. And I know it now."

"Thank you," he says softly.

Fifteen minutes later, both our tests negative, we head

our separate ways, to our separate lives. My dad back to an office he hasn't been to in a year and a half. Me to a school I'm just getting used to.

On our walk to school, Bodie and I quiz each other for our first science test of the year. Science is the one subject we both struggle with the most, and we've vowed to master it together. Bodie being Bodie, he woke up early and prepared note cards for us. Holding one up, I read, "How much of the earth's surface is covered by water?"

"That one's easy. Seventy-one percent. You want to know my trick for remembering that?" he asks. When Bodie asks if you want the answer to a question, he's usually going to answer it anyway. "Über-hottie Murray Bartlett was born in 1971, and he's a Pisces, which is a water sign. Seventy-one percent water."

"You have a truly strange mind, Bodie," I say, smiling at him. But it's more than strange, it's incredible. Were it not for Bodie, I likely never would've come out to my parents. He's the brave one. The outspoken one. He's the one who decided we'd come out on the same Sunday morning, first to our moms so they could lay the groundwork before telling our dads. Both our moms begged us never to tell the dads, but Bodie wouldn't stand for that. He chose another Sunday morning for us to come out to our dads, so they could commiserate about their queer sons together that night at their card game. Bodie's dad said he didn't care if he was gay as long as he went to law school. My dad told me electroshock therapy was safer than people thought. But that's all in the past now.

"Okay, I'll ask you one. Did humans and dinosaurs ever exist at the same time?" he asks.

I shake my head. "These are easy ones."

"It's the first quiz of the year. We're not going to be asked to cure cancer."

"Yet," I say.

"How can we be sure what dinosaurs looked like?" Bodie asks.

"What do you mean? Fossils."

We reach the steps to school. Crowds of our fellow students pour in. "No, I know we reconstructed dinosaurs using fossils. But think about it. Let's say in millions of years, human beings are extinct—"

"Jesus, Bodie, can we not go there in the middle of a global pandemic?" I plead.

"All pandemics are global," he reminds me. "It's kind of baked into the definition."

"Yeah, I wish I didn't know that, but I do."

"Just hear me out, okay? We're in some future world. Humans have become extinct, and some new form of sentient beings find fossils of us. They reconstruct human beings based on those fossils, right? But, like, how can they know what we *really* looked like based on those fossils? And what would the humans they reconstruct even look like? Would they look like Beyoncé or Vladimir Putin?"

I laugh. "Why are those the only options?"

"I just picked the best and worst of current humanity to prove my point, which is that maybe dinosaurs had just as much variety in what they looked like as we do. Like dogs."

"Dogs?" I echo. "You're telling me every poodle doesn't look like every other poodle, and every golden retriever doesn't look like every other golden retriever?"

"Every dog looks different," Bodie argues. "How else would they start looking like their owners over time? I swear Gaga and her dog Koji look exactly alike."

"You're truly absurd." I laugh.

"Okay, look at that dog across the street." Bodie points to the same dog I saw lick Ash's face that morning not long ago. "On the count of three, we'll each say what celebrity the dog looks like. Ready?"

"Not at all," I say.

"Well, get ready, 'cause ONE. TWO. THREE." At the count of three, he says Angelina Jolie and I say Scooby-Doo. Bodie looks annoyed by my answer. "First of all," he says, "Scooby-Doo is a cartoon, not a celebrity. And also, he's a Great Dane and that dog is some kind of German shepherd mutt. We're playing this game again. Maybe at a dog park." This is what life as Bodie's best friend is like. We don't play games designed by other people. We make up our own games, with our own rules. When we were kids in Toronto, we turned the long basement hallway of his apartment building into the setting for a game called Otnorot, which was basically backwards dodgeball with Frisbees and blindfolds. Nobody ever won or lost that game. The point wasn't even to compete, because Bodie and I don't compete with each other. We do with the rest of the world, but when we're together, I know I'll always be a winner.

We throw our masks on our faces as we enter the threshold from safe outdoors to the aerosol-full indoors, and the fun ends. We head to our lockers to start the day, and when I open mine, a thick piece of paper flies out and lands on the floor. Bodie leans down to pick it up. One knee on the ground, he hands it to me.

"What is it?" I ask.

"How would I know?" He stares at it for a moment. "It's from him, isn't it?" He stands up and hands me the paper. We both look at it together. It's a colorful drawing of a pink sunset, just like the one I saw yesterday. That's why he asked me my favorite color. Scribbled into the sky are words inside the clouds. As I follow the path of the letters, I realize they're the lyrics to "God Knows I Tried," slightly altered to include the color pink.

Sometimes I wake up in the morning to pink, blue, and yellow skies.

At the end of the hall, I see Ash, watching me. He waves. I wish he could see how big I'm smiling.

"Kam, you're not . . . into him, are you?" I don't respond. I know Bodie won't like the answer. "We both agreed not to let boys distract us from our goals." I never agreed to that. I just stayed silent. "It's just . . . he's really strange. And old."

"Oh my God, you just called Murray Bartlett an

über-hottie and he was born in 1971!"

"See, you remembered," he says with a smile. "All I'm saying is that Ash is a senior and you're a freshman. It's creepy."

"Well, he's the youngest senior and I'm the oldest freshman. Technically a week older than you."

"Still creepy. And people think he's weird."

"Since when do you care what *people* think?" I ask aggressively.

"Yeah, no, I don't. But I'm just looking out for you. That's why I asked a few people about him last night."

"What people?" I ask.

"That's not important," he says. "But no one knows why he transferred here this year. And don't tell me starting a new school your senior year isn't suspicious."

"*Suspicious?*" I echo. "What's your suspicion?"

"I don't know." He lets the silence linger, waiting for me to voice my own reservations. When I don't, he says, "Maybe he got expelled from some other school."

"So what if he did?" I ask. "That doesn't make him some horrible person."

"It could make him a bad influence on you," he says.

"Right, because I'm not strong enough to be my own person." I feel my body tense, because I suddenly realize how much I've been influenced by Bodie all these years. Maybe the reason I've never dated anyone is simply because I've been following Bodie's lead like I always do, writing guys off before I can even get to know them.

"That's not what I meant," Bodie says apologetically. His eyes travel to the drawing Ash made for me. "It's a cool drawing, though," he acknowledges. "He's talented."

"Yeah, it's a cool drawing." Ash disappears into his homeroom. I place the drawing in a folder in my backpack, careful not to crease it in any way. The burst of pink fills me with joy. I love that it's not a sunset like I thought it was. Of course it's not. A sunset is the end of something. It's the sunrise of a beautiful morning. A new beginning.

JUNIOR YEAR

"Kamran, get out of bed. Farbod is here!" My mom's voice is so loud that it cuts through the sound of Ash speaking to me through my headphones. I've spent the morning watching videos of him, wishing I could capture him one more time.

Ash's face in blurry close-up: "I love you, I love you, I love you."

A low-angle shot of Ash blowing out the swaying flame of a candle: "No more candle in the wind, baby."

A frenetic tracking shot of Ash climbing a huge, ancient-looking tree: "I want to know what it feels like to be a tree. Kam, can you imagine what this tree has seen?"

An extreme close-up of Ash's thin fingers covering his face: "Okay, stop filming me now. These moments belong to us, not to some tech company. Our relationship isn't data. I mean it, Kam. Stop or I'll say goodbye."

"KAMRAN!" my mom yells louder. My mom is so contradictory sometimes. When my dad was still living with us, she hated how he would scream at me across the house. But now that he's gone, she does it all the time.

"I'M AWAKE!" I yell back. "BE RIGHT DOWN."

I watch one more video. A wide shot of Ash in Joshua Tree, his face lit by the desert sun: "Solitude is the ultimate luxury."

I close the video. Take my headphones off. I can hear my mom speaking in Persian to Bodie and his mom downstairs. I'm not surprised Bodie's mom is here. She usually picks my mom up on Sundays, which is their busiest workday. Sunday is the day they host open houses for the properties they're trying to sell. But Bodie usually sleeps in on Sundays, and it's still early. My mom forces some barbari on him, then pleads with him to get through to me before I destroy my future.

I want to drown them out and go back in time, to Ash and me staring at those red and black rocks, promising each other we'd be together for eight million years.

"Kamran, hurry up!" My mom's impatient authority is one of the few constants in my life, always telling me what to do and inspiring me to do it immediately. She and Bodie keep me on track. Like coconspirators, they do everything in their limited power to keep me going, moving, surviving. I can hear them conspiring right now.

"I'm coming!" I yell. I figure I have at least five minutes before anyone barges into my room, but nope, they invade together. All three of them. My mom opens the curtains. Sunlight streams in through the leaves and branches of the humongous ficus that has practically become a part of our house. When we bought the house, my mom wanted to tear the tree down. She said it looked like a monster. My dad loved the tree, though. He said it made him feel safe. Cocooned. When they did the required inspections on the house, my dad was proven right. An arborist said the tree's roots made the house exceptionally safe in an earthquake. She also said the roots were now a part of the home's foundation. Cut the tree down and the house would fall down alongside it. The natural world had fused itself to the created world.

"Hi, everyone," I croak out as I rub my eyes and look at them. My mom and Bodie's mom are all dolled up for their showings. Bodie looks like he's dressed to go out. He's wearing one of his nice cashmere cardigans with suede elbow patches. His dad wears the same exact style.

"What do you think?" my mom asks Azam.

Bodie's mom looks around my room like she's seeing it for the first time. I guess it has been a while since she's seen it. My room is my sanctuary. No one enters except my mom and Bodie. Azam looks at the drawings I've taped onto all four of my walls. "Well, these are . . . a little disturbing," she says softly. "We might want to consider removing them."

"I'm sorry, what's going on here?" I ask. "Are we painting the walls?"

Bodie shrugs. He's just as lost as I am.

My mom sits at the edge of my bed and brushes my hair with her long red nails. "Nothing is going on. I'm just thinking of selling—"

Before she can finish, I say, "What? No!"

My mom squeezes my hand. "We haven't made any decisions."

"Who's *we*?" I snap. "It's just you making the decision. Dad's gone and you didn't even mention it to me until right now."

"Nothing's happened yet," she says, with a concerned eye toward Bodie's mom. "I'm just considering all our options, and I wanted Azam's professional opinion on what we could list for."

"Why are we getting professional opinions before we've even discussed it?" I ask.

My mom's body collapses out of its usually perfect posture. "Because we need money." I wish I could erase the shame from her voice. I can tell she blames herself for our situation, even if she'd never admit to it. If I didn't feel so bad for her in this moment, I'd point out that we need my dad's permission to sell the house. But then I wonder if she's already discussed it with him.

Azam looks down at my dirty carpet as she says, "Maybe Farbod and I should give you two a little time."

I hop out of bed. "No, it's fine. I have to get ready anyway. I'm going to a tennis match with Ash's parents today. You know, the guy who made all these *disturbing* drawings."

Azam whispers an "I'm sorry" and my mom absolves her

with a quick look. I want them all out of my room immediately. They feel like invaders as they eye me with pity. Even Bodie looks concerned as he gazes from me to the new drawing we found in the library, now taped above my bed. Concern is the worst expression of all. I'd rather have people's scorn. It's easier to hate other people for thinking I'm evil than to hate myself for causing people I love to worry.

"There's barbari downstairs," my mom says, like bread can make everything better.

"I'll be right down," I say, pulling the sheets tight to my chest.

My mom grimaces when she sees my bare foot pop out from under my crumpled sheets. We used to send the sheets out to be ironed, but that was back when my dad was around and we were a two-income household. She can't help saying, "Your toenails look like they haven't been cut in months. I can—"

"I'm seventeen, I can take care of myself." I yank my feet up so they're under the covers again, embarrassed by how disheveled I am. Even more embarrassed by how my mom just infantilized me in front of Bodie and his mom. Bodie's mom has her issues, sure, but she doesn't offer to clip his nails for him in front of other people.

"Of course you can. I'm sorry." She speaks the words, but she doesn't believe them. "And I won't flunk out of school," I assure her. "I'm getting by. You don't have to keep begging Bodie to fix me. You can just . . . trust me, okay?"

"Of course I trust you." But she's lying. Why would

she trust me when I've done nothing but hide from her? Then again, she's the one who taught me how to hide my emotions, bottle them up, pour them obsessively into achievement, goals, grades.

"Please give me a few minutes," I beg.

My mom raises her hands up in surrender. "Message received," she says with a smile.

The moms leave, but Bodie lingers behind. "Want me to cut your toenails for you?" he asks.

I say, "Asshole," before breaking into a smile.

Bodie reaches under the covers for my feet. "Give me those dirty feet right now," he demands.

His fingers tickle me as they worm their way across the soles of my feet and up to my toenails. "Ouch," he says, feigning hurt. "Those are sharp."

"Stop making me laugh when I'm annoyed," I say.

"Stop being annoyed," he counters.

"Easier said than done."

He digs his fingers into my arches. I feel my feet tense in response. "What are you doing?"

"Giving you a foot massage to chill you out." He closes his eyes and digs deeper. The pain quickly turns to pleasure as some of the tension releases. "I learned how to give a foot massage from that guy I hooked up with once in junior high."

"*That guy?*" I laugh. "You don't remember his name?"

He smiles. "Of course I do. Paul Thompson. He had really flat feet so his mom used to give him foot massages when he was a kid, and then he gave me one when we hung out that one time."

"You never told me that," I say quietly. "You just said it was horrible."

"It *was* horrible," he says. "We had no chemistry. Now shut up and let me do my job."

He moves from my right to my left foot. We don't speak as he digs his knuckles into my knotty arches and soles. The warmth of his skin relaxes me. When he's done, he squeezes himself next to me on my small bed. I move over to make room for his height and his width. His feet dangle off the mattress. We might have started out at the same exact birth weight, but now he's so much taller than me.

"Did you know my mom was thinking of selling the house?" I ask in a hush.

"I swear I didn't," he says, his tone serious. "I obviously would've told you. I know how much this place means to you. I know this room is where—"

I cut him off. "Yeah, I know you know." Sometimes, I can finish Bodie's sentences and thoughts for him. He was going to say this is the room where I lost my virginity to Ash. The room where Ash first said he loved me, and where I didn't say it back.

I can't relive all that right now. "I need to shower," I say, hopping out of bed.

He moves to the center of the mattress, the memory foam molding itself to accommodate his body just like it once did for Ash. He props himself up so his head rests on the new drawing Ash made for me. "I got a ticket for the match," he announces. "I'm coming with you. If you're going to ask his parents about Joshua Tree, you'll need some support."

"Bodie, you don't have to do that."

"I know I don't have to," he says. "But I want to."

"Okay. Then thanks." I stand by the door, waiting for him to leave. When he doesn't move, I say, "Bodie, I have to shower now. I need some privacy."

"Right, sorry, see you downstairs." When he's gone, I take off the shorts and T-shirt I slept in and throw them into my overfull hamper. Laundry is one of my chores, and I've been behind on chores for two years now.

When I head down to the kitchen, they're all eating bread with fresh herbs and Persian cheese.

"I'll never understand why people spend so much to live in a place that will be underwater in our lifetime," Bodie says as he reads a flyer for the Malibu house they're showing today.

"Please don't say that to our clients," my mom says with a laugh. "Besides, Malibu might be underwater in your and Kam's lifetime, but not in mine."

"Stop being so pessimistic." I grab some bread and cream cheese from the fridge. "You're still young."

"Cream cheese?" Azam asks. "On barbari?"

"Fusion!" Bodie declares. We all laugh, so Bodie takes the opportunity to push a little further. "Maybe I'll open a Persian fusion restaurant someday. Has anyone ever done that?"

"No, because Persian food is perfect just the way it is," Azam says firmly.

"Maybe I want to be imperfect," Bodie replies.

Azam rolls her eyes. "Anyway, cooking is just a hobby for you."

Bodie throws me a look of profound exasperation, and I offer him all the support I can without saying something that will add to the tension.

Thankfully, my mom cuts in. "I think Malibu will never sink. My prediction is that the future is brighter than we think it will be." The way her gaze is fixed on me tells me we're not talking about climate change anymore. This is how my mom approaches the subject of the missing men in our lives. Through coded messages. She shakes her perfectly coiffed hair. Even at our lowest, when I was mute with grief, when my dad was wild with rage, she kept her hair meticulous, her lashes curled, her eyes on the prize, which to her is enough money to keep us afloat and send me to college. That's who she is. A woman who never gives up, not on herself, not on me, and definitely not on the future. She'll sell our house if that's what she has to do to get me the education she thinks I need.

"Your *prediction*?" I echo. "Are you a fortune teller now?"

She catches my despondent gaze and meets it with fire. "You'll see. Maybe the tech people will find a way to save the oceans and the planet and the—"

I shake my head. "Technology caused climate change. How can the problem also be the solution?"

"Humans have fixed the unfixable before," my mom argues. "And we can do it again."

We both look toward the door at the same time, like my unfixable dad might just appear in the doorway.

"I don't think human hubris is getting us out of a changing planet," I say.

"Hubris?" My mom speaks English incredibly well, though there are moments—when she slips and pronounces a *w* as a *v*, when she doesn't know a word like *hubris*—that I'm reminded she's not a native English speaker like me.

"It means . . ." I remember Ash telling me what it meant. "It means an excess of pride or confidence. It tends to get people into trouble."

My mom shrugs. "Maybe our excess of pride and confidence is exactly why humans have gotten to where we are, both the good and the bad. In any case, we can't see the future so let's not argue about it."

Bodie leans in. "Maybe we can't *see* the future, but aren't we the ones who create the future?"

"Yes we are," his mom says. "That's a beautiful way to put it, Farbod joon."

"I'm so glad you agree, Mom." The smile on Bodie's face is boastful as he adds, "Then you no doubt agree that everyone should get to create their own future."

"Of course," she says, unaware she's stepping directly into his verbal trap.

Bodie smiles. "We're on the same page, then. If I don't want law school in my future, so be it. And if I want to take a gap year with Kam—"

"What is a gap year?" Azam asks, like she's talking about something shameful.

Bodie rolls his eyes. "It's a year off to explore the world, work, figure out who you want to be—"

Azam laughs. "A year off? Did I get a year off from building our life? A year off from being your mother?"

Bodie shakes his head at her overdramatic reaction. "I'm not asking for a year off from being your son. I'm just saying I want to take time to travel, work in restaurants around the world to learn from lived experience, and then go to culinary school."

"*Culinary* school?" Azam's eyes narrow. "Don't you dare say a word about this to your father. It will break his heart."

Bodie turns to me. I want to find the right words to support him, but all I'm thinking is that if Bodie's dad's heart hasn't been broken yet, he's a very lucky man.

"This gap year isn't a serious idea, is it?" my mom asks, her eyes on me.

I shrug, trying to downplay it. "We're still juniors. We have time to think about it. Besides, if me and Bodie get jobs in restaurants, I can send money home to help."

"Aziz joon, why would you work in a restaurant? You don't even like cooking." My mom's steely gaze challenges me to contradict her. She's right, of course.

"All I'm saying is that if I help out a little and if I don't use the money you saved for my college tuition, then maybe we won't have to sell the—"

She waves a hand in the air to cut me off. "You're going to college if I have to sell everything I own."

"And so are you, Farbod," Azam adds firmly. "We didn't move so you could give up on the American dream. You're both going to college and you're both becoming American citizens when you turn eighteen."

I let out an anxious chuckle. "I don't know that I want to be a citizen of this country."

"What?! Why wouldn't you want to be a citizen?" my mom asks. "You live here. You'll be working here."

"I just don't know if I *feel* American," I say.

"Personally, I can't wait to vote against fascists," Bodie says.

His mom pushes her chair back and stands up to indicate it's time to go. "If only you knew what life was like under actual fascism, perhaps you wouldn't be so willing to throw your future away to make Persian enchiladas."

My mom tousles my hair. I know she's thinking I need a haircut. "Turn the alarm on and lock up when you leave, okay?"

"Don't worry," I say, knowing full well she'll be worrying. It's not like she can't check the status of our home alarm and door locks on her phone. My mom loves tracking everything. I wonder if she can still track my dad's location. Maybe he finally feels free without us.

As the moms leave, Bodie yells out, "Admit Persian enchiladas sound delicious!"

* * *

Bodie drives aggressively toward the UCLA campus in his dad's car. As he does, he replays the conversation with his mom, analyzing its every nuance.

"Bodie, we're not in a rush," I say as he swerves from one lane to another.

"All things considered, it wasn't the worst way to float the idea of a gap year past the moms, right?" he asks.

"What is this gap year?" I ask, trying my best to nail an impersonation of his mom.

Bodie laughs, then sighs. "Well, at least now they understand the concept, and they have almost two years to get used to the idea."

"Yeah, sure," I say. "But we both know your dad's going to be the real problem. He wants you to follow in his footsteps."

"By representing drunk drivers in court?" He honks loudly at the guy stopped at a green light in front of us. "GET OFF YOUR CELL PHONE, ASSBRAIN!"

"Breathe, Bodie," I suggest calmly.

"You know what really bothers me?" He thankfully slows down the car as he accelerates his words. "That following-in-his-footsteps means picking-the-same-exact-job. Not, like, making my own choices the way he did, you know."

The rest of the ride is more of the same. Bodie ranting against his parents while taking time to also curse out other drivers, who all seem to be on their phones.

When Bodie and I get to the college courts, I text Ash's

mom to ask where they're sitting. We push past rows of students and families until I see his parents from the back. It's been months since I've seen his family, and my heart skips a beat because his dad's long red hair, pulled into a ponytail, looks exactly like Ash's hair from the back. "KAM!" Mrs. Greene yells over the commotion as she waves her arms up in the air.

"Hey!" I lead the way toward them, and Bodie follows. Mrs. Greene hugs me first. I let myself melt into her arms. Into the familiar scent of the Greene home on her clothes and in her hair. Mr. Greene pulls me into one of those hugs that start with a firm handshake before morphing into a tight embrace. "Is there room for Bodie?" I ask. "He decided to join."

Mrs. Greene offers her hand to Bodie. "Yes, of course. So you're the famous Bodie." I suddenly realize Bodie has never met Ash's family. It's hard to believe, but it also makes perfect sense. For the months I had with Ash, I became an expert at keeping him and Bodie apart.

"I'm definitely Bodie, but if I'm famous, I'm not sure what for." Bodie shakes her hand, then shakes Mr. Greene's. "It's really nice to meet you both and, um . . ." I sense Bodie's hesitation. He feels he should say he's sorry about their son, but he isn't sure how to say it. If he says he's sorry for their loss, it's like saying Ash is dead. If he says he loved Ash, he'd be lying. I can almost hear the spinning wheels of his brain.

Before Bodie can say any more, a ridiculously tall,

annoyingly hot guy stands up. "You can take my mom's seat. She can't make it," the guy says. He looks our age, but he has a very deep voice. He looks like the living embodiment of the California surfer ideal. Shoulder-length blond hair. Sickeningly broad shoulders. Golden skin. He wears shorts even though it's November, like he can't go a day without blessing the world with his toned calves.

"Kam. Bodie. This is Louis. His brother is Dawn's mixed doubles partner. He came in from Long Beach for the match."

"Oh, you're from Long Beach," I say. "Did you know that there's a tunnel under Ocean Boulevard?"

Louis looks confused by me. "I mean, yeah, of course. I think everyone from Long Beach knows that."

"Ignore him," Bodie says. "He thinks the whole world can speak in Lana Del Rey code."

"Oh, right, she's obsessed with Long Beach, isn't she?" Louis says. "So random. Most of us want to escape the place and she glamorizes it."

Bodie laughs. "She's hard at work on her follow-up, *Did You Know That There's a Dog Park in San Bernadino?*"

Louis smiles. "*Did You Know That There's a Pumpkin Patch in Fresno?*"

I feel oddly defensive. "She sees beauty where others don't," I explain.

"Please don't get him going on Lana. He'll never stop. Trust me." Now it feels like Bodie is putting me down to ingratiate himself to Louis.

82

"Should I trust you?" Louis asks flirtatiously. "I mean, we just met."

Bodie smiles impishly. "I don't know, maybe ask my best friend."

Louis turns his gaze to me. My face feels flush. "Yeah, I mean, Bodie's the best," I say, tamping down my annoyance at how he was just making fun of me.

"See, I'm the best." Bodie offers Louis his hand.

Louis hesitates before touching Bodie. "Full disclosure, my mom has COVID. She's on day nine and I've been testing myself every day and I've remained negative. But if you don't want to shake my hand, I totally understand. No, you know what, don't shake my hand. Not that hand-shaking is how you get it. But still, it's a gross habit. And so impersonal. At least hugging feels good." Louis finally takes a breath.

"Bring it in, then," Bodie says with open arms and his most charismatic smile. Louis gives Bodie a strong hug. They seem to fit together perfectly, like magnets. When they let go of each other, Bodie softly says, "I'm sorry about your mom. Is she okay?"

Louis nods. "She had two bad days, but she's much better now. Thank God for vaccines."

"Amen to that," Mr. Greene says. "If it weren't for the brilliant scientists who worked so hard, this would've been so much worse."

"Let's talk about something else," Mrs. Greene says anxiously.

Mr. Greene puts an arm around his wife. "One of her clients just died," he explains. Mrs. Greene shakes her head. "She was old and had underlying conditions, but still . . ."

None of us say anything. Eventually, Mrs. Greene keeps going. "People love to say the pandemic is over, but it's not. If we don't protect the most vulnerable among us, then who are we?"

"We're assholes," Bodie says. "Humans have always been assholes. It's the defining characteristic of our species." That gets a laugh from everyone.

"On that note, let's sit and talk about something more upbeat," Mrs. Greene says. "I can't take any more sadness." As I sit, I wonder how I can tell them I'm thinking of going back to the desert. If she can't handle thinking of losing one of her clients, how will she take being reminded of her missing son?

Mr. Greene sits on the aisle, next to Mrs. Greene. I sit next to her, then Bodie, then Louis at the end. Bodie and Louis both have absurdly long legs that barely fit in the tight bleacher seats.

"Let's talk about tennis," Mr. Greene suggests. "Who's excited to see Dawn and Nick whoop some ass on that court?"

"Is this a safe space for controversial opinions?" Bodie asks.

Louis very quickly says, "Depends on the opinion."

Bodie smiles. "I'm not sure I get tennis."

Louis laughs. "I can teach you the rules."

Bodie and Louis are having their own private conversation now, their faces turned toward each other. We're just spectators. "No, I know the rules. I just don't get why people love it. Like, with team sports, the dynamic between the players is what makes it all so exciting. But tennis isn't like that."

"Sure it is. Dawn and my brother are a team. They've got big-time chemistry. You'll be excited when they win. You'll see." Quietly, Louis adds, "Tennis also has the hottest players out there. I mean, if watching Berrettini take his shirt off after a match doesn't get you into the sport, nothing will."

Bodie sits up a little straighter. I know Bodie too well. He was wondering if Louis is gay, and now he has his answer.

Bodie flirts back. "I don't know, dude," he says. I give him a look when he uses the word *dude*, which is not usually in his vocabulary. "I would argue that soccer has the hottest players out there. I'm especially proud of the physical perfection of the Iranian team."

With a smile, Louis nods. "No arguments from me there. Who doesn't love a hot Iranian?"

The Greenes can't hear Louis and Bodie over the voices of the crowds. I'm the only one close enough to catch the cringe of their conversation.

When the players come out, the crowd begins to cheer. Dawn's opponents come out first, and a big group of people sitting behind us cheer for them. Then Dawn and Louis's brother Nick walk onto the court and accept their applause. Dawn looks even more like her mom than she used to. It's like she's the keeper of her mother's genes, and Ash was the keeper of his father's.

The crowd quiets down when the match begins. Dawn serves first. The match is exciting.

The score is close, the points dramatic. But it's hard for me to focus on the game when Louis and Bodie won't stop chatting next to me. "Okay, a tennis court is kind of like a courtroom," Bodie says to Louis. "Like, each side has to make their argument over and over and over again until one side comes out on top."

"Or on bottom," Louis responds with a smile.

"Well, the world needs tops *and* bottoms," Bodie says. I've never heard him be so obvious about his interest in someone before. It makes me deeply uncomfortable.

Bodie and Louis make small talk between points. When Louis tells Bodie about his TikTok dance videos, Bodie lights up. "Wait!" he says as he pulls out his phone and scans through his videos. "That was you in the video where you're dancing to 'American Teenager' with a Marjorie Taylor Greene mask on your head! I watched that so many times." I remember that video too. Bodie showed it to me. He thought it was hilarious, and a perfect fuck-you to the ultra-right-wing's anti-trans policies.

"Yeah, that was me." I'm impressed despite myself. That video was genuinely cool and smart. Maybe he is worthy of my best friend. I tell myself I won't do what Bodie did to me when he wouldn't support my relationship with Ash. I can tell Bodie is into this guy, and I'll support him.

After Dawn and Nick lose the match and graciously congratulate their opponents, the Greenes invite us all to an early dinner at their place. Louis turns toward us. "I have a car, if you guys need a ride."

I glance toward Bodie. I can tell he's tempted to ditch his dad's car in the UCLA parking lot so he can ride with Louis and get a peek at his car to see if there are any deal-breakers in there. "That's really nice of you, but I shouldn't leave my car here. We'll see you soon."

When Bodie drives us out of the parking lot, he opens up Spotify and turns on Lana. "I'm sorry about what I said about you going on and on about Lana. As penance, I will play her for you on the ride there."

A minute later, I turn "Born to Die" off.

"Hey, I actually love that song," Bodie protests. "It's one of the few songs she's made with a beat."

"She doesn't need a musical beat because her heart beats through every song she's ever recorded," I say.

Bodie rolls his eyes. He doesn't know I skipped the song because I'm too superstitious to listen to a song called "Born to Die" while I'm searching for Ash.

"Hey, Bodie . . . ," I say, unsure how to begin the

conversation I want to have.

"Yeah?" He brakes fast when he sees a barely visible stop sign peeking out from behind a wild branch. Bodie pushes a protective arm into my chest when he brakes. I feel a rush of love for my best friend.

"I think you should ask Louis out," I suggest quietly.

He quickly places his hand back on the steering wheel. "Really?"

"What do you mean, *really*? He's beautiful and smart."

"Yeah, I mean, I agree. He seems great, but . . ." For the first time in his life, he can't think of a deal-breaker.

"I mean, he lives in Long Beach and you hate traffic, but so far, can you think of one other red flag? The guy seems amazing and he's clearly into you, and you were obviously into him too."

"No, I mean, I was, but . . ."

"But what?" I ask.

"He's a senior. I'm a junior."

I can't help but laugh. "Bodie, that's a *one-year* age difference. You're really reaching for a problem here."

"I just meant that next year, he'll be in college. He'll probably move even farther away. Why would I set myself up for heartbreak?"

"What's the cliché?" I ask. "Better to have loved and lost than never to have loved at all . . ."

My words, and my loss, linger in the air between us.

"Do you think he's the one for me?" he counters. "Like, really, truly. Or do you think there's someone better for me out there?" He holds my gaze.

"Like who?" I ask.

He shakes his head. "I don't know . . ."

"What I don't know is why you won't just date someone for more than a day," I say emphatically. "I know you're focused on your goals and all that, but learning how to have a romantic relationship should be a goal too, right?"

"That's an interesting way of looking at it," he says. "Let's think this through—"

"Or let's *not* think it through," I argue. "Let's just follow our hearts. What does your heart want?"

He looks at me with a longing in his eyes I've never seen before. "My heart wants love," he confesses.

"And maybe you found it," I whisper. "But you won't find out if you don't at least try to get to know him. You can't love someone you don't even know."

"That's so true," he says in a quiet voice. There's hesitation in his eyes. "But . . ."

"Another but?" I ask.

"I mean, we only talked for a few minutes," he says.

"I knew I liked Ash after two minutes of talking," I respond. "That's all it takes to know there's potential. And you talked through the *whole* match!"

He smiles. "Yeah, I guess we did. And he didn't say a single thing that annoyed me, which I recognize is shocking given my history." Shaking off the vulnerability, he jokes, "Hey, speaking of butts, did you see his ass?"

I laugh. "I did. It was intimidating."

"It was inviting, is what it was." An impish grin forms on his face.

"See, a match made in heaven." I feel myself tense when I speak the word *heaven*. I don't want to think of heaven, or hell for that matter.

"I guess when I imagined my first love, I never imagined a guy like him," he utters.

"How could you have imagined someone as flawless as that guy?" I ask, and he laughs. "You know I can read your mind, right?"

"Oh, please. You have no idea what goes on inside my fucked-up brain."

I turn toward him. "Yeah, right. I'll give you an example. When Louis offered us a ride, you wanted to say yes, didn't you?" He doesn't deny it. "But then you remembered the insane hourly parking rates, and you realized how pissed your parents would be if you spent sixty dollars on parking just so some cute guy would give you a ride. You thought through all of this in the half a second it took you to say no to his offer."

Bodie's eyes open wide. "Who are you?" He pulls up to the curb outside the Greenes' house and puts the car in park.

The branches of the jacaranda trees are bare, waiting for spring to come to life in otherworldly purple. Ash said they were *the* LA trees, not the palm trees that don't even belong here. I push Ash out of my mind and refocus on Bodie. "I'm your best friend and your own personal mind reader. And

I'm telling you to ask that guy out. He seems . . . perfect. And that's what you deserve. What does my mom always say? Never settle for less than *what*?"

"Perfection," he says with a smile. With a voice laced with drama, he adds, "I do deserve perfection, don't I?"

I pull out my phone and open up TikTok. "Let's watch a few more of his videos to see if we can find something wrong with him," I say. The first video to pop up on the app is Bodie doing a kookoo sabzi cooking tutorial. I can't help but watch the whole thing. Bodie's charisma leaps out of the screen, even if he's backlit. "Okay, what's his handle?"

"I think it's at-longest-beach-bum," Bodie says with certainty. The fact that he remembered it tells me a lot.

I go to Louis's account, and we watch videos of him dancing, surfing, sharing well-researched opinions about everything from pop music to global politics to skin care. By the time Louis and Nick pull up and park behind us, it's become abundantly clear there's nothing wrong and everything right with Louis. We watch as the two brothers knock on the front door, as Mrs. Greene welcomes them in.

"Come on," I say as I put my phone away. "You have a cute guy to flirt with, and I have to ask my boyfriend's parents how they feel about me going back to the place where he disappeared. How fair is that?"

"He's your . . ." Bodie was going to say Ash is my *ex*-boyfriend, but he stopped himself.

He knows I don't think about him as an ex. Not when there's a chance he's alive.

* * *

Dinner conversation begins awkwardly. We dance around the absence of Ash at the table, doing everything we can not to bring him up. Tennis feels like the only safe topic. "Great match," I say.

"Best tennis match I've ever seen," Bodie adds.

"*Only* tennis match he's ever seen," I tease.

Louis laughs, then turns to Bodie. "He didn't even know the rules to tennis when the match started!"

Bodie clearly doesn't mind being ribbed. "Okay, you know that's not true. I knew the rules, I just didn't get why people cared about the game."

Mr. Greene smiles as he changes the subject. "Who can guess the secret ingredient in my vegan loaf?"

Bodie take a bite of the loaf. Eyes closed like a psychic, he begins to list off ingredients. "Lentils. Pine nuts. Onions. Carrots. Shiitake mushrooms. Coriander. Cumin. Garlic. Olive oil." Opening his eyes, Bodie asks, "Which one was the secret ingredient?"

A deeply impressed Mr. Greene says, "Coriander. That was remarkable."

"I want to be a chef," Bodie tells them. "Not that my parents think it's a viable career goal."

"I'm sorry they don't support you," Mrs. Greene says.

Dawn throws a knowing look toward Nick, but stops herself from saying anything. I know that the Greenes don't support her dream of being a tennis coach. They feel it would be a waste of her brilliant brain.

"Bodie, you have to do your impressions of your parents when you cook for them." Turning to the others, I add, "Trust me, this is the best."

Bodie turns away from us. When he rolls his head back to face us, his lips are pursed tight just like his mother's. His eyelids look heavy, frozen in a critical squint. "Bodie joon, what is next? Ballet? Sewing? Are you going to knit me a winter hat?"

"What do you think, Mr. Omidi?" I ask, cuing Bodie.

Bodie lets out a gruff noise and crosses his arms. "Kitchens are for old ladies, not young men. Men belong in boxing rings. In courtrooms. In places where we can fight. Where's the fight in cooking?"

Everyone laughs again. The rest of the dinner is dominated by Bodie talking about his dreams. "I want to be more than just a chef," he declares. "I'd like to change the way we eat."

"Sounds like your career goal is to be a food revolutionary," Louis says.

Bodie smiles. "I love that. Bodie Omidi, food revolutionary. That's what my business card will say, if you'll let me use the term."

"It's all yours," Louis says flirtatiously. "Just thank me when you get your first Michelin star."

After dinner, I offer to help Mr. and Mrs. Greene clean the dishes, which gives me an excuse to be alone with them. I stack the plates as Dawn, Nick, Bodie, and Louis head to the living room and plop themselves down on the L-shaped couch. I can't hear them, but I can tell that Bodie is charming them all because they're cracking up.

Whatever he's saying, it inspires Louis to scoot a little closer to him. I feel a twinge of jealousy. His love story is just beginning. Mine is in limbo. I close my eyes and remind myself to be happy for my friend.

When I reach the kitchen, Mr. Greene is placing silverware in the dishwasher and Mrs. Greene is cleaning a pot. "Just put the dishes by the sink," she says.

"Anything else I can do?" I ask.

"If you remember where the plates are, you can put seven dessert plates on the table," Mr. Greene suggests.

Seven. An odd number. If Ash were here, we'd be even. "Of course I remember." I reach for the dessert plates and count them, but I don't move. I have to ask them now. "Mrs. Greene. Mr. Greene." I take a breath. This is harder than I thought.

"Come on, Kam," he says. "You know you can call us Beau and Diana."

"Right. Beau. Diana." I try to sound as calm as possible, though my hands are practically shaking. "I need to ask you something. It's not easy . . ." I trail off, but they stay quiet as they eye each other, wondering what's coming. "The thing is, every year, our school's GSA takes a school trip, and it's really special." I look out to the living room, where Louis and Bodie sit even closer to each other now. "Anyway, this year, the GSA . . . Well, they're going to Joshua Tree."

The Greenes hold each other's gazes for what feels like

an interminable moment. They seem to be having some silent conversation with each other. "You're thinking of going," Mr. Greene says. It's less a question than a statement of fact.

"Maybe, I mean, I don't know." I put the plates down because I suddenly feel too weak to hold seven tiny dessert plates. "What I really mean is . . . I won't go if you think it's a bad idea. I want your blessing, I guess." In my romantic fantasies, I imagined proposing to Ash someday.

Asking for his parents' permission first. That's the blessing I wanted. Not this.

Mrs. Greene puts the pot down and moves close to me. She takes my hand and squeezes it. "Kam . . . we would never stop you from living your life in whatever way you choose."

"I know." Her hand is still warm from the hot water. "But this isn't just my life. It's your grief. And my grief too, I guess. And I also, well, you're a therapist. I wonder if maybe, I don't know, going back could be good for me. Healing or something."

She pauses and then says, "Everyone grieves in their own way. What helps one person might not help another."

"Yeah, I get that." She's treating me like one of her clients. Ash said she would do that to him and his sister. It bothered him sometimes—and bothers Dawn all the time. "It's just . . . I don't want my way of grieving to cause you any pain."

"Sweetie . . ." She shakes her head like she's unsure she

should say this next part, but she does. "Nothing you could do could ever cause our family any more pain than we've already known." That's when Mr. Greene puts his left arm around her, and his right hand on my shoulder.

I quietly accept the truth in her words, the narcissism of me thinking that going back to that desert would have any impact on her. And yet, I know that she would never go back there. Not anymore. Not once it became clear that all the police officers, local volunteers, posters, phone calls, rewards, search dogs, and helicopters couldn't help find him. On the one-year anniversary of Ash's disappearance, Mr. and Mrs. Greene donated all their camping gear. They moved on. They haven't forgotten him, but they don't believe he's coming back like I do. I want to reach the stage of grief they've reached. Maybe I should follow their lead and stop searching for him. "Can I see the portfolio books again?" I ask.

"Kam, why?" The misty look in her eyes tells me everything I need to know. She doesn't want to live in the past.

"I thought maybe, if I could see those last drawings, the ones that were found, it would help me decide . . . if going back is a good idea, or . . ."

She has a haunted look in her eyes now. I know she doesn't want to go back to that emotional state again. Maybe that's why she's stored Ash's art on the highest, deepest shelf of their bedroom closet.

"Mrs. Greene, I know you want to forget—"

Her expression changes. A flicker of anger passes

through her face. "I never want to forget. I never *will* forget. I want to . . ." She takes a breath. "Accept. I want to accept. I have to . . . I have had to . . . practice what I preach."

"I'm sorry, that was a bad choice of words. I know you'll never forget Ash." She closes her eyes when I say his name, like she's saying a silent prayer.

"I've grieved." Her eyes are still closed. She's still with us, but she's also somewhere else. Somewhere deep and private, a place inside her that I feel terrible for invading.

I know she's grieved because I've seen her go through all five stages of it. Denial came first. She didn't believe anything I said. Didn't believe her son could be gone. Then anger, most of it aimed at me. She used to address me with the composed serenity of what Ash called her "therapist voice." I once asked him if she ever got mad, and he said of course she did, but even then she retained her composure. But when she screamed at me, she was out of control. I can still hear her desperation on the day he went missing, the earsplitting howls no one knew she had in her.

I told you kids not to leave our campground.

How could you be so stupid?

Why didn't you just listen?

And then came bargaining, in her case literal bargaining. All the rewards she offered. The posters she and Mr. Greene and Dawn put up all over the Coachella Valley and handed out to the strangers in the mysterious desert towns north of it that feel stuck in time, those towns Ash called Westworld.

Depression came next, and lingered longest. And now I suppose, acceptance. "But . . ." I look down and realize my foot is tapping anxiously. I steady myself. "What I meant is that . . . Well, it doesn't matter what I meant, it's just . . . Mrs. Greene—I mean, Diana, I'm so sorry, I didn't want to—"

"Kam, I can't control what you do," she says softly. "Nor do I want to. It's your life. But . . ."

"But?"

"I worry about you, that's all. I think Ash . . ." She closes her eyes and releases a heavy sigh. "He would want you to be happy, to live a full life. He would want you to do well in school and go to a great college and . . . to date someone new. He wouldn't want you chasing his ghost."

I nod because I know she's right. Except he might not be a ghost. He might be alive. And until I'm sure he's not, I can't let go. I won't give up.

"So it won't hurt you, or Mr. Greene, or Dawn, if I do go?" I ask.

She shakes her head. "We're already hurt, Kam. There's nothing you can do to make the pain go away. Live your life. It's precious."

I try to say thanks, but it comes out more like a sob.

She lets go of me and smiles. "We should bring out some tea. Those two sweat so much on the court. They need to hydrate."

"Yeah, good idea," I say. "I can make some."

"Thanks, sweetie." With a decisive nod, she says, "You

know what? You two bring out the dessert and the tea. I'll go get the portfolio books. We can all look at them together. I don't think Nick has ever seen Ash's art." She gives me a bittersweet smile. "Don't feel bad about bringing him up, Kam. Never, ever feel guilt for that. You're one of the only people who loved him as much as we did. That means a lot to us."

It takes me and Mr. Greene less time to serve up homemade lemon bars and ginger tea than it takes Mrs. Greene to grab some portfolio books. My gaze travels around the room. Photos of him are everywhere. Baby Ash. Toddler Ash. And of course, the Ash I knew. They don't want to forget him. Of course they don't. They just refuse to spend their days and nights like me, asking questions that can't be answered. Living in a constant state of longing.

"Here we go." I look over and there she is, holding a stack of portfolio books. "I thought, since Ash isn't here with us tonight, we could include him by showing Nick and Louis his art."

Dawn stands up in shock. She moves close to her mom with a tremulous smile on her face. "That's such a good idea, Mom." Turning to Nick and Louis, she says, "My brother was kind of a creative genius. He made art and then he layered poetry into the imagery."

I feel myself flinching at the way she talks about Ash in the past tense. But then, everyone talks about him like he's gone.

We all huddle around the portfolio books as Mrs. Greene turns the pages. Nick and Louis ask questions about his style, and Mr. Greene reads one of Ash's poems out loud. When Mrs. Greene reaches the end of the last book, revealing the final drawings Ash made, the ones that were recovered from the park, I feel my heart race out of my chest. We all searched for him. Searched and searched and then searched some more. He never turned up. But these drawings did. Along with a few other items of his.

His hand-painted sneakers.

The matte-black hairband he used to pull his long red hair back.

And then everyone forgot about him. Everyone but us. The people in this room. The ones who loved him.

There's a quiet reverence in the house as Mrs. Greene shows us his last drawings, torn out of the art journal he brought to the park with him. He said he was always inspired in the desert air. He sketched me, sleeping in the sun. He sketched his parents, gazing up at the sky. He sketched horned lizards and roadrunners and desert tortoises. He showed me everything he was working on, always.

But then there were the things he sketched that I never saw, the things he must have drawn when he was alone.

Trees that look like people, arms outstretched to the sky in desperation.

Rocks that look like monstrous formations, with craters for eyes.

I run my fingers along the plastic that covers a tormented image of a boy with seven arms, each of them the branch of a Joshua tree. His limbs twist around each other. The boy's face isn't visible. He looks up to the sky. Searching for answers. Maybe praying for help from a helicopter, a UFO, God.

I close my eyes at the pain and fear in these images. When these drawings were found, the Greenes were still in their anger phase. The sketches scared them. Whatever happened to Ash, these drawings were undeniable proof that he suffered.

I can still hear their voices, their words, daggers aimed at me. Who else did they have to blame but the last person who saw their son alive, the only one who might have any answers?

What was the last thing he said to you? What was his state of mind?

I turn to Mrs. Greene. "There's a part of me that thinks that if I go back . . . maybe . . . I mean, what if . . ." I realize how awkward this is, having this conversation in front of so many other people, but I can't help it.

She seems to read my thoughts. "It's been two years, Kam. He's gone. You can't survive two years in that desert. A couple of days would be difficult. Two years is . . . it's just not possible."

She closes up the portfolio books. "Okay, that was a beautiful trip down memory lane, but now it's time for Celebrity."

"Oh my God, we're playing Celebrity?" Bodie asks. "It's my favorite game."

"Me too!" Louis squeals brightly. He's really into Bodie. He's not even trying to hide it or play coy.

As Dawn hands out pieces of paper for everyone to write celebrity names on, I think that Mrs. Greene must be right. But then I remember Ash's remains still haven't been found. He could be out there, somewhere. He could be in some awful man's secluded house. Or abducted by aliens. Missing people have come back. And even if he doesn't, if I retrace my steps . . . I could remember something that helps us all find peace. Or maybe it's just me who needs peace. Maybe the Greenes don't need my missing memories that disappeared along with him. Those final moments that could answer everything.

As my mind wanders, we split up into two uneven teams and the game begins. It's Dawn, Nick, and Mr. Greene against me, Louis, Bodie, and Mrs. Greene. Dawn holds a piece of paper. "Oh, okay, I know this one! She's a nepo baby. Well, not really, because she's not famous yet."

"Why is she in the game if she's not famous?" Nick asks. "Isn't the game called Celebrity?"

Dawn speaks quickly. "Okay, wait, I remember. It's Gwyneth Paltrow's baby. Whoever wrote this name is on my shit list. First name is a fruit."

I turn to Bodie, knowing it was him. The grin on his face confirms this.

"Kiwi," Mr. Greene yells out.

"Mango," Nick screams.

"No, a more common fruit."

"Coconut," Mr. Greene says.

"Dad, how is coconut common?" Dawn shrieks.

"Is coconut even a fruit?" Louis asks.

"Don't interrupt if you're not on my team!" Dawn yells, her competitive spirit coming through.

"Major fruit," Nick says. "So are avocados, peppers, and olives."

"And so am I," Bodie yells out.

"And me!" Louis raises his hand.

"Coconuts are common in Thailand," Mr. Greene muses.

"Guys, focus!" Dawn begs.

The timer on Nick's phone rings. "Time!" he yells. "Good thing you're better at tennis than at Celebrity."

Dawn shakes her head. "The name was—"

"Wait, no," Bodie says. "You have to put it back in the bowl."

"Put the fruit back in the bowl," Louis cracks, and everyone laughs, no one louder than Bodie.

Bodie goes first for our team, and as he assumes the position in front of us, I have memories of all our past Celebrity games, mostly played with our parents, who royally suck at the game. I think about the time Bodie tried to get my mom and dad to guess Shawn Mendes, and how much we laughed at the way our parents said *Eh-Shawn* with their Persian accents.

As Bodie rapidly gets Louis to guess every name he picks out of the bowl, the memory of Mrs. Greene's voice rings in my head, frantic, screaming at me, begging me to remember.

Think, Kam, THINK.

"La, la, la, la, la, la, la, la."

Where were you?

"Kylie Minogue!"

What did the rocks look like?

"Forty-Four's oldest daughter."

Did he have water with him? Did he?

"Malia Obama!"

This is your fault.

"Benito."

If you hadn't come, our son would still be alive.

"Mussolini. No, wait, Bad Bunny!"

This is all your fault.

Sometimes, I think the worst moment of my life wasn't the moment I woke up to Ash being gone, but the moment when I was blamed for his disappearance by the only people who loved him more than I did. I don't care how many strangers and classmates think I killed him. But when his parents thought I might have been their son's murderer, it broke me.

"Wow," Dawn says when the game is over. "Bodie and Louis, you guys were really in some kind of mind meld."

"Wait, are you a Trekkie?" Louis asks excitedly.

"Are *you* a Trekkie?" Bodie asks Louis with just a hint of judgment.

"I mean, yeah, kind of."

I can feel the wheels in Bodie's head turn. He doesn't get sci-fi. Watching Star Trek would be like torture for him. He's *finally* found a deal-breaker for Louis. And then he smiles and says, "Cool."

After we've cleaned up the dessert plates and said our thank-yous, Bodie and Louis linger in a corner and exchange information. In another corner, Dawn and Nick are in a heated debate. I can't tell what they're arguing about. The only audible thing I can make out is Nick emphatically saying, "Just tell him."

Tell who? Tell what? I look over at Bodie and Louis, both carefree, their bodies inching closer to each other as they watch something on Bodie's phone. The first thought that crosses my mind is that maybe Louis has a boyfriend, and Nick thinks Dawn should be the one to tell Bodie.

But then Dawn marches across the room. Not to Bodie, but to me. "Hey, Kam, can we talk privately for a minute?" she asks.

"Of course," I say, surprised.

"Let's go outside, maybe?" she asks, already heading to the door. I glance back to Bodie, but he's too wrapped up in Louis to notice me. When we get outside, Dawn seems scared to start. "My parents just told me you're thinking of going back to Joshua Tree."

"Oh," I say, almost relieved this is what she wanted to talk about. "Yeah, I mean, I wanted to ask all three of you to make sure you're okay with it. I'm sorry you weren't there when we discussed it. I won't go if it brings up too much stuff for you, or—"

"Kam, breathe." She puts a hand on each of my tense shoulders. "Thank you, but it's not about hurting me or not hurting me." There's a tear rolling down her cheek. "It's about . . ."

"About what?" I ask. There's a sliver of fear in my voice, scared of what she's going to say.

"Ash was happiest when he was with you," she says.

I feel an ache go through my body. "It was the other way around. I was happiest when I was with him."

"But you don't understand how unhappy he was when he wasn't with you," she continues. "How self-destructive. That's why we never told you. We should have told you. My parents love to say they're all about honesty, but they also love their secrets. And when I call them out on it, they're always like, *The only person you need to practice radical honesty with is yourself*, like that somehow absolves them."

"Dawn, I'm not following," I say.

Dawn shakes her head. Releases a throaty laugh. "Remember when we first met you for dinner and you said something about how Ash hated phones and didn't want a phone or something like that?"

"Yeah." I think back to that moment, wondering why

she's bringing it up now.

"I almost told you then, but my parents stopped me."

"Told me what?" I ask.

"My brother *loved* his phone. My parents are the ones who took it away." She swallows hard.

"But why would he lie to me?" A long silence follows my question.

Dawn finally says, "Because he used it to buy drugs. He was an addict."

"What?" I blurt out. "That doesn't even make sense. I never saw him drink once."

"He took pills."

"No!" I exclaim. "I would have seen him. He never took anything."

"He was good at hiding," she says.

"But we didn't hide anything from each other," I protest. "We—were honest. We were . . ." I trail off when I realize I wasn't honest with him. I hid my dad's addiction, the tumult of my home life.

She continues softly. "Listen, go to the desert if you want to be with your friends. Just don't go looking for answers. I know what happened."

"You don't. You can't. You weren't there."

"I was there so many other times, Kam. I was there when he ODed. I was there when we dropped him off at rehab. I was there when he would sneak out of the house at night. All my life, my brother sucked up all the attention because of his problems and his genius, but I loved him just as much as I resented him. And I knew him in a way you didn't."

"But—"

"Listen to me. Ash probably brought something with him to the desert when you guys went. Maybe he took something that was laced with fentanyl, or maybe he mixed them with some weird desert plant because he glamorized all that hallucination bullshit—"

"NO!" I blurt out too loud. I can't hear any more. I repeat the word like an incantation. "No, no, no, no, no."

"Kam, I'm sorry. I should've told you." She holds back tears.

"Maybe you didn't because deep down, you know it's not true. There's some other explanation. I know there is."

She exhales sadly. "I always wanted to tell you. The thing is, when Ash was alive—"

"He is alive." I see the doubt in her eyes. "He *could* be alive."

"He begged me not to tell you, Kam. Begged all of us not to tell you."

"But—"

"All those times he disappeared . . . Where do you think he was?"

I know the answer to this question. "He was making art. He needed to disappear to get into his creative zones. That's why he loved the desert. That's why—"

"Kam, stop. You're doing what we used to do. Believing a lie because it's easier than the truth. The truth is he isolated himself because that's what addicts do. That's how they hide their addiction."

"But he wasn't isolated. He had me." My voice trembles.

"He did have you." She looks at me with a sad smile. "He loved you so much that he didn't want to scare you away. He couldn't believe that someone as together as you would see anything in him, and he was scared of losing that."

"Together as me? I'm not together. I feel like I've completely fallen apart." My eyes are blurring with unshed tears.

Dawn looks at me sadly. "I really am so sorry, Kam. Maybe if I had told you right away, you never would've gotten so serious. Maybe I could've saved you from falling apart."

"No, no, no," I protest. "You don't understand. I was always broken. *He* was the best thing that happened to *me*." Now my tears are starting to fall. "I can't believe this."

"I used to think he was just a wild creative spirit too. But then the pandemic happened. And that made everything so much worse. Maybe the isolation set him off. I don't know . . . We tried two rehabs—"

"But . . . I would've known if he wasn't in school." I'm doing everything I can to disprove what she's saying.

"You weren't at the same school then. Why do you think he transferred as a senior? Clean slate. No one knew what he'd been through."

"Oh God," I hear myself utter.

"We did family therapy. My mom even took him to some kind of experimental ketamine therapy. Nothing worked. But when he met you, he seemed . . . different. And we convinced ourselves you were the solution we never saw. That's why we never told you. And then . . . when he—"

"Don't say *died*," I beg. "Please don't say that. You don't know, you can't know."

"When he disappeared . . ." Her voice quivers. "My parents, they didn't . . . They couldn't . . . They wouldn't face the most simple explanation. Because that would somehow mean we didn't do enough to stop him, to save him." Dawn closes her eyes.

"But he wasn't . . . ," I stammer, trying to find the words. "He didn't seem *high*," I say. "Not when we were together. Not on that trip to the desert. Never. I promise. If he seemed high, if he did something dangerous, I would've stopped him. I would've told you."

"I know that," she assures me. "But maybe you just missed the signs, like we all did in the beginning."

"What signs?" But even as I'm asking, little moments flood back to me. The pain of him ghosting me. The thrill of being around him when he was *on*. The rush of him when he would give me a mixtape or talk rapidly about his favorite succulents. But then there were the other moments when he was off. Off on his own. Hard to carry on a conversation with. I thought he was just moody. Maybe he was coming down from some high.

"I don't want you suffering forever because of this." She pulls me into a hug. At first, I resist. But when I hear a sob come out of her, I clutch her tight. We weep in each other's arms as my mind races. All this time, Ash and his family hid his addiction from me because they didn't want to scare me away. And for the months I had with Ash, I hid my father's drinking from him because I didn't want to scare him away. All this secrecy. All this shame. Maybe if we had just been honest with each other, he'd still be here.

But then I remember that Ash's body hasn't been found. Maybe he struggled with addiction, but that doesn't mean he's dead. In fact, isn't it more likely someone abducted him if he was high? Or maybe he ran away to hide his addiction from us?

I've never wanted to save him more. I know he's out there, waiting for me to find him. And I know that I didn't give him all the love that was inside me because I lied to him. I held back the worst parts of me from him and he did the same. I need to find him and show him the real me, the complete me.

But when Dawn begs, "Please don't go back there. You'll only torture yourself," I hear myself agreeing with her, promising her I won't go searching for him in the vastness of the desert.

FIRST YEAR

"My place or yours?" Bodie asks when the school bell rings.

"Aren't we baking at your place?" I ask.

"Oh, right. I hope my mom picked up the ingredients we need." Bodie texts his mother as we head out into the hallway.

I see Ash standing at the very end of the hall, like an apparition. He waves to me.

"Ingredients confirmed," Bodie says.

"Actually, can I meet you there?" I ask.

Bodie looks over at Ash, annoyed. "I can wait for you," he offers.

"I mean, yeah. But . . ."

"But you want to be alone with him," he says. "Right. I totally get it. I'm being an idiot."

"Bodie," I say urgently as Ash walks toward us. "Go."

He looks at me with a quick flash of hurt. "Yeah, right.

Just . . ." He doesn't finish, but I know he's thinking I should *just* be careful because Ash is strange and older.

"Where'd your friend run off to?" Ash asks when he reaches me.

"Bodie? He went home and I'll meet up with him. We're gonna bake rainbow cupcakes for the next GSA meeting."

Ash nods. "You like baking?"

"Not really; baking and cooking are Bodie's thing," I explain. "But it's fun being his sous chef."

"What's your thing?" Ash asks with pure curiosity.

"I don't know." I shrug. I wish I was full of passion like Bodie. I'm so afraid of coming across as boring, so I quickly put the spotlight on Ash. "The art you made for me. The sunrise. It's so cool."

"Yeah?" he asks, holding my gaze.

"Yeah," I say. I glance at the clock on the hallway wall. "I have to get to Bodie's soon."

"I can walk you there, if that's of interest to you," he says.

I giggle nervously. "Yeah, that's very of interest to me."

We take our masks off when we head outside. I'm shocked at how happy I feel at the sight of his unmasked face. The unique curl of his lips. The wisps of ginger hair on his cheeks. "Lead the way," he says.

I head down the stairs, loving the sound of his footsteps behind me.

"*I'll follow you into the dark,*" he sings.

I smile. "You weren't at the show where she covered that song, were you?"

He shakes his head. "I mean, I wish, but I don't have the money to go to Denver for a Lana show. I've seen her once at the Hollywood Bowl from the cheapest seats they have. I went with my sister. It was magic. You?"

"Never. And now concerts aren't even a thing anymore."

"Fuck COVID for depriving you of seeing Lana live." We both laugh. I wish Bodie could see that Ash does have a sense of humor.

I try to think of a joke to keep the conversation flowing, but I can't. "It's not far," I say. I look down at his hand-painted shoes, bright yellow on the dark concrete. I remember seeing him paint them in the bathroom.

"I wish it was far. It would give us more time together."

I smile. I wish that too.

"Is Kam your full name or a nickname?" he asks.

"Kamran," I say.

"Kahm-rahn," he repeats deliberately. "That's beautiful."

"When it's pronounced correctly, which it never is."

"Did I butcher it?" he asks.

"No, no, you did good. But I don't have the patience to sound out my name for everyone a hundred times before they learn it. Anyway, my parents call me Kamran, and Bodie's parents too. But pretty much no one else does."

"Do you feel more like Kamran or more like Kam?" he asks.

"I don't know . . ." No one's ever asked me that before. Maybe if someone had, I would have an answer by now.

"So you're close to Bodie's parents too?" He picks up a flattened soda can and holds on to it.

"Oh, yeah. Our parents are best friends. We formed a pod when the pandemic hit with them and some other Persians, mostly so the parents could keep gambling together, honestly."

"That's some real commitment to gaming. The only game we play is Celebrity when we have dinner guests."

"We play with our parents sometimes!" I say, excited to have found a point of connection. "Bodie's so good at it."

"You talk about him a lot," he observes.

I laugh nervously, trying to decipher his tone. Is he criticizing or just commenting? "I guess it's inevitable. We're best friends. Our moms work together too. They're a real estate team."

"Do they take out ads on bus benches with photos of them smiling in power suits?" he asks playfully.

"I wish, that would be iconic. My mother, bus stop superstar."

"Do you get your beauty from her or your dad?" he asks. I feel my face get hot with embarrassment. I want to say that I'm not beautiful, but I don't want him to think I'm some insecure mess. Then he bursts out laughing. "That sounded so skeezy, ew. I'm so sorry. I'm genuinely terrible at this."

"At what?" I ask.

"I don't know. Flirting. Banter. What are we doing?" he asks.

"We're talking about how hot my parents are," I say. Thankfully, he laughs as he skips toward a nearby recycling bin and throws some stranger's litter inside it. That little action impresses me so much. It feels like a clue to the generous soul he is. "So is Ash your full name?" I ask.

"Asher," he says. "Asher Rainer Greene."

I stop walking for a moment, maybe because the melodic sound of his full name stuns me, maybe because I don't want our walk to be over too soon. "Nice to officially meet the full you, Asher Rainer Greene." I offer him my hand.

"Nice to meet the full you, Kamran Khorramian." He shakes my hand.

I hold on to his hand. "You know my last name?" I ask.

"Yeah, I mean, it's in the school directory, and I one hundred percent butchered it."

"No, you actually pronounced it correctly. Probably because of the Kardashians."

He laughs. "You clearly don't know the real me yet. I've never heard a Kardashian speak. Who are they anyway?"

"Are you being serious right now?" I ask. "They're inescapable."

He looks up to the sky, and then down to the ground. "I'm a terrible Celebrity player, obviously. And I'm very good at escaping." There's something I can't quite place in his tone. A loneliness I recognize from my own.

I turn toward him and ask softly, "Where do you escape to?"

He lets go of my hand, picks up a crushed purple flower,

and places it behind my ear. "My favorite flower."

The flower has probably been stepped on by hundreds of dirty shoes. Probably been pissed on by dogs. And yet, somehow, I don't mind. "What's it called?" I ask as I start to walk again.

"Are you kidding?" He waves his hand excitedly toward some bare trees. "It's a jacaranda. I'm sure you've noticed them. The purple flowers that bloom in the spring and line the streets. *They're* what's inescapable."

"I . . . I don't really notice trees," I say. "I mean, I notice them, except they mostly look the same to me."

"I'm going to have to enlighten you about the magic of trees." There's no judgment in his voice. "There's a line in a Tori Amos song I love, where she basically says that the jacaranda trees are warning her that her friend is in trouble. I feel that, you know. That trees talk to us. Send us little warnings."

"What are they warning us about?" I ask.

He closes his eyes. "Right now, they're warning me not to scare you away by being too weird."

"Is that why you started at a new school your senior year?" I ask. "Because kids at your last school didn't get you?"

"Yeah. I figured I had one more year to do high school right." He bites his lip nervously.

"Tell me more about these jacaranda trees you love so much."

Now he lights up. "Well, like palm trees, they're not even native to the region. Which I don't mind. Some people think trees being imported into Los Angeles proves how fake the city is, but I don't see it that way. I see the trees as dreamers. Like we are. They wanted to come here and chase their own gold rush, you know."

"Where are they native to?" I ask.

"South America," he says. "Mostly Brazil and Argentina. My mom loves those trees. She says they look like a real-life Impressionist painting."

"Your mom's right," I say. "They really do. Like, if you look at them long enough, they get all fuzzy."

He smiles. "Double vision."

"What?" I ask.

"Nothing, sorry. See how weird I am!"

"Maybe I'm weird too." I close my eyes, trying to preserve this moment in my memory. When I open them, I add, "And maybe I'm happy other people don't get you, 'cause that means I'll get you all to myself."

"Cute play on words there, fellow weirdo."

We walk quietly for a few steps. "Were you born here?" I ask.

"Born and raised," he says proudly. "And I'll probably stay here my whole life. There's no place like it. Where else can you be this close to beaches and mountains and deserts too? Where else do you get all the art and culture urban life has to offer but also see coyotes crossing the street?"

I laugh. "I've never seen a coyote crossing the street."

"People who don't like LA don't get it. You know who

gets LA?" At the same time, we both yell "Lana!" and laugh.

"People say it's vapid, but that's because they're too surface to explore its depths. Usually when people criticize something, they're really just criticizing themselves." I realize how right he is.

"This is Bodie's place," I announce when we get there. Bodie peers out at us from the kitchen window, like a detective.

"Have you ever been to the Huntington Botanical Gardens?" he asks.

I shake my head.

"If you're free this weekend, I'd love to take you."

"I'm free this weekend," I blurt out too fast. "Sorry, am I supposed to play hard to get? I've never, um . . . you know, dated."

He smiles. "You're not supposed to play at all. This isn't a game. Just be yourself."

"Yeah, that's easier said than done." I smile nervously. "But yes to the gardens. I'd love to go with you."

His eyes light up. "Wait until you see this place. They have an Australian garden, a Japanese garden, so many camellias you'll never look at a camellia the same way again." I've never looked at a camellia at all, but I don't dare interrupt him to say that. "My favorite is the desert garden. The succulents!" I have no idea what a succulent is.

After we say goodbye, I take my shoes off and leave them by the front door of the Omidi house. The soles are sticky with the crushed violet flowers that I'll never not notice again.

When I walk into the kitchen, where Bodie has laid out the ingredients we'll need, he doesn't ask about my walk with Ash. Instead, he hands me his phone. It's open to a DM he's drafting to Jack Spencer. *Can a boy change his mind about that date?*

"What do you think?" he asks me.

I look up at him. "I mean, sure, it works. But maybe you should spell *boy* b-o-i so he feels seen."

He swats me playfully. "I hate you."

"I hate you too. And I thought you didn't like him."

"I judged him too harshly." I arch a surprised brow at him. He presses send on the message, then glances up at me. "Stop looking at me like that. I know I'm a judgmental jerk sometimes." Within seconds, Jack sends back a winky-face emoji and a hot-face emoji. Bodie holds the phone up. "What do you think that means?"

"That he's happy and horny?" I suggest. "Or that he has pink eye and he's in a sauna?"

"If I get pink eye from him, I'll be so pissed." Bodie quickly texts back two brown-fingered thumbs-up signs to Jack.

"You got pink eye from me and it was the best, remember?"

He laughs. "That's 'cause we got to stay home from school and watch *South Park* through crusty eyes."

"And our moms left us alone since they were too scared

to be around us."

"God forbid they can't put on mascara for a day!" Bodie does an impression of his grossed-out mom saying "I curse pink eye" in her Iranian accent. We laugh until another text comes through from Jack. It's not an emoji this time. It's a picture of Jack, shirtless in front of a streaked bathroom mirror. Bodie stares at it a beat too long. He's either lusting after him or searching Jack's body for some deal-breaker.

"You want me to take a picture of you flexing for him?" I ask dryly.

He rolls his eyes, then puts the phone away.

"You should at least give the text a thumbs-up," I tell him.

Bodie pulls out his phone and hearts the photo of Jack. "This is why I didn't want to be distracted by boys," he explains. "There's so many rules with boys. When it's just us, it's so simple and easy. Like a recipe you know super well and won't ever mess up. Okay, baking starts now!"

I know what he's thinking. He didn't want *us* to be distracted by boys. Now that I ruined everything by letting Ash into my life, he had to balance the scales.

Ash asks me to meet him on Sunday morning at the Huntington Gardens. Bodie comes over that morning to help me get ready. Our moms are already staging some house, and our dads are playing cards. As I throw on one outfit after another, Bodie pecks at his phone on my bed. "You don't have to rush," he says. "The gardens don't even open until ten."

I fling an old button-down shirt at him. "He said he wanted to get there a half hour early so we could be the first people inside."

"The gardens are inside?" Bodie asks with a grin.

"Stop being a smart-ass and help me choose what to wear. I want to look good, but not like I put too much effort into it. Long sleeves or short? I don't want to sweat."

"Sweat is sexy and you need to chill out." Bodie leaps up and picks out a pair of joggers and one of my dad's old T-shirts.

"Joggers?" I ask.

He raises an eyebrow. "These hug your butt just right."

I smile. "I don't know what I'd do without you."

"I don't either." As I go to the bathroom to change, he calls out, "You want me to come with you?"

"To my date?" I ask incredulously.

He stammers. "No, I don't mean—I wouldn't join, but—I could be nearby, in case the date's a disaster and you need to be saved."

I emerge from the bathroom in the joggers and T-shirt. "Hot?" I ask.

"Sizzling." He pulls out his phone and opens up an app. "They're showing the Bond movie in Pasadena near the gardens. I kind of need to see it again, because my parents talked through the whole movie when we went." In a thick accent, he imitates his mom. *"Eh–Sean Connery vas so much more handsome."*

"Bodie, you really don't need to—"

He cuts me off. "And since I've seen the movie, I won't care if you call if the date sucks. I'll leave my phone on vibrate."

I don't bother arguing with him. It's decided. Bodie's coming with me. He even calls the Uber to drop me off first before it takes him to the movie theater.

When the car pulls up to the gardens, I see Ash standing outside. He's holding an old-school boom box. I roll the window down. Wave to him. He presses play and holds the boom box over his head. Lana's voice serenades us from the speakers. *I'm on the run with you, my sweet love. There's nothing wrong, contemplating God.* I melt into the beauty of this gesture. He's giving me my very own rom-com moment, like I'm the love interest in some new version of an old story.

I almost forget Bodie is there, until he says, "Making a song about chemtrails at a time when people believe vaccinations are microchipped is so dangerous, no? And country clubs, really? They're racist institutions that—"

"Bodie, stop," I demand. "Please."

"Fine, I'll see you later." Through the window, he yells out, "Hey, Ash. Have fun!"

The car drives Bodie off to the theater as I approach Ash. He puts the boom box down on a bench, but he doesn't turn it off. The Lana song ends, and a new song I don't recognize begins. Ash pulls a cassette case from his pocket. "I made you a mixtape," he announces. "It's my analog way of saying that . . . well, that I can't stop thinking about you when we're apart."

I feel like I'm floating. "Then let's spend more time together." I pull my phone up and videotape the moment. "When did you make this?" I ask, performing the role of newscaster.

"I made it very late last night, or very early this morning, depending on your definition of night and morning."

I zoom in on Ash's smile, giving him the close-up he deserves as he rattles off the list of artists on the mix. I beam as I realize we already have inside jokes, a shared language that's just ours. "I tried to pick some artists you probably know, like Bowie and Ethel Cain and Nick Cave and Joan Baez," he explains. "And some you most likely don't, like Happy Rhodes and Black Belt Eagle Scout."

"I don't know what to say. Thank you."

"How about you stop filming me now?" he asks.

"But this is all right out of a movie," I counter. "How could I not film it?"

On that note, he lifts the boom box back up and recites, "Don't forget. I'm just a boy, standing in front of a much cuter boy, asking him to like the same music as me 'cause music is one of the keys to my weary heart."

"I really didn't think you were a rom-com kind of guy," I tease.

"It's one hundred percent my sister's influence," he explains. Bodie sends me a text asking if everything's okay.

I swipe it away and keep filming. "She's made me watch the early canon of Ryan, Roberts, and Bullock countless times."

"You say it like you're *not* a romantic," I point out.

His eyes flicker. "I didn't think I was, but maybe you've changed me because . . ." He goes back into his stage voice as he says, "You. Complete. Me." Then he drops the act. "Now can you please stop filming? I feel so self-conscious."

I zoom in on his eyes. I need to capture the way they shine before I silence the phone and put in my pocket.

He moves closer to me. "Thank you. I can finally relax and stop pretending to be Hugh Grant now." He takes my hand into his. "Is this okay?" he asks.

"Yeah," I say. "It's great."

He squeezes my hand. His grip feels a little clammy. I can feel his pulse racing. I was so focused on my own nerves that I didn't think he might be nervous too. "Hey, the mixtape is for you, okay. Just you."

"What do you mean?" I ask.

"I mean . . . Don't listen to the mix when you're studying with him."

"Who, Bodie?" I ask. I can hear the defensiveness in my voice.

"He'll just make fun of it. I know he thinks I'm—"

"I'll listen to it alone," I promise, cutting him off before he can say another negative thing about Bodie.

"Cool." He kisses my hand slowly, holding his lips on my knuckles. "Is that okay?"

"It's great," I say, gazing into his eyes. "You're great."

For a moment, I think he might lean in and kiss me, but then the song changes and we both turn toward the boom box. The moment's gone. "Come on," he says, clutching the boom box by its handle. "Let's be the first ones in. I want you to see the gardens without crowds of people ruining them."

Something happens to me in those gardens. To us. As we wander, we bloom like all those flowers and plants he teaches me about. I've never felt more alive, more curious, more stimulated. My dad once told me that time can feel elastic. He said time moves slower when we're young, speeds up as we get older, draws itself out when we're bored, accelerates when we're lost in the joy of the new. I didn't understand what he meant before, but I get it as Ash guides me through the gardens. When I'm with Ash, everything feels new, and time moves too fast. Maybe that's why I film him again as he tells me about the Buddhist monks who introduced bonsai trees to Japan, and about Arabella Huntington's orchid collection. I can't help it. I want to remember his every word, mannerism, smile.

We linger longest in his beloved desert garden. He tells me that if he were a plant, he'd probably be a cactus.

"Why is that?" I ask, still filming him.

"I'll only tell you if you stop filming me," he says.

I put the phone away just as another text from Bodie comes through. All he sends is three question marks.

Ash exhales. "I guess I identify with cacti because they're prickly on the outside but they have a lot of healing properties for those who are willing to look deeper."

"So you have healing properties?" I ask.

He moves closer to me. There are some tourists milling about, but it feels like we're all alone in a real desert. "Yeah, I'm high in antioxidants. But you have to kiss me to get the benefits."

"Is that how a cactus asks if it's okay to kiss whatever plant I am?" I ask quietly.

"You're a red camellia," he says. "Because it's the rarest flower in the world."

I begin to sing Lana. *"You said I was the most exotic flower—"*

He shuts me up with a kiss. My first kiss. Hesitant initially, and then both bolder and softer as our lips and tongues relax and explore. My hands find their way to his shoulders, his back, and finally his chest. I hold my palms there, and he does the same for me, like we're holding each other's hearts as we kiss.

I never want it to end, but it does. Breathless from the rush, I ask, "Ash, are we . . . boyfriends?" I immediately regret asking the question.

"I don't know . . ." His eyes suddenly look haunted. "I'm afraid I'll disappoint you."

"You won't," I say.

"I don't know if I'd make a very good boyfriend," he says quietly. "I'm . . . I don't know . . . my sister calls me mercurial, but that's just another word for unreliable. Boyfriends are reliable. Steady."

"But you said you think of me all the time." I try not to sound like I'm pleading.

"I do. You know I do." He closes his eyes, lost in thought. When he opens them again, his eyes sparkle. "How about this? Let's not use the word *boyfriend*. It's generic and comes with too many expectations. Let's be our own thing. Let's be each other's lucky ones."

"My lucky one," I say with a smile. "I like it."

"I like you," he says before kissing me again.

That night, I close my eyes and listen to the mixtape from beginning to end to beginning to end, and on and on until my mom knocks on my door and asks me to turn the depressing music off. I tell her that the music isn't depressing. It's beautiful. Like the videos of Ash I can't stop watching, it makes time slow down and lets me replay each fleeting moment as many times as I want.

On Monday morning, Bodie speed-walks ahead of me as we head into school.

"Bodie, slow down," I beg from behind him.

"I don't want to be late," he says.

I run to catch up with him. "Or maybe you're pissed 'cause I never texted you back from my date?"

He scoffs. "No, I obviously figured out the reason you weren't responding is because the date was a big hit."

"It was a big hit," I confirm. "It would be nice if I could talk to you about it. I mean, we kissed."

He freezes. "Your first kiss," he says softly.

"Yeah." I smile. "And it was great. Like, we just fit together, you know."

There's a faraway look in his eyes. Then he shifts his gaze to me and forces a smile. "That's so great. I'm really happy for you."

"Yeah?"

"Yeah." He breathes out a weary sigh. "Jack and I hooked up."

"Wait, what?" I ask, shocked. "When did you hang out?"

"Yesterday." His voice is nonchalant. "I had already seen the movie so I texted him to see if he was around. My parents weren't home so he came over, and then he came over me." Bodie wants me to laugh, but I don't.

"You didn't tell me," I say quietly.

"It was yesterday," he points out. "And you weren't returning my texts or calls, so I'm telling you now."

"Right. Well, that's great. I'm happy for you too." My face feels frozen, unsure how to be in this moment. "Is he a good kisser?"

"Oh, I didn't kiss him," he says. "I kept it PG-13. Hands only." In a silly French accent, he adds, "Some light frottage."

"Okay, got it."

"Kissing is intimate." He turns serious. "I don't want to kiss someone unless I actually care about them."

"Well, I do care about Ash." I hear myself getting defensive.

"I mean, you barely know him," he counters.

"Well, I'm getting to know him," I snap back. I take a

calming breath and ask, "Why does it feel like you're not rooting for me and Ash? Like maybe you're . . . I don't know . . . jealous."

Bodie scoffs. "Please." He pulls out his phone and sends Jack a text. "I'm so not jealous. I just worry you're moving too fast with him and it'll burn out. I'm looking out for you."

"Are you sure?" I ask. "Because if there's something else, I'd rather talk about it than—"

"I'm sure," he huffs. "I just want you to be happy."

"I am happy."

"Then I'm happy you're happy." He must realize he sounds petty because he softens his tone as he says, "You know what? Let's all have lunch together. You and me and Ash and Jack. A double date." He pronounces *double* with a French accent, trying to lighten the mood.

"That sounds . . ." I can't find the words to properly convey how awkward and awful that sounds. ". . . fun!"

"Great, I'm going to find Jack and tell him. You tell Ash. This is great. Our first double date." He doesn't wait for me to say anything. He just puts his mask on and heads inside, his steps too fast.

I hear Ash call my name and see him walking toward the entrance with Carla Pacheco, another senior. When they reach me, Ash gives me a quick peck on the lips, and Carla smiles. "I see we've graduated to public displays of affection," she observes.

"Hey, Carla," I say, my cheeks hot from Ash's touch.

"Oh good, you guys know each other," Ash says. "You're my two favorite people at this school so that makes me happy."

I turn to Ash. "Hey, so I know this may not sound all that fun to you, but Bodie suggested we have lunch with him and Jack. I guess they hooked up over the weekend."

Ash looks at Carla, then at me. "Carla and I were going to spend lunch in the art room . . ."

"We can do that anytime," she says.

"Then you should join us," Ash suggests.

"And be the fifth wheel to two sickeningly adorable gay couples? Hell no." Carla puts a bright pink mask on. "Come on, the bell's about to ring."

Ash lingers behind. I can tell there's something he wants to say. "What?" I ask.

"Nothing." It's not nothing, because he quickly adds, "I just think it's kind of hilarious that your best friend immediately found himself a boyfriend when you became mine."

I want to defend Bodie. I also want to remind Ash that we're not boyfriends. We're lucky ones. But I don't say anything. Because the bell rings. And also, I like that Ash just called me his boyfriend.

When Ash and I get to the cafeteria, Bodie and Jack are waiting. They've got four trays of food ready at the table as they stand up to greet us. Bodie points to a tray with nothing but rice, vegetables, and beans on it. "That's for you,

Ash. You're vegan, right?"

Ash sounds surprised that Bodie knows this. The thing is, I've obviously told Bodie so much about Ash. The people I haven't said anything to are my parents. I guess I don't want to risk ruining things. And yet, Ash *has* told his family about me. He even put me on the phone with them as we were leaving the gardens. As I think about how much closer Ash seems to his parents than I am to mine, Ash says, "Oh, thanks, but I don't eat veggies either."

"Sorry, you don't eat . . . vegetables?" Bodie asks as we all sit.

"Of course not." Ash's voice is deadpan. "They're living things too. They have feelings."

Jack forks one of the long, limp carrots on his tray like he's contemplating its inner life.

Bodie is, perhaps for the first time in his life, completely speechless.

"Plus, a lot of veggies are members of the queer community. Haven't you heard of asexual propagation?"

"Um, no," Bodie says, confused.

"Wow," Ash says. "You have a lot to learn about artichokes." Then, suddenly, Ash laughs, letting us all know he's joking. To my surprise, Bodie laughs too. I let out a breath of relief.

"I literally thought you were serious," Jack says. "I'm literally dying of laughter right now." I catch the sudden tension in Bodie's body. He desperately wants to correct

Jack for misusing the word *literally*, twice. He's twitching with the desire to tell Jack that if he were *literally* dying, we'd be dialing 911.

But Bodie stops himself, showing impressive restraint. "See, you do have a sense of humor," Bodie says to Ash.

"Wait, I get that you were joking about not eating veggies," Jack says. "But are artichokes literally asexual?"

I glance at Bodie, who looks pained by Jack's third misuse of the same word in the span of a few seconds.

"They do indeed reproduce asexually," Ash explains. "That doesn't make them part of the queer community or anything."

Bodie turns to Ash. "I get why artichokes don't show up to our GSA meetings, but why don't you? We need more members."

Ash shrugs. "I'm not good with big groups. I guess I think people are cool until they huddle up and form corporations or governments."

Bodie looks utterly confused. "I mean, our GSA isn't a corporation."

"I get that," Ash says. "I guess I'm just a loner."

"It was only a suggestion," Bodie says, clearly ready to move on.

"I know," Ash says. "Honestly, I don't love that it's still called a gay-straight alliance. The word *gay* excludes too many people, and—"

"I agree, actually," Bodie says. "I pitched a name change

to the QSA. Queer-straight alliance."

"I hate the word *queer*," Jack says. "I don't think of myself as odd or different."

"Yeah, well, you are." Bodie sounds exasperated. "If you're gay, the world automatically thinks of you as odd or different, so just embrace it."

"Nobody's ever treated me as odd or different," Jack says innocently. I can see Jack's life flash before me. Always loved and accepted by family and friends. Never knowing what it feels like to be fractured, unloved, desperate for belonging. Of course he doesn't like the word *queer*. He's not queer. I am. I suddenly feel scared of telling my parents about Ash. It'll be like coming out to them all over again. It's not like either of them has even acknowledged me being gay since I came out. They just pretend the conversation never happened.

"Lucky you," Bodie says.

"Maybe it should be called the LGBTQIA+S alliance," Jack suggests. "That's more inclusive, right? Better than suddenly reclaiming *queer*, a word invented by straight people to bully us." It's clear from the way Jack says it that he's never been bullied.

"I can't tell if you're being serious," Bodie says flatly. "The whole reason we use the word *queer* is because it's more inclusive."

"Is it?" Jack asks. "It literally excludes people like me who don't identify as weird. Who just want to be normal."

"Normal?" Bodie parrots. "Please tell me you didn't just use that word."

I kick Bodie under the table, because I can feel him about to erupt.

"Personally, if it were me, I'd just remove the word *straight* from the group completely," Ash says. "I get that when schools started GSA groups, it was all about making straight people feel comfortable with us. But now . . ."

Bodie nods thoughtfully. "Yeah, times have changed."

"I agree," I say. "And let's be honest, there are no straight people in our GSA. Everyone's queer." I quickly turn to Jack. "Sorry, I know you don't like that word."

Jack smiles. He doesn't seem genuinely bothered by the word, or by anything.

"The thing is . . ." Bodie pulls his computer out. I can tell he's preparing for an argument. He's not going to let this go. "The word *queer* was *not* invented by straight people to bully us. That's just not true. The word goes all the way back to the 1500s or 1600s, we aren't sure." Bodie clicks a button on his computer. His wallpaper is Van Gogh's *Starry Night*. He opens up some notes he took during a GSA meeting. "And if you came to GSA meetings—"

"I can't," Jack says. "They're always during basketball practice."

Bodie's nostrils flare. He doesn't like being interrupted during a debate. "Well, if you did," Bodie continues, "you'd know that our community isn't *suddenly reclaiming* the word. ACT UP used the word back in the 1980s. We've been chanting 'We're Here, We're Queer, Get Used to It' for decades. These are all notes I took during a GSA meeting, by the way. See what you can learn from Ms. Robin and Mr. Byrne if you just showed up."

Jack puts a hand on Bodie's cheek. "You're cute when you're angry."

"Seriously?" Bodie asks.

Ash flashes me a look that tells me this is exactly why he wanted to spend the lunch hour making art with Carla.

"That's cool," Jack says, pointing to the *Starry Night* wallpaper of Bodie's computer. "Did you make it with one of those digital art apps?"

Bodie looks incredulous. "No, it's . . . Vincent van Gogh's *Starry Night*."

"Oh, I thought you painted it yourself, or whatever you call it when it's digital paint."

Jack giggles anxiously. He can tell he's being judged. "Listen, I have to hit the gym. My buddies and I like to use half the lunch hour to make some gains. They're all straight, so it's like my own gay-straight alliance." Bodie squirms in his seat. "I'll see you guys later." Jack slaps Bodie playfully on the back before he leaves. Bodie flinches like he was just punched.

When Jack is gone, I can feel Bodie's desire to chase him down and dump him immediately. There's no way Bodie can stand another moment with him.

"Bodie, it's okay," I say, trying to be supportive.

"It's obviously not okay." Bodie puts his computer away and throws his head into his hands, dejected. "He's a self-hating gym queen who doesn't know who Van Gogh is. And I jerked him off!"

"Lesson learned," Ash says with a smile. "Next time, test a guy on art history before putting your hand on his cock."

I laugh, but Bodie doesn't.

"Too soon?" Ash cracks.

"Maybe you should give him another chance," I suggest, trying to soothe him. "I bet a lot of people don't know who Van Gogh is. It's not like knowing some nineteenth-century Dutch Postimpressionist who cut his ear off is an indication of a person's worth, right?"

Bodie is unconvinced. "There are posters for the immersive Van Gogh exhibit all over the city. If he hasn't noticed them, it means he's not an observant person. I can't be with someone who doesn't pay attention to the world around them." Leave it to Bodie to take what seemed like a frivolous argument and turn it into an undeniable one.

"Did you guys read about that experiment where they realized that pigeons can tell the difference between a Van Gogh and a Chagall?" Ash asks.

"How do you ask a pigeon if it recognizes a painter?" Bodie asks. "Are birds suddenly able to speak?"

"I can't remember exactly, but they were given some kind of treat when they pecked at Van Goghs, I think. But nothing when they pecked at Chagalls. Then they were shown images by the two painters they hadn't seen, and they performed almost as well as a group of college students."

Bodie lets out a wry cackle. "Wow, so you're basically saying the guy I made the mistake of going out with is dumber than a fucking pigeon."

"That's not what I was saying at all," Ash says. "I was just trying to share something I found really cool. And birds might have small brains, but they're pretty smart. Did you know that a crow can remember thirty thousand hiding places?"

"Yeah, cool fun fact, but I'm still stuck on the fact that a pigeon recognizes a Van Gogh, but Jack doesn't." Bodie, perhaps realizing he's coming on too strong with Ash, softens his tone. "Did you go see the immersive show?" he asks Ash.

Ash shakes his head. "It's so not my thing."

"Aren't you an artist?" Bodie asks.

"Exactly why it's not my thing. As an artist, I'm not into the idea of altering someone's work when they're dead and can't consent to it."

"So you're judging the whole exhibit without even experiencing it," Bodie says. "Got it."

"I don't need to experience it," Ash says. "I've been to other immersive exhibits and I reject the whole concept. It's just a marketing ploy to sell people an *experience* when staring at a Van Gogh is already an experience. As is going to a park or a beach or a mountain. The world is an immersive experience!"

"I mean, okay, but maybe Van Gogh would've loved it," Bodie argues.

"Yeah, sure," Ash concedes. "But maybe he wouldn't. And that's my point. We can't know, so we shouldn't turn his art into some kind of theme park ride."

"Yeah, no, you're right." Bodie deflates. I can tell how badly he wants to find a way to win this argument. But he can't come up with a winning strategy. He knows Ash is right, even if Bodie and I loved that immersive Van Gogh show. We went with our parents. Took countless photos. Bought overpriced junk from the gift shop. It was after that show that Bodie made *Starry Night* his screen saver. Having given up the debate, Bodie resorts to taking me down with him. "Kam loved that show," he says, a hint of spite in his voice. "So it's not like I'm the only one who enjoys corrupt art."

My cheeks burn up with embarrassment. I'm prepared to defend myself, but Ash saves me.

"That's cool," Ash says to me. "You're free to like things I don't like. Doesn't make you a bad person."

Bodie shakes his head in disbelief, annoyed that his romantic prospect is a dud while mine is both wise and forgiving. He moves back to hating on Jack. "I mean, even if there weren't posters of *Starry Night* everywhere right now . . . it's still, like, one of the most famous paintings in the world." He snatches his phone up. His wallpaper is a photo of us when we went to New York together, leaping up into the air in Times Square, illuminated by all the LED and neon lights.

"What are you doing?" I ask Bodie, who pecks at his phone urgently.

"I'm googling what the most famous paintings in the world are," he says.

Ash shakes his head. "You don't need a phone to tell you that—"

But Bodie cuts Ash off. "And there you go. According to CNN, it's number three, after the *Mona Lisa* and *The Last Supper*. Should I run after him and see if he recognizes the *Mona Lisa*?" Ash laughs to himself, then abruptly stops. "What?" Bodie asks.

"Nothing," Ash says with a shrug.

"What's so funny?" Bodie asks. "That my romantic life has been one failure after another? That I'm clearly incapable of having a relationship?"

Ash turns his gaze toward Bodie with an iciness that makes me hold my breath. Choosing his words deliberately, he says, "No. It's just funny that you needed to look something up on your phone that you already knew was true. That's all."

Bodie opens his eyes wider with anger. "Oh, okay. Sorry I'm not above having a cell phone like you are."

Ash's face tenses up. "I didn't mean it as an insult."

"Well, it sounds like one. It sounds like you think I'm some cell phone addict who doesn't have a brain—"

"I wouldn't really mock addiction like that," Ash says quietly.

"Oh my God, I'm not mocking anything. I'm just saying I'm not tied to my phone the way you think I am." Just then, Bodie gets a notification. It's a text from Olivia. The words *LET BERNIE MACAW HOST DRAG RACE YOU COWARDS* pop up on screen. Bodie's fingers twitch to see what she sent.

"It's okay," Ash says. "Let's move on."

Bodie checks Olivia's text. It's a link to a video of her parrot saying "sashay away" on a loop. He puts his phone down. "Fine. Maybe I do love my phone. But so what? I use it to connect to people. During the pandemic, it was a lifeline to other people, and I love people. You're the one who's always alone, shutting other people out."

"Bodie, come on . . . ," I say. My stomach churns nervously. I want so desperately for them to like each other.

"No, it's okay," Ash says. "Bodie is right that I shut most people out. I'm working on changing that."

"Stop saying everything is okay when it's obviously not," Bodie says. "It's not okay if the two of us don't get along. We need to get along for Kam. I'm his best friend and you're his . . ."

Ash smiles. "His lucky one."

Bodie looks confused as he continues. "Okay, well, all I'm saying is that we're both important to him so we should make an effort. Okay?"

"Okay," Ash says. I hope that puts this conversation to a reasonably amicable end. But then he adds, "If I can say one more thing, though. Sometimes putting in too much effort ruins things. Sometimes, the best way to connect is to stop trying so hard."

Bodie nods thoughtfully. "Yeah, I get that. I was going

to try again and see if you'd consider coming to this afternoon's GSA meeting with us, but maybe that's trying too hard. I just think you might like it. It's a very small group."

Ash shakes his head. "Thanks, but I really am better one on one. I'm sorry."

Bodie thinks about this reasoning for a moment. "If you're better one on one, then there's no room for me."

"Wait, what?" Ash asks. "I'm not sure what you're saying."

I know exactly what Bodie is saying. That my relationship with Ash is going to be the end of our friendship. That's the fear that's eating me up too. That I'm going to have to choose one of them.

"You just said you want me to leave so you can be one on one with Kam!" Bodie turns to me. I can feel him wanting me to take his side. To break up with Ash just like he'll dump Jack, so we can go back to being us. Part of me is tempted to do just that, but then I'd be running away just like Bodie always does from guys. And I don't want to run away from love or from friendship. I want to run toward both.

"I didn't say that," Ash says. "I'm sorry if you feel that way."

"I can't with this passive-aggressiveness anymore," Bodie snaps. "I'm out. Kam, I'll see you later?" he asks.

"Of course," I say with as much warmth as I can muster. I watch Bodie walk away, tapping at his phone as he does. I already know he's sending a breakup text to Jack. Classic

Bodie. He's done with Jack. And I'm afraid he might be done with Ash.

Ash pushes his head into my chest. "That sucked," he says.

I push myself away from him. "Yeah," I reply coldly.

He scoots closer to me again. "Are you mad at me?"

I look away from him, at all the less-interesting people we go to school with. I am a little mad at him. But I'm also head over heels for him. "I don't know," I say. It feels like the truth.

He holds me. His long hair falls over me, like a veil, protecting me from the outside world. "I'll try harder next time we hang out with him. I promise."

"If there's a next time," I say, unsure Bodie will ever want to spend time with Ash again.

"I get it." Ash sighs. "Friends grow apart all the time. Maybe you and Bodie just don't have as much in common as you used to. You're so different."

"Wait, what are you saying?" I ask, pulling away again. "I'm not growing apart from Bodie."

"Right, sorry. I think I heard you say something different. I'm like that sometimes. In my own world." He sighs. "Is this our first fight?"

"It's not a fight," I say. "I'm not fighting. Are you?"

He shakes his head. "I don't deserve you, Kam. The truth is that I—" The bell rings before he can finish. Everyone rushes toward their classes.

"The truth is that you what?" I ask loudly over the chaos.

"Truth is that I'm so into you," he says. "And I don't want to lose you."

I move toward him now. Kiss him tenderly, aware that we're in public, at school, probably being watched. "You're not losing me. I'm yours."

We are the lucky ones. I feel that every time I spend time with Ash. I feel it when I let his mixtape transport me. I feel it when I join him and Carla in the art room one day. She's so welcoming. She makes room for me in their world. I wish Bodie could be the same way. But the best is when I join the Greenes for dinner. His dad cooks us some kind of vegan stew that tastes incredible. His mom asks me more questions about my interests than my own parents ever do. And his sister, Dawn, brings out a new side of him. They're clearly so different. He's a brooding artist. She's a carefree jock. But there's something funny and sweet about the way they tease each other.

"Okay, now that my mom's gotten the basic questions out of the way, I have to ask the important questions," Dawn says. "Like . . . how did my brother brainwash you into dating him?"

"Dawn!" Mrs. Greene says.

"Did he use some kind of mysticism?" Dawn asks. "Hypnotize you with art?"

Deadpan, Ash says, "All I did was boil up some eye of newt and toe of frog in my cauldron."

Mr. Greene laughs. "Wouldn't be an effective brew

without some wool of bat and tongue of dog."

At the same time, Ash and both of his parents recite something from memory. *"For a charm of powerful trouble, like a hell-broth boil and bubble!"* They all laugh. Dawn rolls her eyes.

"Do you see what I've dealt with my whole life?" Dawn asks. "I'm surrounded by people who quote Shakespeare and Rilke and Jung. You should escape while you can." Dawn's phone dings and she pulls it out to check a text.

"I like it here," I say brightly. "Really. Thank you for having me."

"Dawn, no cell phones at the dinner table," Mr. Greene says.

"Oh my God, it's one text," she says. "I'm in college now. I should be granted a little freedom."

Mrs. Greene shakes her head. "You are free. Doesn't mean you should be rude."

I want to ease the tension. My eyes on Ash, I say, "Well, at least Ash's cell phone won't ding at the table because he's the only teenager in the world who doesn't want a phone."

The family members all look at each other, like I'm not even in the room. Ash shifts uncomfortably in his chair. Dawn gives her parents a sharp look before speaking. "It's not that he—"

Before she can finish, Mr. Greene interrupts. "You know what it's time for? My least favorite game. Celebrity!"

"Okay, fine," Dawn blurts out. "But I swear to God, if every name in there is some obscure philosopher, I'll lose it."

"Better than obscure tennis players," Ash says.

Dawn laughs. "Maria Sharapova is not *obscure*."

"Neither is Kant!"

"What did you call me?" Dawn asks, and everyone laughs. The tension disappears as quickly as it appeared. I wish my family could get over our issues this quickly.

After the raucous game, Ash walks me back to my place and asks when he'll be able to meet my parents.

"That's . . . complicated," I say.

"Because of my septum piercing?" he asks, only half joking. "I can take it off."

"I don't want you to change for them," I insist.

"It's just an object. It's not some core part of who I am." He smiles. "Why haven't you told your parents about us?"

"Why'd you get that piercing?" I ask.

"I don't know." He shrugs. "It's kind of a reminder to be in touch with my senses. To really smell what's around me." He pauses, then asks his question again. "Your turn. Why haven't you told your parents about us?"

"I guess I'm scared," I admit.

"In my experience, fears are less scary when you express them. So what are you afraid of?"

I could tell him the truth. That I'm afraid my dad's homophobia will sprout up again like a weed. Afraid of my dad's erratic intensity, and of my mom's quiet judgment. Afraid they'll scare Ash away, or that telling them will upset the delicate balance of our family. But instead, I just say, "I'll tell them soon. I promise."

He doesn't push any harder than that, but I can tell that meeting my parents means something to him. Maybe it's because he hasn't managed to get close to Bodie. Not that I've tried to get them to spend more time together. If anything, I've done everything I can to keep them apart. Ash and Bodie feel like central but opposing forces in my life, like parallel lines that will never intersect. I accept that. I guess I'm used to leading a compartmentalized life.

On a rare Friday night when my parents are both home for dinner, I work up the courage to finally tell them. I've practiced the words aloud a million times. Written them in my journal. *Mom, Dad, I need to talk to you. I've been dating someone for almost a month and I really like him. I've already met his family and it would mean a lot to me if you would meet him too.* Before I can begin my monologue, my mother says, in a grave voice, "Kamran, we stayed home tonight so we could talk to you."

My heartbeat's rhythm quickens. I worry that they found out about Ash. Maybe Bodie told his parents, who told them. I fear they'll be angry with me, accuse me of lying to them, sneaking around behind their backs. I worry they'll tell me I'm not allowed to see Ash anymore. Maybe Bodie told his parents Ash is bad for me. I need to preempt them. I need to tell them how much Ash has already done for me. How important he is to me. But before I can begin, my dad pours himself a tall glass of whiskey and lets out a heavy sigh. "I lost my job," he announces.

"Oh." I shift in my seat. They don't know about Ash.

And now I feel like I can't tell them. I feel like a jerk for thinking this was all about me. I had figured if my dad hadn't been laid off by now, he was safe.

"They're replacing me with a robot." He takes a way-too-big sip of alcohol. He doesn't even flinch as it goes down. He hasn't touched the plate of food my mom prepared for him. "I won't even be getting any severance pay because they structured my deal as an independent contractor. This country is evil."

"Bahman . . ." My mom doesn't say anything, though.

My dad continues his tirade. "It was bad enough that I made my living moving money around for the same wealthy Americans who destroyed Iran with their coups and their corruption. I could accept that. But this . . . This is . . ." His voice breaks and he finishes his glass. Pours another. I've never heard him sound this . . . small. My dad doesn't let himself be vulnerable. It rattles me.

"We'll get through this as a family," my mom says firmly. "There are other jobs out there."

"We're in a pandemic and I'm old." There's a haunting resignation in my dad's voice.

My mom raises her head up high. "Look at what we've already survived, Bahman. A revolution. War. Moving from country to country to country. For us. For our child." My mom offers me a determined nod and smile. It's meant to calm me. But it does the opposite. She's trying too hard, even for her.

"I'm really sorry, Dad." His nostrils flare. I know immediately I've said the wrong thing.

My dad doesn't want anyone's pity, especially not his son's. He wants me to look up to him.

My dad finishes his whiskey, then empties the rest of the bottle into his glass. Gets up and dumps his food into the trash. "I'm not hungry," he huffs.

"That doesn't mean we need to waste food," my mom admonishes.

He laughs too loud. There's something almost sinister in it. I wish he'd blast some Dean Martin and dance with me. Let me film silly videos of him. "Why can't we waste food? Because your deadbeat husband is unemployed? Huh, Leila? Is that why?"

My mom remains shockingly composed. "Of course not. I just spent a lot of time making the ghormeh sabzi."

"Well, I never asked you to make it," he snaps. I feel exactly the way I felt eating lunch with Bodie and Ash, caught between two forces, one hot, one cold. I can tell my dad wants a fight, and my mom won't give it to him, and that drives him into a frenzy. "I never asked for any of this," he yells. "This whole life. Always having to earn, earn, earn."

"Bahman, stop. Please." My mom stays seated. The wilder he gets, the stiller she remains.

"And for what?" he asks. "It never ends. We're expected to keep working like dogs forever with no end in sight, while the rich manipulate the world to their advantage.

Maybe I should have quit before they fired me. I was their accomplice, wasn't I? Now I can finally get off the treadmill and enjoy my life!"

"Get off what treadmill?" my mom asks. "Aren't you going to be looking for another job? We can't count on my commissions."

I eat as they keep going like this. My dad loudly rages. My mom gently pushes. I bring my empty plate to the sink. And when there's an opening in the conversation, I say, "Guys, I think I'm going to go out for a bit."

Both my parents turn to me. My dad barks out, "Where are you going? Bodie is at the theater with his parents."

I freeze. Fuck. If things had happened the way they were supposed to, I would've told them about Ash tonight, and I could tell them the truth. But I can't do that. If I tell them about Ash now, there's no chance it'll go well. My dad will forever associate Ash with his layoff—his humiliation. "I'm just going for a walk. To clear my head." Not a complete lie. Ash's house is a fifteen-minute walk away.

My mom stands up and kisses my forehead. She holds me for a brief, heartbreaking moment. "Go." There's a whole world of melancholy in that one uttered word. She holds me for a few more seconds, like she's trying to steady us. This quiet version of her scares me. She told me to "Go," but what I heard was, "Save yourself."

Mrs. Greene opens the door when I ring the bell. There's a look of concern on her face when she greets me. "Ash isn't home," she tells me.

"Oh. Sorry I bothered you."

She must sense how much I need him because she asks, "Is everything okay?"

"Yeah, of course." I don't want her to think I'm some troubled kid who's bad for her son. I force a smile. "Just tell him I stopped by, and maybe he can call me tonight if he has time? I'll be up late."

"I will." But there's a hesitation in her voice. When I turn to leave, she blurts out, "He went camping. He'll be back tomorrow."

"Oh, okay." It seems strange that he would go camping without letting me know. I can't help but wonder if something else is going on. Is he over me? Is he into someone else? My mind reels with all the awful possibilities.

Saturday morning, Dawn answers when I call the Greene home. She tells me Ash isn't home yet. I ask her to have him call me.

Sunday morning, he still hasn't called and I haven't slept all night. Neither has my dad, who sits in the living room like a zombie, gambling online as he drinks from the bottle. He doesn't even bother with a glass anymore. I call Ash's home again. No one answers. I go to the house and knock. No one's there. The curtains are drawn. The house is dark. I check my messages again, wondering if I somehow missed a message from him. I check my spam folders, my social media DMs, thinking he must have communicated with me somewhere, somehow.

But he hasn't. Now I'm certain that he's over me. He probably didn't go camping. Maybe he was in his room the whole weekend, telling his family to say he was gone because he's too chicken to break up with me.

I have no one to turn to but my best friend. I need him. I make my way to his house, a short walk in the opposite direction from Ash's place. I almost turn back at least a dozen times on the way. If I tell Bodie that Ash is ghosting me, it will prove Bodie right. It'll give him the ammunition he needs to tell me Ash was always going to break my heart, so maybe it's better that it ends now before I get any more attached than I already am.

"Hey," Bodie says when he opens the door. "You didn't text that you were coming over."

"Sorry, I've got a lot on my mind," I say.

"No worries. I love a pop-in . . . when it's you. If *literally* anyone else pops in, I'd be so annoyed." He makes room for me to enter the house.

"So we're literally allowed to laugh about Jack now?" I ask.

"Literally, yes." I can tell he's alone because there's electropop blaring through the speakers. He silences the music from his phone. "Is it about your dad?" he asks.

"No." I head to his bedroom and throw myself onto his single bed. The corkboard on his desk is in my eyeline. On it is a chaotic mix of images he cut out of magazines and snapshots of us through the years. Next to the corkboard is one of many poems Bodie's family has around their house, rendered in Persian calligraphy neither of us can read. But we both know what each poem says because Bodie's parents have recited them to us so many times. This one is Rumi.

There is a voice that doesn't use words. Listen. "It's Ash. He's . . . not returning my calls."

Bodie picks up some clothes from the floor and throws them into his laundry bin. "So go to his house," he suggests.

"I've done that. He's not home." I pause before adding, "His mom said he went camping and would be back yesterday. But maybe that was a lie. Maybe he was home the whole time and he told her to lie because he didn't want to see me. Because he's done with me. What if it's over between us?" Tears start to flow down my cheeks.

Bodie lies down next to me. He lets me cry onto the soft cashmere cardigan he's wearing. "Hey, it's okay."

"How is it okay?" I sob. "He made me a mixtape. He introduced me to his family. This doesn't make sense. I really like him. A lot. He's the first guy I've liked."

Bodie wraps me in his arms. "Yeah, but not the last, right?"

"I don't know if I can handle this, Bodie. It's too much. The stuff with my dad is bad enough. I haven't told you all of it. His drinking is getting out of control."

"I know." I look at him curiously. "My parents are concerned about him. Your mom was over the other day and my mom asked if she's ever seen that show *Intervention*."

"Oh my God, the thought of my mother staging an

153

intervention is the most hilarious and depressing thing in the world." I sigh. "Wait, they're not really planning an intervention, are they?"

"Hell to the no!" Bodie laughs. "When my mom explained the show to your mom, they both laughed and laughed about Americans and their touchy-feely rituals."

I nod. "Probably for the best anyway. My dad doesn't take well to being told what to do. Hey, you want to hear something fucked up?"

"Always," he says.

"I convinced myself that my dad losing his job was, like, the price I had to pay for being with Ash. I know this doesn't make sense, but, like . . . I told myself I can't have too many good things. So because I got this amazing thing with Ash liking me, I had to be punished somehow."

"You don't deserve to be punished, Kam," he says warmly. "Don't think that way. Authoritarian leaders deserve to be punished. You deserve the world."

"Whatever, it doesn't matter, because now Ash is done with me, and my dad's just getting worse, and my mom is freaking out, and it turns out, I don't have *anything* good going for me."

He kicks my foot with his. "You have me. You'll always have me."

"Yeah." I nod. "I don't know what I'd do without you."

I take his hand in mine and squeeze it gratefully. We both stare up at the ceiling for what feels like an eternity.

"Do you think I should confront him tomorrow at

school?" I finally ask. "Like, should I break up with him before he has a chance to break up with me?"

In his eyes, I see something I wish I didn't see. A glimmer of happiness. He's happy it's over between me and Ash. Of course he is. I wish he wasn't.

"My dad says he should've quit his job before they had a chance to fire him. This is the same thing, isn't it? I should quit Ash before he fires me."

Bodie hesitates, then asks, "If I say that sounds like a good idea, will you accuse me of being jealous?"

I shrug. "I'm sorry I said that."

The warmth in his eyes tells me my apology is accepted. But he doesn't stop there. "It's not that I don't want you to be with someone. It's just that I don't want you to be with someone who'll hurt you. Ghosting you like this isn't a red flag. It's a full-on stop sign. It's horrible."

"Bodie, I get it, thanks." I can hear the annoyance in my voice. I wonder if maybe Bodie wasn't jealous. And maybe he's not happy we're breaking up. Maybe all along, what he really wanted was to save me from feeling this awful pain.

"Sorry." His eyes light up. "Hey, let's cheer you up with greasy food and deliciously trashy television. Your options are *Top Chef*, *Iron Chef*, or wait, have you seen *Salt Fat Acid Heat*?"

I shake my head.

"Oh wow, that's what we're watching. It's not trash. It's a legitimately amazing documentary series about an Iranian chef."

He whips out his phone and starts ordering Chinese food for us. We half watch the show as we distract each other with hilarious things our parents have texted us recently. Our favorite is his mom recently asking him, *Farbod joon what is woke?* And also, my mom recently texting me, *I forgot to turn the sexily system on*, then quickly correcting herself with all-caps *SECURITY SYSTEM. Turn me on when you get home please.* Then again with, *Turn IT on. I hate my new nails. I can't tip with them.*

I must fall asleep because the ring of my phone jolts me awake. My head is on Bodie's chest. I've drooled onto his sweater. And we're on the third episode. I look at my phone and see it's Ash calling. A picture of him standing next to a cactus pops up on screen. "Do I answer?" I ask.

"Definitely not," Bodie says decisively. "Break up with him tomorrow." He waits for me to silence the call, but I don't.

I stare at Ash's photo on my screen. It's from the day he took me to the Huntington and showed me his beloved succulents. I was so happy that day. He told me trees are connected by underground roots. And that's how he felt about us. After six rings, the picture of Ash disappears.

"Ah, silence." Bodie sighs. "Now let's go back to the show."

I croak out a sad laugh as I lie down and let him put his arms around me. He makes me feel safe. But when my phone rings again, it's not safety I want. It's Ash. I leap up and answer it. "Hello?"

"I'm so fucking sorry, Kam," he says. "I was in the desert."

"Okay," I say, waiting for more.

"I just . . . I had this idea for a new series of poems and imagery, and I needed some peace to create it, you know." I don't know, so I say nothing. "I meant to tell you but totally spaced, and by the time I was there, I had no phone or anything. Not that there's service in the desert."

"Your mom said you'd be back yesterday," I say icily.

"Well, that was the plan, but then I was so inspired that I stayed, which didn't really make my parents very happy, but sometimes you have to do what's right for you and not for the people you love, you know."

I stop myself from saying anything. I'm not ready to forgive him, no matter how much I want to.

"I made you something," he says. "I can't wait to show it to you. I think it's really good."

"I want to see it. But Ash . . . I was worried." I try to sound like my mom does, cool and composed. I think I succeed.

"I'm so sorry, Kam. Please give me another chance. Please come over. I can show you what I made and we can eat. My dad made his chickpea stew, which is honestly the best-tasting thing in the world. Minus your lips, of course."

I can't help but grin. "So I taste better than chickpea stew, huh?" I ask. Bodie looks both grossed out and annoyed as he impatiently waits for me to dump Ash.

"Just come over, my beautiful lucky one," Ash says. "I have another surprise you won't be able to resist."

"What?" I ask.

"You'll hear it soon enough," he says, a smile in his voice.

Bodie's face falls when I tell Ash, "I'll be there soon," and hang up the call. "Please don't be mad," I say to Bodie. "We'll finish the show later?"

Bodie sits up straight. "Kam, what are you doing?"

"I know how this looks, but he wasn't ghosting me. He was working on his art." I'm already putting my shoes on and cleaning up the take-out containers.

"But he *did* ghost you. And you're running back to him," Bodie seethes. "Where's your self- respect?"

I stand at his door, holding the plastic bag of used containers. "It wasn't about me and I made it about me. Maybe that's the lesson here. That it's not always about me. That's a good lesson, right?"

"Yeah, I guess it's a lesson I need to learn too, 'cause it's definitely *not* about me right now. It feels like I don't matter at all." His strong jaw clenches, but it's the hurt in his eyes that feels like a gut punch.

"Bodie, I'm sorry," I plead. The last thing I want to do is hurt him. "I freaked out for no reason, and you're such a good friend for taking care of me through—"

"But it wasn't for no reason," he says. "If you ever disappeared for a weekend without telling me where you were, I'd demand your head on a platter."

"Yeah, well, maybe that's the problem right there. Maybe we need to stop expecting people to be reachable all day, every day, right? We don't own people."

"No, but we make commitments to them," Bodie spits out. "We don't hurt them for no reason."

"He had a reason," I argue. "He was—"

"Making art. Whatever, I give up." Bodie shakes his head. "Go enjoy your time with him. But the next time he ghosts you, don't come crying on my cashmere."

"It won't happen again," I say with certainty. "I know him better than you. You'll see."

"Famous last words," he says, his voice weary and withdrawn.

I think about Bodie as I head to Ash's place. I feel torn. A piece of me longs to turn back and be with my best friend, earn his forgiveness, prove to him that I do have self-respect.

But I don't turn back. I go to Ash. When he opens the door, he looks more alive than ever. His eyes glow like they have their own internal light. "I missed you so much," he almost yells. "Two days without you is too many." He scoops me into his arms and kisses me.

"Then don't disappear like that again," I plead. I clutch him with all my strength, like he might disappear again if I don't grip tight enough.

"I won't. I promise. Come on, I have surprises!" He leads me inside. As we head to his room, he yells out, "Mom, Dad, Kam's here."

Mrs. Greene's voice comes from the kitchen. "Kam, do you want—"

"We're going to my room. Bye!" Ash yells. He's radiating

energy and excitement. That's how much he missed me. So much that it's making him jittery. He hands me a sketch. "I made that for you in the desert," he explains.

I stare at the image long enough to realize that what looks like a rock is actually a lizard blending into a rock, like an optical illusion.

"You see it?" he asks.

"The lizard?"

"Yeah." He smiles. "When I was in the desert, I saw this lizard on a rock. It blended in so well it was almost invisible. And it reminded me of you and me for some reason. How we were in the same choir, in the same hallways, for weeks before really seeing each other, you know."

"I do know." I can't help but be charmed by him.

"Okay, close your eyes for the second present," he orders.

"Um, okay." I close my eyes. He puts something cold and hard in my hand. It feels like a CD. "Did you make me a mix CD?" I ask.

"Open your eyes."

When I do, I can't believe what I'm holding. It's a plastic-wrapped CD of Lana's upcoming album. "Wait, but it's not out for another week."

"I know! Crazy, right?" He smiles proudly. "Dawn plays tennis with some girl whose mom works at Interscope."

"I love your sister!" I squeal, giddy with excitement. "Wait, are we allowed to open it?"

"Yeah, of course. We're not allowed to leak it. But we can listen. I thought maybe we could just lie in each other's arms and experience the music together."

And that's exactly what we do. We hold each other and listen once, and then a second time. I'm giddy from the music, from kissing him for hours. The second time we listen, we stand atop his bed when "Dealer" comes on. We hold hands as we jump on the mattress, flying high and screaming "I DON'T WANNA LIVE" with every bit of our lungs and hearts. So loud that it's clear what we really mean is that we want to live like *this*, fully, deeply, with more meaning and passion than the surface world wants us to. Forever.

JUNIOR YEAR

"My name is Jared, grateful member of Alateen." I look around the dozen or so people seated on folding chairs, in the back of a Lutheran church. Everyone's eyes are on Jared, who picks at a zit on his face as he speaks. His own eyes are swelling with buried tears.

"Hi, Jared," we all say.

"I'm not doing great today. I'm really not doing great." Jared looks at Byrne, one of two adult sponsors in the room. Byrne gives him a smile and a nod that tells him to keep going. "I miss my mom," Jared croaks out. "I know how messed up that sounds. I mean, who would miss a mom who . . . well, you all know what she did. But tomorrow's her birthday and she'll be spending it in jail, and that makes me so sad."

A newcomer pulls her hood over her head and sinks into

her chair. It squeaks loudly. I can feel her unease, the way she wishes she were anywhere else but here.

Jared heaves a few wet breaths and lets the tears out. I don't know what school Jared goes to, but I know he has the body of a football player and the mannerisms of the boys who bully me at school. He could easily be a part of Ken Barry's goon squad. And yet he's not like them. He's sweet, and sensitive, and broken. It's a reminder that I shouldn't judge people too quickly. "On her last birthday, she got so mad at me for putting her blow-dryer in the wrong drawer. She begged me not to make her hit me on her birthday. And then she hit me with the blow-dryer."

We all lean in, trying to show him our support through our body language. There's a loud chirp from our time-keeper's phone.

"One minute. I hear that, thank you." Jared sighs. "The thing I keep thinking since she's been gone is that a piece of me is gone. Like we were one person, you know. Or maybe it's just that I didn't know where she ends and I begin. That's what it feels like."

I feel that in my bones. I feel it about my dad. And about Ash too. I wonder if that's a human thing, a love thing, or maybe only an addict thing, like we want to be their missing piece, the thing that completes them. I have a flash of my dad reading that book to me when I was young. He would put on a silly western accent when he sang, *"Hi-dee-ho, here I go, I'm lookin' for my missing piece."* He loves cowboys. He was probably drunk.

"Anyway, well, that's what's on my mind." Jared pushes his sadness back in. "I don't want to go over my time, but I do want to say to the newcomers . . ."

We all look at the two newcomers, sitting close to the door, just in case they want to escape.

"I've been coming here for almost a year now. And it's the one place where I feel, I don't know . . . seen, I guess. It's not always easy. And it's okay to struggle your way through it. But keep coming back. Thanks for letting me share." Everyone claps as Jared sits down.

Byrne says, "We have time for one more share before newcomer time." Everyone but me and the newcomers has already spoken. Byrne's eyes find their way to me, urging me to speak. I don't move. I know by now that all our problems are relative. Still, I can't help but feel that whatever I've gone through will seem insignificant compared to the problems of people like Jared. "Okay then, now it's time for our newcomers to share if they'd like to."

One of the two newcomers raises her hand. "Hey, everyone, I'm Holland."

"Hi, Holland," we all say.

"I just want to say thank you to everyone for their shares. It's weird how scared I am to speak. I'm a mock trial assassin. Public speaking is my thing." A few laughs. "But this is different. I can debate foreign policy or defend a fictional criminal, but talking about my sister is . . . It's hard. It feels like I'm betraying her by sharing this with you guys."

Her words bring me back to my first meeting, which my therapist suggested I attend. My mom thought I was in therapy to deal with Ash's disappearance. And I was, at first. But then my dad left six months later. And therapy became less and less about Ash, and more and more about my dad, and my mom. My dad was gone a year by the time I made it to a meeting. I didn't say anything but my name in Alateen for a full month, which was when I stumbled into a meeting led by Mr. Byrne. He made me feel safe enough to share. He helped me see that speaking our family secrets aloud wasn't betraying my parents, it was taking care of myself.

"Whoever would like to can now stand for the serenity prayer," Byrne says at the end of the meeting.

We all stand and hold hands. I feel self-conscious about how clammy my palms are, how fast my pulse is racing. We close our eyes. "God grant me the serenity to accept the things I cannot change. The courage to change the things I can. And the wisdom to know the difference." Every time I say the prayer, I have the same thought: How the hell am I supposed to know the difference between the things I can and can't change?

"Keep coming back. It works if you work it, and you're worth it." Those words hit me hard. I do keep coming back. To meetings, yes. But also to the same thoughts. Of my dad, wondering where he is. Of Ash, wondering if he's alive. Willing him to be alive.

* * *

Outside the meeting, as all the teens leave, Byrne calls out my name. I find him leaning against a jacaranda tree, its branches bare. "Hey," I say quietly.

"How are you doing?" he asks.

"I'm sorry I didn't share." I bite my lip. "I know I don't speak in meetings as much as the others."

"I didn't say anything about that. I asked how you're doing." Byrne waves goodbye to the other adult sponsor as she gets into her car.

"My dad never hit me. He's not in jail. I feel like such an asshole comparing my problems to kids like Jared. He went through hell." I'm talking too fast.

"Why do think your therapist recommended Alateen for you?" he asks, taking me by surprise.

I think back to my last therapy sessions. My therapist was amazing. I chose her from a list of names Ash's mom gave to me. My therapist helped me through my darkest moments, but after a year and a half, she said I needed something different. "She said I needed community. That what would help me most was knowing I wasn't alone."

"Right." Byrne smiles warmly. "In a community, your pain is not in competition with anyone else's pain."

I know he's right. And yet it's hard not to compare myself to others, usually in ways that make me feel less than. Less beautiful than Bodie. Less talented than Ash. Less traumatized than Jared.

"I know it's not the victim Olympics in there," I say, but even I can hear the hurt underneath my bravado.

I wait for Byrne to say something, but he doesn't. That's one of his strategies. Letting the silence become so uncomfortable that I'll fill it with truth.

"I guess in some ways, I have a lot in common with Jared. I mean, I miss my dad too. It makes me feel sick sometimes, but I do. I miss the moments when he would be silly and . . . fun. I know it was probably the alcohol that loosened him up, but still . . ."

Byrne just nods.

"And also, what Jared said about not knowing where his mom ends and he begins . . ."

"That resonated for you?" Byrne asks softly.

I nod. "Yeah, but not just with my dad. With Ash too."

Byrne nods. "Have you made a decision about Joshua Tree?"

"I'm still debating." I feel the tremor in my voice. Tears form in my eyes and I let them fall. "I guess it's bringing up a lot of stuff for me. Like, it's making me remember what life was like two years ago, back when my dad still lived with us. When my parents would fight all the time. I keep wondering why I never told Ash my dad was an alcoholic. I hid it all from him because I was so . . . I don't know, I guess I was ashamed. And scared that Ash wouldn't want to be with me if he knew how messed up my family was."

I swallow hard. This is where I should tell Byrne what I just found out. That Ash also had problems with substance abuse. But revealing this somehow feels like a betrayal of his family, and of Dawn, who confided in me against her parents' wishes. I haven't even told Bodie yet, and I know he'd be so pissed if he found out I confided in someone before him, even if it was Byrne. I'm afraid that if I utter it out loud, the information will get out somehow. I can only imagine what Ken Barry and his goon squad would do if they had the ammunition to call Ash a druggie, to blame him and his family for what happened.

"I wish . . . I just wish I could go back and be honest with Ash about everything . . . And I'm scared that the fact that I wasn't totally honest with him means I didn't really love him enough, because love is trust, right?"

I don't speak my other suspicions aloud. Like, could I have helped Ash if I had just told him about my dad? Maybe knowing how messed up my own dad is would have made him feel safer with me. Safe enough to reveal his full self to me. And maybe, just maybe, being completely honest would've helped him stop.

Then I think of another scenario. What if he told me the truth and I felt betrayed? Lied to? Well, in that case, I would've broken up with him, never gone on that trip. And if I wasn't there, maybe he'd still be here.

It's my fault he's gone. That's the only conclusion I come to.

"Love is complicated," Byrne says.

"But I didn't trust him with my secrets," I say. "And he didn't trust me with his either. Does that mean he didn't love me?"

"Of course he loved you," Byrne says. "We could all see that."

I shake my head, unsure. "I wish I wasn't like my mom," I confess. "She'd fight with my dad when I wasn't in the room, then pretend nothing happened when she saw me. I would hear her crying alone in the bathroom, and a few minutes later she'd be off to work with a smile, or at some party dancing. I'm like that. I pretend things are okay when they're not."

"That's not what you're doing right now," he says. "Doesn't feel like you're hiding at all."

"Maybe the program is working." I shrug. "I don't know, though. I still struggle with the Higher Power thing sometimes."

"God can be anything," Byrne reminds me. "God can just be love."

"I know all that," I say. "But if God is love, then why is there so much hate in the world? I guess it's hard for me to put my life in the hands of a Higher Power because if I accept that there's a God, then it has to be the same God that took Ash from me. What kind of cruel God is that?" I take a deep breath.

For once, Byrne is at a loss for words.

"No wisdom to share?" I ask, only half joking because I really want more wisdom.

"I've been where you are. Not the same situation, but the same questioning." His body deflates. His shoulders hunch. "All I can say is that the program helped me through it. It reminds me every day to focus on the things I *can* change, not the things I can't."

I think of the Greenes. They believe finding out what happened to Ash is something they can't change. But me, I know in my heart that's not true for me. Maybe I can remember more of what happened that night. Maybe I can find some clue everyone else missed. Maybe I'll prove everyone wrong if I go back to that desert.

"Keep coming back," I whisper to myself. "It works if you work it, and you're worth it."

"That's right," Byrne says.

I let those words float around my brain. I have to keep coming back to that desert, because Ash is worth it. Maybe it's too late for my honesty to save him from disappearing. But it's not too late for me to find him, out there, somehow. I feel that in my heart.

"Mr. Byrne," I say. "I think I want to go back to the desert."

He nods. "You'll need one of your parents to sign the permission slip."

"I know," I say. "It'll be okay. I hope."

"ABSOLUTELY NOT," my mom says when I ask for her signature the night before it's due.

"The whole GSA is going!" I plead.

"Then let them go." She won't even look at me. "They didn't . . . go through what you went through there. You're too young to go back. It's too soon."

"Fine, I can ask Dad. They just need one signature." I pull out my phone threateningly. "Should I call him?"

"Go ahead. He'll be too drunk to read the permission slip." Her eyes challenge me to defy her.

"I don't need him to *read* it," I say, unwilling to give up. "I just need him to *sign* it. Which he'll probably do just to piss you off."

That clearly gets her attention because she finally looks at me. Really looks at me. Not like the conversation is over, but like a new one is beginning. A shift. "Kamran, these last two years, there's one thing I've never said to you. And I've had to work so hard not to say it. I've wanted to say it so many times."

"What?" I brace myself for some secret revelation about my dad.

"I've never said *I told you so*. I've never said I was right."

My heart breaks, not just because of her words, but because of the way she says them. With resignation. My mom is never resigned. There's always fight left in her. But not now. Not as she grabs the paper out of my hand and signs it. She's given up. She's letting me win.

"Sometimes I wish you *had* stopped me from going," I say. "Maybe then things would be different." I look at her, my heart in my stomach. "You *were* right last time, Mom. But you're not right this time. I have to go back."

She hands me the signed paper. "You're my whole life." Her voice is free of its usual pride. "And you're so young. I just want to protect you. Does that make me so awful?"

"No." I give her a hug. Because she signed the paper. And because I love her. "Mom, I don't think you're awful. Is that how you think I feel about you?"

"I don't know," she says. "You never tell me."

"Because you hate talking about feelings," I say.

"And this is why I hate talking about feelings! It's painful," she shoots back. She runs a hand through her hair and laughs. "I'm sorry. You're my whole world."

"You said that already," I say with a smile.

"Because I don't want you to forget it."

Part of me wants to tell her that it's not healthy to make someone else your whole life. Wants to beg her to let go a little. Of me. Of controlling everything. But then again, who am I to ask her to let go when I'm the one who won't let go of Ash?

"I hope . . ." She pauses. Chooses her words carefully. "I hope you take care of yourself out there. Just promise me that. And if something goes wrong again, promise it won't take you two years to tell me I was right."

I want to keep talking to her. There's still so much unsaid. I want to tell her that my dad leaving and Ash disappearing are versions of the same thing. But are they? I can already hear her saying that she shared two decades of her life with my dad. They had a child together. I dated Ash for a few heightened months. There's no comparison, and maybe she's right. Maybe she's always right. I hope not, because I'm defying her advice again. I don't say any of this. I just say, "I promise."

PART 2

JUNIOR YEAR

"Okay, let's review our General Safe Space Guidelines."
Byrne is in the passenger seat of the RV Ms. Robin is driving. "Who can recite them for us?"

Bodie raises his hand, his painted nails waving in the
air. He has the fuzzy white scarf Louis gave him wrapped
around his neck. Louis drove all the way from Long Beach
to say goodbye to Bodie and to meet the rest of the GSA. I
could tell how much Bodie loved showing off his beautiful
boyfriend to everyone. "Go ahead, Bodie," Byrne says.

"None of those assumptions," Bodie begins. "Always use
those 'I' statements. Less of those generalizations, more of
that specificity. Make that space, take that space. Welcome
that discomfort."

We write and refine the rules at the beginning of each
year, that way new students get to be a part of creating
and understanding them. Then we begin every meeting by

reading the rules out loud, usually very loud.

"I'm wondering about the whole welcome-that-discomfort thing," Danny says.

"What about it?" Ms. Robin asks.

"It's about emotional discomfort, right? Which I'm totally fine with welcoming. Bring on the emotional discomfort. You guys have basically watched me transition and counseled me through the worst of it, so it's not like I'm scared of raw emotion." Danny swallows hard. He's a junior like me and Bodie. Sometimes I feel like I have no friends other than Bodie, but then I look around this group and I realize I really do have other friends. "I guess it's the physical discomfort that worries me," Danny continues. "Sleeping in a tent in the middle of the desert in winter? I'm a bit scared, to be honest. My parents' version of the great outdoors is a patio table at Cheesecake Factory."

I let out a sad laugh, because of course, I was once just like Danny. The thought of sleeping outside frightened me. But what scared me were snakes and mountain lions, all the creatures my mom warned me about—not my boyfriend vanishing.

"Wait, who told you we're sleeping in tents?" Ms. Robin asks. "We've set up special glamping yurts just for you with cashmere blankets, your own personal port-a-potty, memory foam pillows—"

"I think you're joking . . . ," Danny says.

Ms. Robin smiles. "Of course I'm joking. But we did rent this RV, so you won't be freezing in a tent, and you'll be safe from the snakes."

"We're basically going to be *Troop Beverly Hills*," Bodie says, getting a few laughs since we all watched the movie at our last GSA movie night.

"More like *Troop Mid-City Los Angeles*," I say, getting even more laughs.

"Well played," Bodie says, but the bright smile on his face feels forced. Maybe he doesn't like me getting a bigger laugh than him. But I think he's a little upset with me for coming on this trip, for not listening to him.

"What kind of animals live there?" Olivia asks. "I mean, I love animals. You guys know we have two dogs, three cats, and a weirdly eloquent parrot named Bernie Macaw."

"We know," a whole group of us says in unison. Olivia talks about her pets constantly. She shows us pictures all the time. She has a semi-popular TikTok account devoted to all the adorably absurd things they do.

Olivia laughs. "Okay, I get it. But despite my animal love, I do have a really weird fear of bears. I think it's because I saw that Leonardo DiCaprio movie."

"You should've watched *Paddington 2* instead," Danny jokes. Another GSA movie choice. That bear is so gay.

"Bears are very rare in the park," Byrne says. "I wouldn't worry about that."

"Rare?" Olivia asks. "How rare? Like, get hit by lightning rare? Or, like, Nina Simone winning a Grammy rare?"

"Wait, which one is more rare?" Lincoln George asks.

"Bears aren't native to the park," Byrne clarifies. "I do

believe they've been seen, rarely."

With a sly smile, Bodie says, "Unlike in West Holly-wood, where bears are everywhere!" Everyone laughs. Bodie is in his element at GSA meetings.

Ms. Robin enters the carpool lane. "Thank you for that, Bodie." We giggle. "The most important ground rule is we arrive as a group, and we remain a group. No wandering off alone. There's no cell phone service in the park so you won't be reachable. But your phones will otherwise work, so you can take pictures. And hopefully Kam will be our official videographer."

"Why me?" I ask.

Ms. Robin laughs. "Because you're always filming every-thing," she explains. "I teach the senior filmmaking class. I know a budding director when I see one."

I feel myself blush. I don't feel like a budding anything.

"What if someone needs to reach us?" Fiona asks. "Like, what if there's an emergency at home or something?"

Ms. Robin takes a breath and gives Byrne a look of gen-erational solidarity. "Then you might miss an emergency. But you know, that's what life was when I was a kid. And when Mr. Byrne was young too. You left your house, you were unreachable. End of story."

"That sounds . . . awful." Fiona clutches the phone in her pocket like it might disappear.

Byrne laughs. "I suppose in some ways it was."

"But there were good things about it," Ms. Robin says. "People didn't bail on you."

"People were more present," Byrne sighs.

"Is that really true?" Bodie asks. "Or is that just you guys romanticizing the past?"

"I honestly don't know," Byrne says. "Maybe a bit of both. Any other questions?"

I want to ask what happens if I panic when we get there. What if I can't take it? What if the memories torment me? But I don't go there. I can't give Bodie a reason to whisk me back home. Not after I begged my mom to sign the permission slip.

"I have a super important question," Olivia says. "Are we allowed to throw cold water on Fiona's face if she snores too loud?"

"I do not snore," Fiona snaps.

"Wait, more importantly, Olivia, how do you know Fiona snores?" Bodie asks. "Have you guys been—"

"Oh my God, we've been having sleepovers since we were eight." Olivia, who's sitting behind me and Bodie, swats Bodie's head hard. "What about that slice of perfection you're dating?" she asks. "Does *he* snore?"

Bodie glances my way nervously. Since he started seeing Louis, he's tiptoed around telling me any details about their time together. I know it's because he doesn't want to hurt me by talking about his present boyfriend when he knows I'm not over my missing boyfriend, but in a way, the evasion is worse. It creates a painful distance between us.

"Of course he doesn't snore," Fiona says. "Louis is perfect."

"He's not perfect," Bodie argues unconvincingly. "Nobody's perfect."

"Then he's as close as someone gets. As are you." That's Olivia again. "The two of you are disgusting, honestly. That video he made for you is, like, so sweet it's sick."

Bodie glances my way again. I have no idea what video she's referring to, and he knows it. He's keeping secrets from me.

"My question is, when's the wedding?" Fiona asks.

"Guys, stop," Bodie begs. I know he loves the attention. It's me hearing all this he doesn't love.

"Can't stop, won't stop." Olivia smiles. "At least I'm not as embarrassing as your mom and her search for a doctor that'll get you on PrEP."

"Wait, what?" I turn to Bodie, trying to read his face to see if Olivia is joking.

He shrugs it off like it's no big deal. "You know my mom. Louis and I are getting serious, so she wants to be sure I'm as safe as—"

"How many doctors did she consult?" I ask. What I really want to say is, *Why didn't you tell me? Why does Olivia know? I'm your best friend.*

"She started by asking our Iranian family doctor."

"Dr. Javaherian?" I ask, because of course we have the same one. "There is no way that dude has heard of PrEP."

"That is correct."

Ms. Robin keeps her eyes on the road as she speaks. "The fact that there are doctors who haven't heard of PrEP tells me everything I need to know about how much the medical establishment cares about our community."

"And in Los Angeles!" Byrne exclaims.

"Well . . . in Tehrangeles," I say, which gets a genuine laugh from Bodie. My joke is a reminder that there's a whole piece of his life none of these other friends can ever truly understand. "It's a different city than the one you guys live in."

Danny leans forward. "We went through five doctors before we found one who didn't sound skeptical every time they talked to me. Our OG family doctor said I was too young for puberty blockers."

"That's exactly what good old Dr. Javaherian said when he finally figured out what PrEP is." Bodie puts on a thick Iranian accent and says, "Farbod joon, why rush into sex with another boy at your age? Wait a while and see if you change your mind."

"Straight cis people never have to wait to start their lives," Danny mutters sadly.

"They think protecting us from STIs will turn us into shameless sluts," Bodie says. "Like, gimme my PrEP and my HPV vaccine, you cowards!"

"I have never been so happy to be asexual," Tucker cracks. "Enjoy the human papillomavirus, friends."

We zoom by a billboard for a casino, another for a personal injury lawyer.

"Grown-ups love to say we're too young for this or that," Danny says.

"My mom said I was too young to go back to the desert," I say quietly. "That I didn't know what I was getting myself into."

Everyone looks at me with concern now. They weren't expecting me to bring this up.

"How did you end up convincing her?" Olivia asks, breaking the uncomfortable silence.

I look at Bodie. He knows threatening to call my dad is how I convinced her, and he also knows I don't want to talk to everyone about my dad. He swoops in to save me from answering by whipping out Ziploc bags full of scones. "I think it's time for you guys to be my scone testers. I tried out a bunch of new recipes. We've got leek, dill, and feta scones. Orange blossom and rose water. Gruyère and broccoli. And my personal favorite, sriracha, prosciutto, and crème fraîche." Bodie passes the bags around.

Olivia grabs the sriracha one as she says, "Okay, back to how Kam convinced—"

Once again, Bodie saves me. "What we really need to talk about is the Hinge profile me and Kam created for his mom over dinner last night."

"Wait, really?" Olivia asks. "I wish my mom would date again."

"My mom hard-core resisted," I explain.

"You should have seen the response she got," Bodie says. "She had ten messages the minute her profile went live. Like, bam-bam-bam." I let Bodie take over the conversation. He amuses everyone with stories of the men who messaged my mom. I wonder if she'll actually go out with one of them while I'm gone, but my guess is she's probably deleted the profile by now. She just let us do it to shut us up, I think. I do want her to find love again, though. Which leads me to another thought.

I hope I find love again. The thought sends a chill of surprise through me.

As we get closer to Joshua Tree, we're faced with snowcapped mountains in the distance and rows and rows of windmills, their blades spinning softly in the breeze. Ms. Robin parks by a small strip of shops. There's a coffee shop, a vintage clothing shop, a vegan restaurant, an apothecary, a bougie place that sells undyed clothes. "Quick stop for supplies before we go to the desert," she says. "We'll meet back at the van in thirty minutes, okay?"

"Remember, your cell phones won't work when we get to the park," Byrne says. "So if you need to call your parents—"

"Or your brutally hot boyfriend," Olivia says with a wink to Bodie.

"If you need to call *anyone*, do it here," Byrne says.

We get out of the van into the cold desert air. We walk the streets as a group at first, taking in an old-style saloon and a facade for a shuttered bordello. The whole place feels both frozen in time and oddly modern. At Ms. Robin's urging, I film it all, swooping my phone around to capture a tree trunk painted with a happy face on it. Then artwork on the entrance of a place called Art Queen with paintings of Jesus and Leonard Cohen and another that reads *R.I.P Ego*. I zoom in on the sign for a beauty salon that's also a "Beauty Bubble Museum." I stop filming as we enter the cramped space together. It's right out of the 1950s, like the beauty salon Frenchy in *Grease* would've opened. "I think we've finally found the gayest place on earth," Bodie jokes.

One of the men setting a woman's hair says, "I'll take that as a high compliment. Feel free to look around. I've been collecting this stuff since long before you kids were born."

"It's amazing," Olivia says.

"Thank you," the man says. "You kids heading out to the park?"

"Yeah," Ms. Robin says. "This is our school's GSA group."

One of the women getting her hair done smiles. "My grandson is a gay," she says. "And nobody seems to care. In fact, he says that at his school, gay is old-fashioned."

"It is a little old-fashioned," Fiona says. "I'm genderflux and pan, which is *very* hip."

"I don't know what that means, but I support you all," the woman says as her hair dries.

We explore the place together. The front is a gift shop, with old books and records and heart-shaped sunglasses for sale. In the back is the museum, which consists of dolls and blow-dryers, framed advertisements for beauty products with Bette Davis and Elizabeth Taylor on them, old magazines and beauty care products.

When we leave the bubble of the salon, Bodie has a huge smile on his face. "That place was so cool," he says. "It's kind of wild that it's in Joshua Tree. I always thought of national parks as super hetero places."

"Why do you think that is?" Byrne asks.

"I don't know," Bodie says. "I guess I just think of the queer community existing in cities, you know."

Ms. Robin nods. "It's true that many of us escape to cities in search of our community because we're escaping the hate of our own families or hometowns or religions." Ms. Robin releases the kind of exhale that carries personal history within it. "But that doesn't mean we don't belong everywhere. We do. We belong in nature because we are nature, period."

"Period!" Bodie and Olivia repeat in unison, followed by a quick, unified, "Jinx!"

We keep wandering across the small strip of businesses. Bodie and I enter the apothecary on our own. There are rows of essential oils next to sage sticks and local art and organic chocolate. "Bodie?" I smell a rose-petal herb tincture that reminds me of Persian ice cream. "Why didn't you tell me about your mom and the whole PrEP thing? And what's the video Olivia was talking about?"

Bodie looks out the store window. All the other kids are at an outdoor vintage store, trying on cowboy hats and denim shirts. Taking goofy photos of each other posing like outlaws. "I don't know. There's just been a lot going on, I guess."

"Yeah, I know, but, I mean . . . you can talk to me about Louis."

"I know that," he says curtly. Then, annoyed at the interrogation, he adds, "You're the one who didn't even tell me you slept with Ash until after he . . . you know . . ."

"Vanished?" I ask.

"He didn't *vanish*." His voice is suddenly urgent. "You make it sound like a magic trick. Like he disappeared and might just reappear."

"What do *you* think happened to him?" I ask. "Everyone seems to have a theory. You've never told me yours."

"Kam . . ." He looks over at the woman mixing tinctures behind the aroma bar, begging her with his eyes to come save him from this conversation. "I don't know. Maybe it was dehydration. A snake bite. Maybe he fell off a rock. I don't know. I just know it's horrible. And I'm still not sure going back is a good idea."

"We're already here," I say.

"No, we're not," he argues. "We're not in the park yet. We could turn back. If I called your mom, she'd come pick us up right now."

The woman approaches us. The crystals dangling from her neck jingle-jangle as she walks. "Can I help you?"

"Yeah, actually," I say. "Is there some oil or scent that stimulates memory?" I avoid Bodie's sharp gaze.

"Of course," the woman says. "I could make you a special blend for memory and focus. A little frankincense, some vetiver, sweet orange, patchouli—"

"I'm going to call my mom," Bodie says, clearly uninterested in essential oils. As the woman heads back to the aroma bar to mix my herb tincture, I call my mom too.

"Is everything okay?" she asks breathlessly when she picks up.

"Mom, relax, everything is fine," I assure her. "I'm just calling you from town before we lose cell service."

"Aziz," she whispers. "I could—"

"Stop. Bodie already tried convincing me to turn back. It's not going to happen. I have to go. I have to remember what happened. I have to know why whatever happened to him *didn't* happen to me."

"You're not guilty because you survived," she mutters, her voice soft. She waits for me to say something. I know what she wants me to say, that she also did nothing wrong by surviving, by staying stable and in control even when my dad raged, even when my dad left.

"I wish you got to know him," I say. "If you just knew Ash like I did, you'd understand why I need to—"

"But I did know him," she says. "I met him."

I laugh. "Mom, you met him once and you mocked him—"

"I didn't—"

"I *heard* you." I feel my heart beating out of my chest, like firecrackers are going off inside me. "You and dad laughed about how *American* he was, and made fun of him. You . . . You treated the person I loved like he was a joke, and now you might never know him. You'll never understand how not-a-joke he is. You'll never know a huge piece of my life."

Her voice is soft as she says, "I didn't know you could hear me."

"I could always hear you. The house is small. I heard too much—"

"I'm sorry. Please accept my apology." She hesitates before she keeps going. "With your father . . . Sometimes the easiest way to get along with him was to find a common enemy. I'm not saying Ash was . . . He wasn't our enemy. But sometimes, it was easier to laugh at someone else together than to realize how broken we were as a couple."

Moments come back to me. My parents driving us home from dinner, laughing about how inept our waitress was. My parents in the kitchen, bonding over how awful the president was, how evil the ayatollah was. She's right, common enemies united them. "Maybe this weekend can be an opportunity for you too," I say quietly. "You can go on a date."

"I have no interest in dating," she says. "Every man who's contacted me on that site sounds awful, and you know me. I'll never settle for anything less than perfection."

"Fine, then you can enjoy having the house to yourself."

"You make loneliness sound like a good thing."

"Not loneliness. Solitude." I close my eyes and see Ash by my side. He's sitting cross-legged in front of a cholla cactus, telling me that solitude is the ultimate luxury. The woman has finished my tincture and waves me over. "Mom, I have to go," I say. "I'll be fine. Please don't worry."

I hang up and pay for the tincture. After she hands it to me, the woman says, "Hey, I just want to say, I'm sorry about your boyfriend."

"Oh. You know who I am?" I feel my face get hot, waiting for what she's going to say next. Maybe she thinks I killed Ash. Maybe she's going to tell me she saw him abducted by aliens.

"I remember you and the boy's parents putting flyers up all over town. You put one just down the block."

"Oh, right. Yeah, we did." I close my eyes and remember our feverish search for him. "I guess I thought everybody had forgotten all about it by now. The local papers stopped covering it after a few days. It felt like people stopped caring."

"I'm sure some people did. The world moves so fast these days, and there are so many things to care about." She sighs. "I'm really sorry for what you went through. This is a magical place, but sometimes it's a dark kind of magic."

"Yeah, thanks." I can't help myself from asking, "You haven't seen him, though, have you?"

She squints at me. "The boy who went missing? Of course not." She gazes down at the tincture I'm holding in my hand, like she's finally piecing together what I'm doing in this store. "I hope it helps you with whatever you need to remember. I really am sorry."

When I leave the apothecary, everyone calls me over to the vintage store. "HURRY UP, KAM," Olivia yells. "Group photo." I rush over. Lincoln puts a black cowboy hat on my head and Tucker sets the timer on his phone's camera. We all pose as the screen counts down from ten to one, and then everyone gets on AirDrop so Tucker can share the photo with them. I click accept when the photo pops up. Then my phone rings and when I see who it is my heart skips a beat.

It's my dad.

I haven't heard from him since he left.

I step away from the group, contemplating whether to answer or not. I let the phone vibrate in my hand, like it's him I'm holding. His chaos. The vibration stops. I clutch the phone tight, waiting for a voice mail. Maybe he'll tell me he loves me again. Or that he's sober now. But he doesn't leave a message. I should have answered.

I feel Bodie's eyes on me, wondering what's going on. I want to call my dad back, but I hesitate. I don't know what he wants. I don't know if I'm prepared for whatever he'll tell me before I head back to the desert.

My phone rings again. It's my dad, trying me a second time. Now I'm worried. What if it's not even him calling? What if something happened to him, and—

"Hello?" I say urgently into the phone.

There's silence from the other end. I think I can hear him breathe.

"Dad, are you there?"

Déjà vu. Me waking up in the desert, searching for Ash, unable to remember the details of the night before, screaming up to the sky, to the rock formations, to the expanse of misshapen trees . . . *Ash, are you there?*

"Dad, where are you?"

Ash, where are you?

"Dad, say something."

Ash! Ash!

"Dad . . . Please listen to me. You need to get sober. I know that it's not a thing for us . . . I mean, culturally . . . Therapy and AA and all that . . . I know you don't get it, but please . . ." I feel my throat go dry. "Just go to one meeting, wherever you are. There are meetings everywhere, even on Zoom—"

He hangs up. I clutch the phone to my chest. A piece of me feels like I should call him back. Another piece feels like I should block his number. I don't know what's right, so I do the one thing that can overpower thoughts of my dad. I go to my secret folder of Ash videos.

There he is, reading Rilke to me. *Live the questions now. Perhaps you will then gradually, without noticing it, live along some distant day into the answer.*

I click to another video. There he is, in our school library, at one of the computers because he doesn't have one of his own. *Hey, baby, will you grab my homework assignment from the printer right there, thanks.* I keep the camera on him as I reach for the paper. It's not a homework assignment. It's a page that reads *I love Kam, I love Kam, I love Kam* over and over again until there's no room left on the page.

There he is, saying, *Stop filming me and come kiss me!* Saying, *Put that phone down and be in the moment.*

Bodie is suddenly by my side, watching the video. "What are you doing?" he asks. "Who were you on the phone with?"

"Oh, um, my mom," I say, not sure why I lied. Bodie's my best friend. He knows all about my dad.

"Is she freaking out without you?" Bodie asks.

"Yeah, a little, I guess." Ash is still on my screen. I see Bodie glance over at his image on my phone. "Sometimes I watch my videos of Ash when I'm feeling . . . I don't know . . . When I miss him, I guess."

"Someday we should watch all the videos you've made of us," Bodie says. "You've got years of embarrassing evidence of my awkward phases saved to the cloud."

I think back to all we've been through. I feel terrible for lying to him. "It wasn't my mom on the phone," I blurt out.

"What?" he asks. "Who was it?"

"It was my dad."

He looks at me curiously. "Why didn't you just tell me? What did he say?"

"Nothing. He said nothing. He just . . . hung up. Not a great sign about how he's doing."

"I'm sorry," he says gently.

"Yeah." I release a heavy sigh.

"I still don't get why you lied." Bodie's gaze is sharp. "We're supposed to tell each other everything."

I put my phone away, thinking of everything Bodie and I have shared. And also, of the little things we've chosen not to share. I feel a wave of anger toward him. "That's kind of hilarious coming from you after you didn't tell me about

194

this mysterious video Louis made."

"The video is nothing."

"It's obviously not nothing if you hid it from me."

"I didn't *hide* it from you," he argues. "I was always going to tell you."

"But after you told Olivia and the rest of the GSA." I feel like a blaze that's just getting hotter.

"For fuck's sake, he said he loves me, okay?" he finally blurts out.

"He what?" I ask. I can't seem to keep the sadness from my voice.

"He recorded himself saying he was too scared to say he loves me in person, so he said it on video."

"And you didn't tell me because you love him too." I'm piecing it all together. "Because you're scared that seeing you in love will officially break me, right? Fuck, Bodie."

"I'm sorry," he says. "But—"

"I don't want to hear it," I snap. In the distance, Mr. Byrne and Ms. Robin wave us toward the van. "It's time to go."

"Kam, please!" Bodie begs as I walk away from him. "We don't have to do this."

"No, *you* don't have to do this." I take a shallow breath of mountain air. "*I* have to do it. This is my story. It's not always about you."

"What are you even talking about?" he asks. "I'm here for you. It's all about you."

"No you're not. You're here because of the GSA. You

don't care about Ash. You never did." I feel so many conflicting emotions bubbling up inside me. Fear and rage and confusion. And I'm unleashing them all on him. "And it's always about you. *Your* passions. *Your* friends. *Your* dreams. Sometimes it feels like I'm just tagging along in your life."

"And sometimes it feels like I'm tagging along in your life!" he yells. "Like right now, for example."

I shake my head. "I don't know what's happening," I confess.

"Then let's do what we've always done when things get hard," he says. "Let's watch *The Great British Bake Off* and eat and laugh and be us again. This place is so eerie. Let's just go back home."

I keep my gaze on the mountains in the distance. A smattering of marshmallow clouds opens up from behind them, letting the sun peek out and warm me. I can't go backward. I need to move forward, and in order to do that, I have to travel deeper into the desert. That's where the answers are.

FIRST YEAR

"Please explain to me why you want to sleep in the middle of nowhere?" my mom asks.

"It's not the middle of nowhere. It's a national park. Dad, tell her!"

My dad climbs onto the kitchen counter. He reaches into the highest cabinet for a fresh bottle. He used to be a discerning drinker. He liked his scotch from Scotland. He cared how long it was aged. Now he drinks constantly, often by himself. And we just pretend it's normal that he fills our cabinets with the cheap stuff, the only bottles he can afford to buy in bulk since losing his job. "Tell her what?"

"Tell her it's a national park, not the middle of nowhere," I plead.

My dad shrugs as he grabs a bottle and hops back down to our level. My mom reorganized the kitchen cabinets recently. She moved the alcohol from the pantry into the very top shelf, the one that's too high for anyone to reach without climbing atop the galaxy marble counter, bleached with little white spots from all the times my dad has cut lemons on it. She probably thinks that extra piece of effort might give my dad pause before drinking. Or maybe she thinks it'll give *me* pause, because she's afraid I'll start drinking like he does.

"I've read about it." My mom moves khoreshteh gheymeh around her plate. "It's a dangerous place. People get lost there. Dehydrated."

"We would bring water. Tell her, Dad."

My dad joins us in the kitchen nook where we have dinner. He opens his bottle and pours himself a tall glass as my mom gives him a stern look. "I don't argue with your mother because I never win."

My mom shakes her head. She doesn't take the bait. She never does in front of me. She saves her scorn for when she thinks I can't hear her. "I've done my research."

"What kind of research?" my dad asks.

I can feel my mom trying hard to stay composed. Her lips tighten ever so slightly. "Research into this place Kamran wants to go to with complete strangers."

"The place is called Joshua Tree, and the people are Ash and his parents. They are not strangers," I huff. "He's my boyfriend, and his parents are amazing people. Which you would know if you actually spent any time with them."

"I met Ash," my mom says, curt.

"Once!" I scoff. "And only because I forced you into having a conversation with him after our choir concert." My mom was exceedingly polite when she met Ash. She told him the concert was beautiful. She asked where he planned to attend college next year. She kept her questions short, not expecting Ash's long and winding answers. Ash told her he was still deciding between going to art school or not going to college at all. I saw the look on her face when he said this, like she could never approve of me being with a bad influence who might dissuade me from going to college. He told my mom that he wasn't sure creativity could be taught, so maybe his job as an artist isn't to go to college, but to find ways to get closer to God. That's when the look on my mom's face turned from concern to panic.

Later that night, when my parents thought I was asleep, I heard my mom tell my dad about Ash and his theories about creativity. She said it was the most pretentious thing she ever heard. He said, *This is why therapists and philosophy professors shouldn't be allowed to have children.*

I've always wished my parents could just get along with each other, but I wasn't prepared for the thing that united them in laughter to be how silly they found my boyfriend.

"If you want us to spend more time with Ash, how about we have him over for dinner soon?" my mom suggests. "Just forget about all this camping business."

I roll my eyes. "You're only inviting him to dinner as a negotiation tactic to stop me from going. Meanwhile, his parents have spent hours and hours with me. They *know* me."

My mother ignores me. "Bahman, help me out. There are rattlesnakes out there. One bite and your son is gone. Tell him to stay here with us."

I swallow down hard. I've done my own research too. I know there are snakes out there, and they terrify me. I've read about how I shouldn't put my hand in any dark spaces because it's hands they like to bite. But I also know that a snake bite won't kill me. "That's actually not true, Mom," I explain. "If we get bit, and we won't, we could drive to a nearby hospital and get antivenom."

My dad closes his eyes when the alcohol goes down, like the only way to enjoy it is to drown us out. When he opens them, he says, "When I was a kid, my parents wouldn't monitor our every move. They would let us go anywhere we wanted. They would never even ask where we were when we got home. They'd just feed us and let us live our lives."

My mother's eyes narrow. "Forgive me for not emulating your parents' methods, given how—" She stops herself from saying more. My mother lacks many things, but not self-control.

"Given what?" my dad asks.

My mom walks over to a framed painting Bodie's parents gave us as a gift. She shifts it to the left until it's perfectly even. "It's nothing," she says, her lips rigid.

But it's not nothing. It's *that* moment. The moment when I make my exit because I can sense things are about to erupt. "I'm going to Ash's for a bit." I take my dish to the sink and wash it.

"You can put it in the dishwasher," my mom says quietly. I can hear the regret in her voice. I know she wishes she was raising me in a perfect home, with a perfect dad, in a perfect world.

"There's no cell phone service there," my mom says. "How will I know you're safe?"

My dad laughs, a deep, self-righteous cackle. "How in the world did parents know their children were safe before they could track their every move?"

"I do not track his every move," she says.

"You're always checking his location on your phone." My dad speaks in an accusatory slur. "You told me you'll never let him get a driver's license because you'd rather he use your Uber account so you can track the cars." I hate my dad's drunkenness, and yet, I appreciate what he's saying. I do feel suffocated here. He just wants me to be free.

"I was joking!" she says, trying for lightness.

"No, you weren't."

"I'm leaving. I'll be back before ten." I give my mom a quick kiss on each cheek. My dad offers me a nod. He's never been one for hugs and kisses. Neither has my mom, really. Her kisses are polite, obligatory. Neither of my parents ever tell me they love me, or that they're proud of me. Ash thinks that's unbelievable, but to me, a dad who tells you he loves you every day is the unbelievable thing. Before I walk out, I say, "Joshua Tree is Ash's favorite place in the whole world and I'm going, whether you like it or not."

"Kamran, we haven't agreed to—"

Before my mom can finish, my dad stops her. "Let him go, Leila."

I make my escape. My bike is just outside the front door where I left it, leaning against the humongous ficus tree that's fused itself into the foundation of our home. All the windows are open because it's hot and we can't afford air-conditioning anymore. Since my dad lost his job, we've had to cut back wherever we can. No cable. No air-conditioning. No gardener, which I don't mind because I like feeding the flowers and plants the little water we're allowed to offer them given the drought restrictions. Watching them bloom and die and bloom again.

Through the open windows, I can hear my mom coolly ask, "Would it be impossible for you to support me once in a while?"

"I could say the same to you," my dad responds.

"Could you now? Because the way I see it, I'm supporting you in every way. Who pays the bills?" The cruelty in my mother's voice shocks me. She's never spoken to me with the sharp edge she addresses my dad with.

Bodie bikes up just as my dad is railing that it's not his fault human beings are being replaced with robots. "You coming or going?" Bodie asks me.

"I was on my way to see . . ." I hesitate before saying, "Ash." Ever since Ash ghosted me, Bodie seems to like him even less than he used to. I change the subject to something

202

that bonds us instead of divides us, our parents. "But right now, I'm listening to the beautiful sound of my parents fighting. Hear that?" We both listen for a few seconds. My dad screams. Says my mom treats him like a second child. My mom fights back with steely words. Tells my dad she treats him like a child because he acts like one.

"I'm sorry." Bodie offers me a supportive smile. "I thought we could prep for the math test together, but maybe we need a more relaxing study space than your house."

"I already studied," I say.

"Fucking overachiever," he says with a smile. "You're a Persian parent's wet dream."

"You're one to talk. You study just as hard as I do, and you look like Peak Marlon Brando. You're the ideal Persian child and you know it."

"Except for the fact that I'm a homosexual and that I have no intention of ever going to law school," he says with a sad laugh. "Is it absurd that I'm more scared of telling my parents I want to be a chef than I was to come out?"

"When it comes to our families, it's all absurd."

From inside the house comes the sound of my mom screaming, "Stop, please. I know *why* you're not working. What I don't understand is why you can't help in other ways."

"At least the neighbors can't understand them," Bodie says.

"Yeah." I shrug. "But I'm glad you can understand them. Not just the language. But, you know, the cultural stuff."

Bodie's parents may still love each other. They may not fight the way mine do. But he gets the history my parents carry because his parents carry the same traumas.

"What other ways?" my dad asks.

"With Kamran," my mom yells. "I fix his meals. I do all the school paperwork. The endless forms. I'm the one who got him into this new charter school, and made sure Farbod's family applied too, so he could keep his best friend close."

Bodie hugs me from behind. Imitating my mom's voice, he says, "Keep your best friend close, okay?"

My mom continues. "I take him to the doctor, to the dentist. It used to make sense because of your work schedule, but—"

"My work schedule was never why you did everything and do everything," my dad spits out. "I let you do everything because if I ever try to help, you tell me I don't do it right." He has a point too.

"Like when?" my mom asks.

"I don't know," my dad screams.

Bodie puts a hand on my shoulder. "You know you don't have to listen to this, right? We can ride off and go get ice cream. My treat."

But I don't move. "I need to hear this," I tell him. "It's better to know than to imagine."

"Is it? Why?" Bodie asks.

"Because whatever I imagine will be worse than what they say to each other."

Bodie nods. He puts a head on my shoulder as we listen to my parents fighting.

"The birthday party!" my dad yells.

"What birthday party?"

"The party. You know the one. The trampoline."

"That was five years ago. He was ten. *That's* your example of showing up as a dad. Taking him and Farbod to a birthday party half a decade ago."

My dad's voice becomes deeper, louder, more out of control. "No, that's my example of why I don't dare do anything anymore. Because I took him and Farbod to that stupid party, and you blamed me for his sprained wrist."

"It was a fracture, not a sprain!" My mom sounds just as angry as she did five years ago when my dad brought me home from the hospital. "And yes, I blame you. Because trampolines are dangerous, and—"

"SO WHAT?" my dad screams, and I feel my body recoil into itself. "Life is dangerous. Crossing the street is dangerous. Getting in a car is dangerous. You want him trapped in a cocoon."

"No, I don't. But I also don't want him doing things that could—"

"That could make him a *man*," my dad says, slowly and deliberately.

"What are you saying?" my mom asks.

I can feel Bodie's body stiffen in anticipation of what's coming next.

"You're the reason he's the way he is," my dad accuses.

"You won't let him become a man."

"A man?" My mom says the word like it's an insult. "The men in my life all died being a man."

"You know what I mean," my dad says. "I'm not asking you to send him to war. Just stop coddling him so much and maybe he'll change. Maybe this phase—"

Déjà vu. My dad angrily saying my sexuality is just *a phase*. Turning my coming out into his tantrum. I feel so stupid for thinking my dad wanted her to stop suffocating me so I could be free, when the truth is he wants her to stop so I can be straight.

Bodie looks over at me. "Kam, seriously, let's get out of here. You don't need to relive your coming out. Once was bad enough."

"At least I accept him." My mom speaks in a hush that barely reaches me. "At least I've met Ash once, which is more than I can say for you."

"And you mocked him!"

"I mocked him because he's pretentious, not because he's a boy. If Kam was dating a nice boy like Farbod, I would be thrilled."

Bodie and I both giggle nervously when she says this. "Oh God, of course my mom wants me to date you," I say. "She really doesn't get it."

Bodie bites a hangnail. "Yeah" is all he says.

"I'm going out," my dad yells. "Enjoy having the house to yourself for a few hours. It's your house anyway. You pay the bills."

"I think that's our cue," I say as I hop on my bike. Bodie follows my lead.

"Go," my mom screams as I throw my helmet on and latch it. "Go to your bars and your gambling and wherever else you disappear to." As I start to ride away, I hear her yell, "And don't bother looking for your car keys. I hid them."

"I would've thought you'd want me to drive myself into a tree," he screams. "Then you'd be free of me."

Bodie and I pedal as fast as we can. Away, away, away. From their screams, and their sadness, and their endless cycle of blame. We stop at our favorite ice cream place. I watch our bikes while Bodie goes inside and orders. He doesn't ask me what I want. Bodie has strong opinions on ice cream. He thinks you should always have more than one flavor, and one of them should always be vanilla, because it's comforting. And the other should always be one of the most adventurous flavors available, because it's exciting. Bodie thinks food, like life, is best when it's both comforting and adventurous.

He comes back out with two cups of ice cream.

"We have vanilla and cardamom, and vanilla and lavender honey. Which one do you want?" he asks.

"Lavender honey." I grab my ice cream.

We eat in silence for a bit, taking bites from each other's cups without asking.

"How are things going with Ash?" he finally asks.

I'm shocked he's asking about Ash. Sometimes it feels like my friendship with Bodie and my relationship with

Ash exist in parallel universes. "Great," I say.

"He hasn't ghosted you lately?" he asks with a raised eyebrow.

I sigh. I thought maybe he was ready to support us. "Bodie, don't be like my parents. I know Ash isn't your favorite person, but I love him and—"

"Wait, you love him?" He pushes his spoon too hard into the melting ice cream in his cup. Some of it spills out. "You've never told me that."

"I've never told him that either," I confess.

"Does he . . . love you?"

I pause. "I think so." I feel like he loves me. Maybe that's enough. "I mean, he says it in writing. A lot actually."

"It just feels fast," Bodie says. "I think true love has to be . . . I don't know, earned. It can't be some instant thing."

"Ash and I aren't some instant thing. And not everyone has to experience love the same way. Maybe it happens differently for everyone." I look at Bodie curiously, wondering what he knows about true love anyway, when he's rejected everyone he's ever tried to date.

"Are you going to tell him?" he asks.

I shrug. "I don't know. Somehow it seems so much easier telling you how I feel about him than it is telling him."

He smiles. "Maybe that's because you're so much more comfortable with me."

I shrug. "Or maybe it's because I'm afraid of scaring him off."

"Yeah, well . . ." Bodie hesitates before saying, "We both

know he likes to disappear." When he sees the flash of annoyance in my eyes, he quickly apologizes. "I'm sorry. I'm just protective of my best friend, okay? But I'm happy for you too. And I do want to get to know him better. Not that he makes it easy, but you know, maybe we can all go get a meal. Or go bowling."

"Bowling?" I laugh. "An activity all three of us hate."

"Maybe the hatred will bond us." He laughs. "Isn't hatred of kashk bademjoon what first bonded us?"

I smile at the memory. "In fairness, no four-year-old wants eggplant in their lunch box."

"I used to have such an unsophisticated palate." He shakes his head, judging himself.

"You were four!" I laugh. "Besides, we both love it now."

He nods. "Exactly. People change. If we can go from hating eggplant to loving it, then maybe your parents will figure their shit out, and maybe someday Ash and I will be best friends."

"You're *my* best friend. I don't want that to change. I just want you to not hate him."

He drinks the soupy melted ice cream. "You're free to go to him whenever you want. I really do have to study tonight."

I give him a quick hug. "Thanks for the ice cream, and for being the only person in my whole life who understands how fucked up my family is."

I hop on my bicycle and pedal toward Ash, and toward a family that welcomes me, accepts me, and doesn't erupt like a volcano every night.

I brake outside Ash's apartment building. Crouch down to lock my bike at a parking meter. I feel his hands around my eyes. "Guess who?" he asks.

"Salvatore?"

"No, he's beatboxing and rapping in the summer rain."

"Carmen?"

"Nope, she's too busy walking the streets so mean."

"Norman Fucking Rockwell."

He laughs. "In the flesh." He takes his hands off my eyes.

I can feel his hardness as his body presses against mine. "Norman hard as a fucking rock-well," I say, loving the mischief in my voice.

"Do you think maybe . . . in the desert . . . you'll be ready?" he asks. "Not that I'm pressuring you or anything. I just . . . I'm ready, that's all."

I spin around and kiss him. "I feel ready too, but . . ."

"But?"

"I just . . . I'm not sure I want my first time to be in a desert."

"What better place to make love than under the stars?"

"I love that you call it *making love*."

"What should I call it?" he asks with an innocence that makes me want to leap into his arms. "We can escape my parents in the desert . . . find some private cove—"

"Get bitten by snakes or attacked by a coyote—"

"Okay, fine, we'll do it the traditional way, in a *bed*, with all the windows closed so no wild animals attack us."

"And doors locked so no parents walk in on us," I add.

He kisses me. Then he points up to his bedroom window. "I was drawing when you got here. I saw you turn the corner on your bike, and I asked myself, *Who is that hottie?* And then I realized, *Wait a minute, that's my hottie.* And I ran down to you."

I blush. "What were you drawing?" I ask.

He gazes at me lovingly. "You always change the subject when I tell you how gorgeous you are."

"Let's go inside," I suggest.

He rolls his eyes. "I'm just going to keep telling you you're beautiful until you believe it."

"I'm average," I say. "Bodie's the handsome one."

He runs a tender hand along my cheek. "I know your parents probably compare the two of you all the time, but you don't have to do that."

"Yeah, I know." There's so much more I want to tell him. Like how much I love him. But words don't flow out of me the way they do with him. Neither does love. "I wasn't saying I think Bodie's hot. I think you're hot."

"He's much hotter than me, and I'm not jealous of him at all," he says.

"The truth is, I think . . ." I take a calming breath. "I think you're the most beautiful person in the whole universe."

He smiles. "The universe is vast. There's probably a planet out there where the beings are more beautiful than anything we could imagine." He points to the sky. "What do you see up there?"

"Smog."

"Exactly." He wraps his big arms around me. He's four inches taller than me, thirty pounds heavier, two years older. I like the wisdom those two extra years have granted him. I love the way his body envelops mine when he scoops me up in his arms. "Now imagine the same exact sky, but without all that smog. That's what we'll see in Joshua Tree. Stars. Constellations."

"It sounds incredible," I say.

He kisses my neck. "We're behind that smog, right next to each other. Cancer and Leo, side by side, always."

I close my eyes, imagining us in the desert, under our constellations.

"Come on," he says. "There's dessert inside."

His parents greet me with hugs, vegan peach pie, and rice cream. Mr. and Mrs. Greene throw questions at me as I eat. *Have I spoken to my parents about the camping trip yet? Do I need them to help me with a packing list? Do I have any snack or drink requests?*

"My parents haven't agreed to let me go yet," I tell them. "But I'm going. I just have to get my mom to not be so nervous."

"About what?" Mrs. Greene asks.

"She's not really an outdoorsy person. I don't know that she's ever left a city."

"Sounds like my kind of woman," Dawn cracks.

"Since Dawn isn't joining us, we could invite your parents. We'd love to meet them, and what better place to bond than on a camping trip?"

"No, it's okay. I mean, thank you, but it's not their thing, and . . . well, they're really busy." I don't say that the last thing I want is my parents coming with us. This trip is about being with Ash in the place that makes him happiest, but it's also about having a weekend away from my parents and their eruptions.

I feel Ash's inquisitive eyes on me, like he can sense all the things I'm not saying.

Mr. Greene puts an arm around his wife. "If you need us to talk to your parents, we're more than happy to. We can be a very convincing pair. Just ask Ash about the time we got him to eat beetles."

I grimace, then say, "I guess it depends on which one you ate. I bet Ringo tastes good."

"Ringo is without a doubt the hottest Beatle." Mrs. Greene raises her hand up, and I give her a high five.

"You're both wrong," Ash says. "It's undoubtedly George. No question. No competition. George for the win."

"I hate agreeing with you, baby brother," Dawn says. "But definitely George."

We all look at Mr. Greene now, who shrugs. "I'm as hetero as people come, but if I had to go bi, it would be for John."

I sink into my chair as we laugh and debate who the hottest Beatle was. I wonder what it would be like to live in a home with a dad who talks about going bi for John Lennon, with a mom who treats her son's boyfriend like a member of the family, with parents who show each other physical affection at the dinner table.

When we've cleaned our plates, we move into the kitchen. On the fridge are sketches I've never seen. "Are those new, Ash?" I ask.

"Aren't they incredible?" Mrs. Greene pulls one of the drawings off the fridge. It's undeniably Ash's work, but it's an evolution. The mysterious monsters he loves to draw are there, but they're in a new landscape, in a place that looks like an undiscovered planet. "This is my favorite. I don't know where my son gets his imagination from."

Ash blushes as he grabs the drawing and puts it back on the fridge. "It's nothing."

Mrs. Greene puts the rest of the pie in the fridge. "It's not nothing. It's a whole universe you've created out of thin air."

"Not out of thin air," Ash says. "They—"

"They come from divine inspiration," Dawn says, gently teasing him. "And maybe a little bit from—"

Ash's dad cuts her off. "Dawn!"

Dawn glances at her phone. "I have to go. The tennis team is going out tonight. I'll see you guys later."

Mr. Greene gives Dawn a strong hug. "Please be home by—"

"Dad!" Dawn is incredulous. "We've already covered this. If I were living in the dorms, you wouldn't know where

I was going and what time I was coming home. And since I'm only living here to save you money, you don't get to tell me what time to be home or where to go."

Mr. Greene smiles at his daughter's confident combativeness. "You're right," he says. "Have fun."

When Dawn is gone, I ask, "Mrs. Greene, can I see those portfolio books Dawn mentioned?"

Ash rolls his eyes. "Come on, we don't need to look at the terrible art I used to make."

"Please," I beg. "I just love your drawings. It's like . . ." I want to say it's like looking into his soul, but words like that don't sound natural coming from me the way they do from Ash.

"Okay, fine," Ash says.

Mrs. Greene leaves and returns with a stack of portfolio books. As I flip through them, I find myself drawn into the bizarre creatures and worlds Ash has created through the years, desperate to solve the beautiful mystery of the boy I love.

My parents finally agree to let me go the afternoon of one of their poker nights. I call Ash and tell him the good news. Not only am I going to the desert with him, but I'll have the whole house to myself for the night. Poker doesn't end until at least midnight. He asks if he should show up early enough to see my parents before they leave. "It would be nice to finally meet your dad before whisking you off to the desert."

"You're whisking me, huh?" I ask with a sly smile. "I think I'd like to be whisked."

"Come on, be serious," he begs. "He's your dad. I want to thank him for making you."

It does sound nice to finally introduce Ash to my dad. But I think of all the things that could go wrong. I can only imagine my dad's response if Ash really thanks him for *making me*. Those words would sound so silly and foreign to my dad. "I think it's probably best if you come when they're gone," I say.

Downstairs, I can hear my parents arguing. My mom begs my dad to change his clothes. "You've worn the same shirt for the last four card games."

"Yeah, okay, I get it." Ash doesn't try to hide the disappointment in his voice.

"Ash . . . I . . ." My voice wavers. "I think, if you really did want to whisk me, or if you wanted me to whisk you—"

"We're not talking about baking, are we?" he asks, his voice bright and clandestine.

"No, but we are talking about . . . cream." I immediately cackle. "I can't believe I just said that."

"You have a future writing erotic fan fiction." He switches to a deep audiobook voice. "Ash Greene whisked me until my cream was smooth and my sugar was raw. Then he took his hardening dough and—"

"Not his dough!" I cackle again. "Anyway, maybe tonight might be a good night for it. I feel . . ." I stop myself from saying that I feel needy, because neediness isn't hot. Instead I say, "I feel ready."

"I feel ready too." When he hangs up, I hold the phone close to my ear, like he's still there. I pull up my videos. There he is, holding the boom box above his head. The hero of my very own romantic comedy. And tonight, he'll be the hero of my very own erotic fan fiction.

Downstairs, my parents continue to fight about my dad's shirt choice. My mom's voice is contained but incredulous. "People will think we can't afford new clothes."

My dad chuckles harshly. "We *can't* afford new clothes, but that's not why I'm wearing the shirt."

"Then why?" my mom asks. "It hasn't even been dry-cleaned. Honestly, I'm not trying to be mean, but it smells."

I hear the sound of my dad reaching for a bottle. The climbing onto the counter. The opening of the high cabinet. The waterfall of whiskey that cascades into a tall glass. "You want to know why, Leila? You want to force every little secret out of me until I have nothing left for myself?"

"Bahman, it's just a shirt—"

My dad's voice is seething now. "It's not just a shirt. It's my *lucky* shirt. I win when I wear it. I didn't clean it because I was afraid the luck would wash away if—"

"Bahman, are you listening to yourself right now?" my mom asks softly. "You're talking like one of the religious nuts you laugh at." I feel myself tense like I'm being insulted too. I'm a victim of my own superstitious mind.

"You win, Leila. Here, take the shirt. Wash it. Throw it out. I don't care." My dad must be taking his shirt off. He's

217

probably flinging it at her. "The luck only works when no one knows about it. So now the luck is gone."

As my dad walks away, my mom calls out to him. "I'm not accepting the blame for your losses tonight. If you lose, it's because you make impulsive bets. Not because you're not wearing some dirty piece of fabric!" She marches toward their bedroom.

My parents are still arguing when Bodie's parents come to pick them up. I don't bother going downstairs to greet them. I'm too busy cleaning my room up for Ash. I open up my shoebox of Ash memories, where I keep everything he gave me. The sketches and poems, starting with the sunrise and the Lana lyrics, up to the last one he gave me, a sketch of ravens with a poem about flight winding its way through a cloudy sky. I've kept all the little notes he's hidden in my locker or in my backpack or in my books for me to find. Notes that read, *I love my baby*, or *I love Kam*, or that have his favorite quotes. Like, *Love is space and time measured with the heart.—Marcel Fucking Proust!* And of course, the paper he asked me to grab from our library's printer. The one that reads, *I love Kam. I love Kam. I love Kam. I love Kam.* I close the box and hide it all the way at the top of my closet. I don't need Ash finding it, knowing how obsessive I am about storing my memories of him.

"KAM!" my mom yells from downstairs. "COME DOWN. FARBOD'S HERE."

I feel a surge of panic. Bodie was supposed to be having a movie night with some of the GSA kids tonight. They asked me to join, but I told them I was going to stay home and study. I could have said I was going to be seeing Ash, but I didn't want to answer the follow-up questions about what we were doing. I take one last look at my bedroom, satisfied with how it looks, then head to the front door. "Hi, Mr. Omidi, hi, Mrs. Omidi, you both look great."

Bodie's mom proudly adjusts the collar of her husband's shirt. "I just bought this for him. It's organic."

Bodie's dad laughs. "What makes a shirt organic?"

I glance at my parents, who just argued over an old shirt, who can no longer afford new shirts, let alone organic ones. They say nothing. I turn to Bodie. "I thought you were going to watch a movie with Lincoln and Olivia and—"

"Olivia has a sore throat," Bodie explains. "She tested negative, but out of an abundance of caution—"

Bodie's dad interrupts him. "Abundance of caution. Three words I've heard every day since the pandemic began. It's amazing how much vocabulary has been created in the last year. Social distancing. Quarantine."

Bodie gently corrects his dad. "Dad, people used the word *quarantine* before this last year. Anyway, Olivia canceled our plans because she decided to practice social distancing by quarantining herself out of an abundance of caution." Bodie's dad laughs appreciatively. "And since she was hosting the movie night, we all just decided to do our own thing. I figured we could get some studying done." He holds up his heavy backpack. Sees the ashen look on my face. "Sorry, did you have other plans tonight?"

I feel my pulse race. "No, of course not, let's study."

"Our boys are both so brilliant," Bodie's mom says. "Always working so hard. Who says the next generation is lazy and entitled?"

"*You* just said it, Mom," Bodie says with a laugh.

Mrs. Omidi runs a loving hand through Bodie's hair. "Kalak," she says. It means wise guy or trickster or cheat, but it's a term of endearment in our culture. "Kamran, have you given more thought to what you want to be when you grow up?"

"Oh, um—Yeah. I mean—No," I stammer.

"Maybe you'll be a lawyer like Farbod," Mrs. Omidi suggests.

I see Bodie's jaw clench.

"Wouldn't it be nice if our sons worked together just like we do?" Mrs. Omidi continues.

"Kamran is smart enough to be anything he wants." My mom runs a hand through my hair, like she needs to prove she's just as proud of me as Bodie's mom is of him. "Lawyer, doctor, businessman."

Bodie and I share a smirk at how "anything he wants" really means only three acceptable options for Iranian parents.

My mom claps her hands. "If you kids get hungry, there's leftover khoreshteh karafs in the fridge and enough rice for both of you."

"Wish us luck!" Bodie's dad says lightheartedly before they leave. But it's clear he doesn't care much if he's lucky or not tonight. He has a job. Win or lose at the poker table, he'll be okay.

But for my tortured dad and his secret superstitions, winning is a matter of survival.

Bodie barrels into the house when the parents take off in his dad's car. "We don't have to study if you don't want to," he says. "I brought a little surprise." He pulls out a screener for *House of Gucci*. "I was going to bring it to Olivia's, but we could watch it. My dad has some client who's a producer and he gave him all his screeners as a thank-you gift. We can rewind every time Gaga says, '*Father, son, and House of Gucci.*'" Bodie puts the Italian accent on thick for his Patrizia Reggiani impersonation.

When I don't laugh, he knows something's up. "Is everything okay?" he asks. "Is it Ash?" I look at him and nod. "Oh fuck, he hasn't disappeared again, has he?"

"What? No!" I say defensively.

"Then what is it?" He heads to the kitchen and I follow him in. He opens the fridge and takes a look at the Persian stew through the glass Tupperware it's in. "Your mom's karafs is perfection. Can I heat some up?" He doesn't wait for an answer. He just takes the Tupperware out of the fridge, then grabs the rice too. I feel so annoyed with him for barging in like this, even though we've been barging in on each other since we were kids. We've never asked for an invitation to each other's homes. Never needed to.

"Why do you do that?" I ask.

"What?" He makes a plate for himself, serving ample

helpings of rice and stew.

"You ask a question, but you don't wait for the answer."

"What? I don't do that." He puts his plate in the microwave and sets it to two minutes. "I'm morally opposed to microwaves, but also starving so don't judge me." The plate spins in the illuminated appliance, giving him his very own spotlight.

"I'm not judging you for using a microwave, but Ash—"

"What's going on? Wait, did you guys break up?" The hope in his question feels like a dagger.

"Things are going great. My parents said I can go to the desert with him as long as we all get tested before we go—"

"Oh, you didn't tell me." The microwave dings and he pulls his plate of food out. He eats standing up.

"It just happened," I explain. "I was going to tell you."

"At least you get to go somewhere," he says. "My parents canceled our winter break trip to Hawaii because of the cases going up. It sucks."

I want to tell him what doesn't suck is that his parents can still plan joyful family trips when my parents do nothing but argue about money and my dad's joblessness. But instead I say nothing.

"I'll miss you when you're gone," he says. "How long are you going for?"

"Just five days," I say. "It's a quick trip."

"Five days without you, what will I do?" Bodie asks melodramatically.

Then the doorbell rings.

Bodie looks at me curiously.

"It's Ash," I explain, annoyed at myself for sounding apologetic when I haven't done anything wrong.

Bodie puts his plate down. He looks wounded. "I thought . . . You said you were studying. I thought that's why you couldn't join us."

"I was. I mean, that was my plan when I told you. But then my parents agreed, and Ash and I wanted to celebrate." The doorbell rings again.

Bodie follows me to the front door. "Aren't you nervous about having him in the house? What if your parents come home early?"

"My parents have never come home early." I turn to Bodie before I open the door. "He hasn't even met my dad. I just want him to see where I live. That's it."

"Okay," Bodie says.

When I open the door, Ash is holding a stack of drawings with a book on top of them, and a large stainless steel whisk. He has a huge smile on his face . . . until he sees Bodie. "Oh, Bodie, hey, I didn't know you'd be here."

"Are you guys baking?" Bodie asks, his eyes on the whisk. I know what he's thinking. Cooking and baking are his domain.

Ash glances my way with a wicked grin as he says, "It's just an inside joke."

Bodie receives that answer like a slap across the face.

"Right. Well, in that case, I'll show myself *outside*."

"I didn't mean it that way," Ash says quickly. "I just meant—"

Bodie picks up his backpack and throws it on. "No, it's really okay. I'm going to Olivia's tonight anyway." I wonder why Bodie feels the need to lie about his plans. As he heads to the door, Bodie points to the book Ash has on top of his sketches. "Ugh, *The Alchemist*," Bodie says. "One of my mom's friends made me read it. She said it was deep, but it was so shallow. Do you have to read it for school?"

"No, it's one of my favorite books," Ash responds flatly. "I wanted to share it with Kam."

Bodie takes a deep breath. "Oh, sorry, I guess the book just felt blamey and fake-spiritual to me," he explains. Before Ash can respond, Bodie quickly adds, "Anyway, I should go. Enjoy your inside jokes."

When Bodie leaves, I ask Ash to give me a minute.

I step outside. "Bodie, wait!" He stops and stares at me.

"Why do you have to be like that with him?" I ask.

"Like what?" he asks. "You're the one who lied to me about him coming over."

"I didn't lie. You had other plans. I just—"

"Oh, just admit you lied," he says. "You want him to be all yours, and he is all yours. And you're his. And I'm fine with that, but—"

"But you're *not* fine with that," I yell. "You're jealous."

"Oh please, not this again," he scoffs. "Trust me, I don't want to be with Ash."

"I didn't say you want to be with Ash." I try to soften my tone. "But you want to be with *someone*, and you're jealous because you can't find the right someone for you, and I found the right someone for me. And you never thought I'd find my person first because you're the good-looking one."

"What?" he asks. "I don't think that at all. I've never—"

"Well, that's how it feels," I confess. "And I hope you do find your person, I really do."

"I hate the term *my person*," Bodie says quietly. "It's so silly."

"Well, obviously I don't think so," I say, my voice combative.

"Okay, I'm sorry." But there's nothing apologetic in his harsh tone.

"You know the thing I always loved most about our friendship?" I ask.

"Are you going to answer your own question, or should I guess?" His eyes travel to my bedroom, which we can see from outside. I look over, and see Ash has walked in and turned my bedside lamp on.

"I love that we've never competed with each other the way most siblings or best friends do."

"Yeah," he says. "That's true."

Ash pulls my bedroom curtains shut. "But it doesn't feel that way anymore," I say. "Ever since I met Ash, it feels like we're not on the same side. I mean, I'm on your side, but it sometimes doesn't feel like you're on mine."

"I don't—" Bodie's voice breaks. "I don't want it to feel

that way. I'm sorry. I guess I didn't know what it would feel like. And I guess I always imagined that when we found boyfriends, we'd be like our moms, you know. We'd go on double dates and socialize together and still be *us* even though there were these other people in our lives."

"We can still get there," I tell him. "You'll meet someone soon."

"Yeah, who?" he asks.

"I don't know. I'm not a psychic. But I do know one thing."

"What?" he asks.

"I'll call you tomorrow," I say. "That I know. I'll call you tomorrow, and every other tomorrow."

He manages a smile. "Not if I call you first." I know that's his way of letting me know we're still okay. Still best friends.

When I go inside, I head to my bedroom. "Ash?" I call out as I make my way down the hallway. There's soft music coming from the bedroom. Lana. The *Honeymoon* album. I knock on the closed door, which feels silly, because it's my room. "Ash, can I come in?" I ask.

"Give me two more minutes," he calls out.

"What are you doing in there?" I ask.

"Patience, my lucky one," he says.

I let the music calm me. *Say you want me to, say you want me to,* she sings, and I feel every word. I want to rush into the bedroom and let Ash hold me. Heal me. Make me dream away my dad's history of violence, the fire of Bodie's jealousy.

"Close your eyes," he orders from inside the bedroom. I do as I'm told. The door opens. He presses against me from behind. His palms are on my eyes. I don't open them, but I can see so much. Swirls of lines in the darkness, like the lines of his palms are dancing in my imagination. I open my eyes when he pulls his hands back to his side, and I'm stunned. He's covered my walls in the stack of drawings he had brought with him. "Don't worry," he says. "I used removable putty. Your walls won't be damaged."

"I wasn't thinking of my walls." I take in the drawings. There are huge rocks. Cacti. Clouds and sky. Ravens and lizards and creatures I don't recognize. And Joshua trees, so many, each a different shape.

"You wanted our first time to be in a bedroom, and I wanted it to be in the desert. I figured this was a perfect way of making both of our wishes come true. I've turned the bedroom into a desert. Double vision."

"Double vision?" I echo.

He moves close to me and whispers in my ear, "*For double the vision with my eyes do see. And a double vision is always with me. With my inward eye, 'tis an old man gray. With my outward, a thistle across my way.*" He points to an image of a thistle blooming in the desert dirt. The base of the plant looks like an old man's body. Its leaves like a man's limbs. "That's William Blake. I didn't write it. But I did write that one." He points to a sketch above my bed. A row of Joshua trees. There's a poem scribbled around the trees, but the sketch is too high for me to make it out.

When I pause in front of a colorful sketch of an animal, he explains, "That's a kangaroo rat, which is neither a kangaroo nor a rat." He points to another sketch. To something that looks like a turtle. "Desert tortoise. I like how slow it moves. I like being reminded that we don't have to move so fast, you know."

"The desert tortoise is like our favorite album," I say. "A languid reminder to slow down our lives."

"Yes." He kisses my neck. "And we don't need to go too fast tonight. We can take it as slow as we want."

"Like two desert tortoises," I suggest.

With a smile, he takes his hoodie and T-shirt off. And then his pants and his underwear. "Is this okay?" he asks.

I run my hands on the skin of his backside. "It's much better than okay."

"Your turn," he says.

I hesitate, then I slowly peel off my clothes, enjoying the moment, reminding myself to move like a tortoise. Not to rush past the best moments of my life at accelerated speed. I want to savor him.

"You're so beautiful," he says quietly.

No one ever called me beautiful before him. I feel my body changing. My posture prouder. My heart calmer. I never want to forget how this feels, to actually believe I'm beautiful. Worthy of love.

Our hands lock into each other effortlessly. I love his scent on my sheets. His skin fuses into mine, like we're becoming one. Every time I close my eyes and reopen them, he looks different, like he's changing in front of my very eyes. His skin milkier. His eyes deeper, a portal to a secret place. His freckles glimmer like stars in some undiscovered galaxy.

We laugh. We kiss. We cuddle. We stop sometimes and just face each other.

We ask questions when we need to. Ask each other what feels good and what doesn't. We don't go as far as I thought we might. We choose to stick to just touching each other for now. But we talk about all the things we want to do when the time is right. I hesitate before verbalizing each fantasy, and he tells me never to be ashamed of my desires. When my hand guides his body to a climax just as his hand takes mine to the same peak, I feel the absence of shame, the swelling not just of my body but of my pride.

"Wow," he whispers.

"Yeah, wow." I feel depleted. But it's a beautiful emptiness, because I feel, for this moment at least, weightless and free.

He puts his fingers on my chin and guides my face until it's facing his. "I love you," he says.

Time feels like it stops. I'm overwhelmed with the happiness of hearing those words, but suddenly don't feel like I'm the new person I want to be. I'm the same old Kam, wondering if I can say I love Ash when he'll be graduating soon, when my dad hasn't even met him, when Bodie hates him.

"Don't worry, you don't need to say it back," he reassures me. "Words are overrated anyway. I already feel your love speaking through your soul."

"What does my soul sound like?" I ask, smiling.

"Like a soft wind," he says. "Your soul always speaks in a murmur, but I never have trouble understanding what it's saying."

"So my soul is an it?" I ask.

"Souls don't have a gender." The Lana album has played through and begins again. *Our honeymoon*, she sings. "You know where I'd like to go on our honeymoon?" he asks.

"Joshua Tree?" I'm only half joking.

"Mars!" he exclaims. "Hopefully by then, people could travel to space. Could you imagine?"

"I'm not sure how romantic that sounds," I say. "I was imagining some beautiful beach somewhere. . . ."

"Maybe Mars has a beach," he says. "Unlikely because it's negative eighty degrees there, but you never know. But it definitely has canyons, lake beds, and so much red dust."

"Here's an idea." I nuzzle against his chest. Twirl the smattering of hairs that cover his chest in my finger. "How about you make a bunch of drawings of Mars, and tape them to the walls of some beautiful hotel in Paris or some Caribbean island?"

"I like the way your mind works," he says, laughing.

I pick up the book he brought me. Flip through its pages. My eyes are drawn to a line in the middle of the book. "*The desert takes our men from us, and they don't always return.*" I feel a jolt of dread fill my body. Put the book down.

I stand up on my bed so I can read the poem he wrote into his drawing of Joshua trees. I feel dizzy when I stand, like I'm intoxicated, even though I don't know what intoxication feels like. "*Double Vision,*" I read. "*You asked 'What can I do to help stop the slow apocalypse from coming so fast?' I'm no authority, I said, but maybe we need to close our eyes and see with our souls again. Understand that children are birds, trees are family, liquid is solid, the unforgiven are diamonds.*" I look at him with awe. "I love that."

He blushes, then he finishes reciting the poem from memory. Soon, it feels like we're transported out of this room, into his sketches, deep through the desert.

Later that week, when Mr. Greene drives us to the desert, my heartbeat is going at double speed. We listen to Lana on the three-hour ride. Ash and I crack up when Mrs. Greene says all the songs sound the same.

When we cross the threshold into the desert, it's all so vast, beautiful, captivating, that I have to pull my phone out and film it. It's almost like I can't process it in real time, so I have to create a record to review later. I film the sky, rocks, trees, moving the screen to capture it all, zooming in on little details of the natural world.

It's not just the desert I capture, though. It's Ash too.

He's like a natural wonder to me. I film him as he helps his parents set up our campground. Film him as he leads me to a quiet, sunny spot for some alone time before dinner.

"Stop already," he begs as I zoom in on his face in the light.

"I don't want to forget this," I confess. "Me and you. Us. All alone in this immense place." I look around. Not a soul visible from any direction. Everything feels ours here. Like the world is a secret only we share.

"So you love it here?" he asks with a smile.

"I love it with you." I take a breath. "If I was alone here . . . I don't know . . . I'd probably be scared."

"Why?" he asks.

"I don't know," I confess. "I guess total solitude scares me. Like, who would you turn to if you needed help out here?"

"Solitude isn't scary. It's just being alone and liking it," he says. "If you learn to love solitude, you'll never be lonely."

"I guess," I say from behind my phone's camera.

He hovers his index finger over the spindle of the cactus. Pokes himself gently. Pulls away. Then pokes himself again. Pulls away.

"I guess I never thought of solitude and loneliness as different," I explain, squinting. The sunlight feels blinding.

"Solitude is the ultimate luxury. You know what else is a luxury?" His eyes seem to light up the landscape. He's like the sun.

"What?" I ask.

232

"Not being constantly filmed!" He tackles me to the ground, and we fall onto the dirt next to each other. He wears a tank top and my head rests on his hot shoulder. The smell of his sweat makes me dizzy with lust. "If you want to film people, become a filmmaker and find yourself a muse."

"I'm not an artist," I say. "You are. But if I were an artist, you'd be my muse."

He clutches my hands above his heart. "I know you're afraid of forgetting the good memories, but you won't. There's actually no such thing as memory. Just remembering. That's what my mom thinks at least, and she's a professional at helping people make peace with their memories."

"Maybe I don't think memories are peaceful," I say. "Most times, when I remember something, it's because some piece of it feels unfinished. Like I wish I could go back and change it. Maybe that's why I don't like being alone." I could say more. That when I'm alone, the sadness comes. The worry. About my dad's drinking. My mom's disappointment. The fear of what will happen when Ash graduates. Fear of fire, of nuclear war, of climate change, of this pandemic, and more pandemics. Fear of my own powerlessness.

"Then you need to learn." His voice floats across the dry expanse of land. Over the Joshua trees, across the strange rock formations. "Solitude is the one thing money can't buy. To experience solitude . . . to love it even . . . to not require other people's approval to be okay . . . it's everything. Once you know how to be alone, no one can ever bring you down. Does that make sense?" I've heard him ask that question before, like he's used to not making sense to people. Maybe that's why he keeps to himself so often. It's easier than being misunderstood.

"I don't know that I can ever get there," I confess. "I think of you graduating next year, and I'm filled with dread."

"I'll still be with you. I'll always be with you."

"I know you're planning on staying in LA, but—"

He spins around to face me. "That's not what I meant." His eyes search mine. "You know you're never really alone, right? You just have to learn how to listen."

"I'm not sure I know how to do that. I'm not like you. Being alone scares me. This kind of vastness does too. Maybe nature scares me." I catch glimpses of Joshua trees, imposing rocks, a beady-eyed lizard. "I guess cities make me feel safe. Maybe I prefer people to creatures."

"People *are* creatures." He smiles lovingly. "Cities are what scare me. Nature's a lot more predictable than people."

"But you're a person," I say.

"Hey, I never said I wasn't scared of myself." He sighs gently. "Why do cities make you feel safe?" he asks, no judgment in his voice, just curiosity.

"I don't know. I guess because there are rules, you know. And hospitals. And ice cream shops."

"You really like ice cream," he says with a smile.

"Never enough sweetness for me." I kiss his lips gently. "Never enough." I kiss him again. Deeper this time. "Hey, maybe you can teach me how to be alone."

"I don't think I'm much of a teacher," he says. "But if there is a secret, it's just leaning into your creativity."

"But I'm not creative," I say.

"Of course you are. You sing." He kisses my lips. "Beautifully."

"I sing in a choir. I feed off other people's voices. It's not like I write my own music."

"What do you think songwriters do?" he asks. "They listen to the voices that come to them."

"It's different," I say. "I don't *make* anything. There's no voice from above speaking to me."

"Close your eyes," he commands.

"Why?" I ask.

"Just do it."

Before I close them, my eyes land on a raven perched on a tree, then on a lizard rushing from rock to rock.

"What do you see?" he asks.

"What do you mean?" I laugh uncomfortably. "My eyes are closed. I see nothing."

"No one sees nothing when they close their eyes. We all see—"

"Little black dots," I suddenly hear myself say. "And colors."

"Those are called pseudohallucinations," he explains.

"What are?" I open my eyes and look around, like I'm seeing the desert for the first time.

"What we see inside our eyelids when we close our eyes.

They may not seem like it, but they have all the same qualities as real hallucinations."

"*Real?*" I ask. "Isn't the whole point of hallucinations that they aren't real?"

He shrugs. "Hallucinations are more common than we think," he says. "Artists have relied on them forever. Homer. Yeats. Rilke. And not just artists. People who work alone, doing something repetitive and monotonous, have hallucinations all the time."

"Like who?" I ask. "I want to avoid those jobs."

He squints. "Don't avoid the voices and images that need to come to you. I'm not suggesting you become a truck driver so you can see things. But—" He suddenly stops himself from saying more.

"What?" I ask. "What is it?"

"I'm scaring you," he says quietly.

I clutch his forearm. "You could never scare me."

He smiles. "You know why I love the desert so much?"

"Tell me, please."

"It's because the open space, the visual monotony, the solitude, even the sense of dehydration, it leaves room for ideas to come to me. Sensory deprivation is tied to hallucinations. They call it the Prisoner's Cinema."

"Why?" I ask.

"Because when you put a prisoner in a dark cell, he or she or they will start to see things."

"Okay, that scares me," I say. "I don't want to be a prisoner. I don't want you to be one either."

"I'm not," he says, like I've completely missed his point. "Lie down, I want to draw you."

I do what he says. I always do. "Am I your Prisoner's Cinema?" I ask playfully.

"Shut up," he says, laughing.

"Oh, so you want me to be a silent film?" I cackle at my own joke.

He pulls a spindle off a cactus. "I'm going to prick you if you don't lie still."

"I like it when you prick me." I spread my legs and offer him my most comically seductive gaze. One thing I love about being with Ash is that his seriousness brings out my humor, like I want to earn his laughter. I spread myself out. "Draw me like one of your French girls, Ash."

"You're not very good at staying still, you know that?" he asks. "You would've driven Van Gogh crazy."

"He cut his ear off. I don't think he needed my help." I watch him watch me, his brain figuring out how to draw me. He closes his eyes for a second, two seconds, three. "What are you thinking?" I ask.

He opens his eyes. "Just how, almost a century and a half later, we still don't know how Van Gogh really died. Some people think he killed himself. Others think he was murdered."

"What do you think?" I ask.

"I don't care, really. I'm more interested in how he lived. In the source of his magical gift."

I close my eyes. The sunlight turns the darkness under my

eyelids into a kaleidoscope of pseudohallucinations. Colors swirl across my own personal cinema screen. Red, yellow, orange, violet, like a tie-dye pattern, or a tub of paint, all in my mind's eye. I feel myself dozing off to the sound of his pencil on paper, his voice my breeze. It makes me want to cry.

I exhale a glorious, "Mmm." I think about how his history is here, in this country, in this state, up that mountain, across that desert. Generations of his family tree were shaped here. My own history is in another land, a foreign place where the air must smell and feel different.

Maybe the reason he knows how to be alone is that his ancestors are all by his side here, and the reason I'm afraid when I'm alone is that my ancestors are far from here, wondering where I went and when I'm coming home.

His pencil scratches the paper faster now. "You're so beautiful, lying alone like that." He's figured out how to draw me. "I think that if someone doesn't love being alone, then that's how you know they're truly unhappy. You look happy."

I think of my parents. When my mother is alone, she fixes things, cleans things, polishes things, checks items off her to-do list.

When my dad is alone, he destroys himself.

But I don't say any of this, because the sun is calming me, and because I can't speak the things I've been taught to cover up about my family.

The colors spin under my eyelids, deeper and richer than before.

Silence.

Stillness.

Sleep.

"Babe, look." His hand lands on my cheek, rousing me awake. The portrait is done. I'm asleep in the sketch, lying down on the dirt. Everything about the picture is naturalistic except my fingers, which are branches, growing into the land, like I'm an extension of the desert. "What do you think?"

"You turned me into a tree." I let out a throaty laugh, still groggy from sleeping in the sunshine.

"Trees are connected to each other by underground root systems no one sees. We are too, I think." Ash pricks himself on a cactus again as he speaks. Prick and pull. Never deep enough to draw blood, but too close for my comfort.

I yank his hand away from the cactus and kiss each of his fingers. One at a time. "Please stop."

He laughs, not a care in the world. "Roadrunners live in those plants."

"You're not a roadrunner," I say. "I don't want my baby full of spindles."

"Nature's acupuncture." He laughs. "One of many desert miracles."

I look around. Infinite desert. Endless Joshua trees. Tree after tree after tree, and rocks atop rocks atop rocks, and mountains over mountains over mountains. The mountains that block the water from coming in. He's already explained that to me. We're in a rain-shadow desert.

Those mountains block the western storms from coming.

"You know how old the oldest rock here is?" he asks.

"I don't know. A hundred million years. Two hundred."

"Almost two *billion* years old." I watch him watch me ponder that length of time. It doesn't make sense. That this rock was here before human beings were.

I lean my head on his chest. His heartbeat is loud, but it also sounds perfectly in sync with the birdsong. Everything seems to slow down. The air is still. The sky is cloudless. The branches of the trees are steady, undisturbed by the movement of the lizards that move across the land.

"Let's pick a more manageable number," he suggests. "And commit to being together that long."

"Eight million years?" I suggest.

"A perfect number. We'll be together for eight million years." I kiss his neck. He tastes like dry sweat and pure love.

"Now that we've committed to eight million years together, let's try being alone for just a few minutes," he says suddenly. "I want you to experience the power of this place without me."

"What do you mean?" I ask, hearing the panic in my voice.

"See that rock." He points to a big rock a few feet away from us. "I'm going to go to the other side of the rock—"

"Ash, I don't need—"

"Just for a few minutes. Or longer, if you want. Why don't we see how long we last without each other."

"I can't last a minute without you."

"We both know that's not true." He leaps up onto his feet. The sun shines behind him, its rays seem to bounce off his face back into the sky. "I'll be right behind that rock. If you need me, call to me, like a bird."

"Ash—" But he runs off, behind the rock. I feel his absence the moment he's out of sight. Everything feels different without his presence. No words to fill the empty space all around us. I prick myself gently on the cactus he was pricking himself with. I stare out at the trees, pondering the shapes they make. How unique each shape is. None of the trees look alike. I stare up at the sky. In the distance, the faint outline of the new moon. I close my eyes. My body sounds louder than it ever has before. I can hear my heart beat outside my body. When I can't take any more of myself, I yell out, "Ash!"

And there he is. Smiling. Bouncing toward me, full of life. "So, how was that?"

"Fine, I guess. I mean, I knew you were right there." I hold him close to me again.

"Did you notice anything new?" he asks.

"None of the trees look alike," I say. "I thought this looked so visually monotonous, but when you look at the Joshua trees, they all make such unique shapes."

"Except the juveniles." He points to what look like tiny shrubs. "See, those are baby Joshua trees. They haven't formed yet. They haven't matured into their uniqueness."

"How long do they live?" I ask.

"Around a hundred and fifty years." There's an ache in his voice when he adds, "But by the end of the century, all these trees might be gone."

"That's so sad," I say in his chest.

"*Nothing gold can stay*," he sings softly, quoting Lana, who was quoting Robert Frost, who was probably quoting ancient wisdom, words passed down, so meaningful, and also so meaningless in the grand scheme of two billion years, a time before words. "Which is why we need to make the most of our time together."

He kisses me gently. "Ash . . ." I want to say I love him but I hesitate.

He fills the silence of my hesitation with more words. "You know what I love about this place? It's not a desert. It's two deserts with totally different climates. The Mojave and the Sonoran. This is where they meet." He lifts a finger and traces the shape of my face with it as he speaks. "Sometimes I think . . . we're like this place. We are the place where two deserts meet. You know what Rilke said about love?"

"Of course I don't," I say. "Tell me."

"That love is like two solitudes protecting, bordering, and saluting each other. Isn't that beautiful?"

I nod.

"Two solitudes. Like these two deserts coming together. Like us."

"Maybe we're not two deserts." I mount him. "Maybe we're like those rocks." I slowly run my hands along his chest, unbuttoning his shirt, and then pulling his shorts and mine down. "Smashed together by a mighty geological explosion, or a major cosmic erosion or the—"

He cackles as he grabs ahold of me. "You really know nothing about how nature works."

"I know a little bit," I grunt as he strokes me, and I stroke him.

"Boys!" Mrs. Greene's voice, like birdsong itself. Human voices don't sound the same here. They seem to travel at a different frequency, slower, more poetic. "Boys!"

Ash lies on top of me and just as I'm about to come, he screams, "Coming, Mom!"

We collapse next to each other, in laughter, love, breathlessness.

"Where's the lie?" he says. "I told her we were coming."

"And so we did."

"Boys!" his mom calls out again. "Come for dinner!"

"I did just come," he says. "And it made for a delicious appetizer."

"Stop!" I can't stop laughing.

"Can't stop, won't stop," he says, a smile in his voice.

"Ash and Kam, come on!" she calls out again. "Kids, we went over the ground rules. No disappearing."

We giggle as we rush back to our campsite.

"I hope you're not too much of a carnivore," Mrs. Greene says to me. Ash holds my hand as his parents get dinner ready on the camping stove. I wish we could be like this with my parents. Unafraid to show our affection.

"Not really," I say, remembering Ash telling my mom he was a vegan that one time they met, and the look of confusion on my mother's face. She was probably wondering what in the world she would feed him if she ever invited him over. My mom's repertoire of meals, which was her mom's repertoire of meals, consists of meat-based stews, and meat kotlet, an endless variety of ways to cook beef, veal, chicken. On the ride home that night, she said at least he could eat Persian rice, and I told her, *Not if you put yogurt in it.* She looked horrified.

"Kam does love his meat," Ash says with a grin. "But I think he can handle a vegan camping trip."

"If you think we miss your double entendres, you're wrong," Mr. Greene says.

I blush. I know Ash discusses *everything* with his parents—including sex—but I have no interest in talking about my lust for Ash's meat with his mom and dad. "So what are we eating anyway?" I ask.

"I'm making sweet potato casserole with wild rice," Mr. Greene explains. "And we have a whole host of snacks from Trader Joe's too. And please don't forget to hydrate. Do you need a drink?"

"I'm okay, and the vegan meal sounds perfect," I say.

"Okay, who said this?" Mr. Greene asks. He closes his eyes and recites, "*True human goodness, in all its purity and freedom, can come to the fore only when its recipient has no power.*"

"It's Milan Kundera," Ash says, like it's obvious.

"You didn't let me finish," Mr. Greene says.

"I'll finish it." Ash stands up. *"Mankind's true moral test, its fundamental test, consists of its attitude toward those who are at its mercy: animals."* I smile, not at the quote, but at the way Ash and his dad both love to quote writers and philosophers. If Dawn were here, she'd absolutely be in hell.

"If that quote doesn't convince you to be a vegan . . . ," Mr. Greene says.

"Dad, can we not pressure my boyfriend into living just like us?" Ash asks.

"Is that what I was doing?" Mr. Greene cocks his head sheepishly. "I'm sorry, Kam."

"What makes the world spin is the uniqueness of its individuals," Mrs. Greene says.

"Like the Joshua trees," I say, excited to be able to contribute in some small way to this conversation.

"Kam noticed how they all look different," Ash says.

"That's right," Mrs. Greene says brightly. "That's one of the things I love about those Joshua trees. They mirror your emotions back to you."

Ash smiles. "My mom thinks that what every child needs is for their emotions to be mirrored back to them."

"It's true," she says.

I think about my parents, about how they never seem to mirror my emotional state. They contradict it. They try to change it.

"Tell Kam what you used to do." Ash joins his mom in front of the camping stove. He grabs the spatula from her

245

and moves the casserole around.

"Why do I get the sense you're mocking me?" Mrs. Greene leans her head on her son's shoulder.

"I'm not," Ash insists.

Mrs. Greene turns to me. "When Ash and his sister were babies, I would try to mirror their emotions, so if they cried, I would cry or pretend to. If they laughed, I would laugh."

I smile. It sounds like an absurd way to be a parent. But also very sweet.

"And what would you do if I had a tantrum and threw my blended vegetables at the wall?" Ash asks, laughing.

"See, you are mocking me." Mrs. Greene smiles. She doesn't mind being teased by Ash because there's so much love there.

"I don't mock, I mime." Ash starts gesturing like he's trapped in a box. His mom faces him and mirrors his every move. Ash looks up, she looks up. Ash laughs, she laughs. Ash stands on his tippy toes, she stands on her tippy toes. They do this until they burst out laughing. They hug each other tight. Take a silly bow. "Our second show of the night begins at midnight."

"We will be asleep at midnight," Mrs. Greene says. "Kam, are you sure you don't need a drink?"

"I can pour myself some water, don't worry about me." I grab the pitcher of water and pour myself a glass.

Mrs. Greene has an arm around Ash when she says, "Miming aside, I think the most important thing is for kids, really all people but especially young people, to feel that their emotions are valid."

"Yeah," I whisper sadly. I've never felt that way. Not really.

"That's what I love about nature," Ash explains as he plates the casserole. "It meets you wherever you are. I mean, look at those Joshua trees."

We all look out at the expanse of trees beyond our campground.

"If you're sad, they look sad, their branches desperate. But if you're happy, they look happy, their branches reaching up to the sky. Like they're dancing. Does that make sense?"

Mrs. Greene hands us each a plate and we sit in a circle to eat.

"When we destroy nature, we destroy our inner life," Mr. Greene says before he takes his first bite.

"You know how this place came to become a national park?" Mrs. Greene asks me.

I shake my head as I take a bite of food. "This is really good, thank you," I tell his parents.

"A wealthy socialite who lost both her child and her husband came to the desert searching for meaning and convinced the government to protect the land," Ash explains. "Now let's get to the ghost stories!"

"Minerva Hamilton Hoyt saw beauty where no one else did," Mr. Greene says. "Before her, no one saw this land as beautiful."

I look at Ash. No one in school sees his beauty the way

I do. They think he's weird. A loner. They think his hair is too long and his clothes are too baggy. I see his beauty, though, just like he sees mine when no one else does. Maybe the best kind of beauty is the kind only you can see.

"Let's tell him something more fun," Ash suggests. "Should I tell him about Mormon tea?"

"What's Mormon tea?" I ask.

There's a moment of unspoken communication between his parents.

Ash laughs. "Fine, how about we tell him about Gram Parsons?"

"Who's Gram Parsons?" I ask.

Ash buzzes with excitement. He loves telling me things I don't know. "Gram Fucking Parsons was an amazing singer who wanted to have his ashes spread at Cap Rock here in the desert. He used to come here searching for UFOs with Keith Fucking Richards."

"Can you stop with the constant swearing, please?" Mrs. Greene asks.

"It's just something we do because of Lana's album *Norman Fucking Rockwell*." Ash rolls his eyes. "Anyway, Gram *Effing* Parsons died at the Joshua Tree Inn when he was twenty-six years old because of fucking drugs."

Mr. and Mrs. Greene look at each other quickly.

"But the thing is, his family didn't get him. They didn't honor his wishes. They organized a funeral in Louisiana and didn't even invite his friends. So Gram's manager stole his body from the airport."

"I'm sorry, he did what?"

There's delight in Ash's eyes. "He stole his body from the airport, brought it to Cap Rock. Him and a friend tried to cremate the body themselves."

"How do you even do that?" I ask.

"With a lot of gasoline and a match." Ash cleans up our plates as he speaks.

Mrs. Greene pulls out everything we need to make vegan s'mores. We hold the gelatin-free marshmallows over the stove. They tell me more strange desert stories as we roast and eat. Some Broadway dancer painted a fake audience on the walls of an abandoned theater in Death Valley. I close my eyes and imagine myself dancing alone in an abandoned theater, for an audience of painted people. The only one left dancing. Solitude.

"Psst," Ash whispers to me. "Let's go."

"Go where?" I ask.

"Stargazing."

"Your mom told us not to—"

"We're not wandering off," Ash says. "We're just going to look at some stars. Didn't I tell you I'd show you Cancer and Leo?"

"I'm half-asleep," I groan as he ties the glittery laces of his hand-painted sneakers and pulls his hairband back, revealing the line of his widow's peak.

"That's the best way to see the stars. Like you're in a dream. Come on." He sings in my ear, "*My Cancer is sun and my Leo is moon.*" And then he pulls me out of my sleeping bag. He grabs his art journal and a pencil.

I follow him out into the darkness. He walks farther than I want him to, but he won't stop when I ask him to. Time seems to melt. Maybe we walk for ten minutes, maybe thirty, maybe more. I don't know.

The sky stuns me when we finally stop and lie down on the dirt, side by side. In the darkness, the black sky is littered with stars. They're everywhere, illuminating us. I point up to something moving. "Is that a shooting star?" I ask.

"No, you'll know a shooting star when you see one." He kisses my neck. "That's a low Earth orbit satellite."

"A what?" I ask.

"They're used for military reconnaissance, and by corporations, for communications, for spying."

"I'd rather it was a shooting star," I say.

"Look at the moon," he says, guiding me toward the moon with his eyes.

"Wow." The awe in my voice travels upward toward the sky. I've never seen a moon like this one. The sliver of the new moon is brightly lit, but the entire moon is visible.

"You know what they call this? The old moon in the new moon's arms."

I keep staring up at it. "It looks more like the new moon in the old moon's arms to me."

He smiles. "That works too. They're in each other's arms." He pulls me closer to him. Runs his hands through my hair.

"Is the new moon topping the old moon?" I ask. "Or is the new moon bottoming for the old moon?"

He laughs. "The moon is definitely vers."

"Unlike the sun," I whisper. "The sun is such a power top."

"Hey, you know that the way I feel about you . . ." His tone changes from raunchy to reverent. "It's bigger than that sky up there."

"I don't know if that's possible," I say.

Our eyes are locked into each other when he says, "When we're looking up at the stars, we're looking at the past."

"I . . . I don't understand."

"It takes years for the light of a star to reach us. So when we're looking at a star, we're actually looking at what it looked like years ago."

"How many years?" I ask.

"With some stars, we might be looking five hundred years into the past," he explains. "With others, less. Or more."

"It's too much to make sense of," I say.

"I know, that's why I love it. The guy who built the Integratron out here said he was told to build it by aliens. He said the structure would let people travel through time."

"And?"

"And people were disappointed," he says. "But maybe that's because people think of time travel all wrong. Maybe the only way to time travel is to sit still and go within." I'm not sure what to say, so I just keep staring up at the stars as he continues to talk. "Sometimes I imagine that there is life on another planet, and the beings way out there have figured out a way to see us on Earth. But they're not seeing *us*, because of the time it takes for our light to travel to them. What they're seeing is humans, like, five hundred years ago."

"Or thirty million years ago," I say.

"There was no us thirty million years ago."

"Then the beings on this undiscovered planet probably haven't figured out there's life on Earth yet." I let out a deep sigh. "What's this planet called?" I ask.

"Planet Kam," he whispers.

"I don't know if I want a planet named after me. Feels lonely. How about Planet Kash, with a *K*, for Kam and Ash."

"Yeah, I get it," he says, smiling. "Planet Kash." He points to a star. "See that star?"

"Ash, I see hundreds and hundreds of stars. Which one?"

"The one that's twinkling. I think that's a double star." He takes my hand in his. Squeezes it. "Sometimes stars look like one star, but it's really two stars, so close to each other, shining as one."

"Like two deserts coming together," I say.

"Exactly. Come on, let's find a rock we can climb to get closer to the stars."

I sit up, cradling my knees in my arms. "Ash, your mom said—"

"My mom said what moms have to say. Your mom didn't

want you to come on this trip at all, and look at you now. You're a desert rat."

"Please don't say rat." I feel a shiver in my body. "Rats freak me out."

"Then you better get up, 'cause I see one coming from behind you."

I squeal and bolt up. I look behind me. "You tricked me."

He smiles. "Come." He charges ahead, into the darkness, and of course I follow. What else can I do? I can't let him go alone. I can't miss out on what else this magical night holds in store for us. "Look at that rock formation," he says.

"Which one?" I ask.

"It looks like a face. Like two faces. Side by side."

"I don't see it." I'm having trouble keeping up with him. "Ash, slow down."

"There's no one here. It's all ours. I've dreamed about this. Walking through the desert with the love of my life, just us and the critters and the spirits and the stars."

"Ash, I can't see you. Where are you?"

"Follow my voice."

"Ash, are you there? I'm scared."

"Don't be. It's just like before, when we separated and I was behind the rock the whole time."

"But that was in the daylight. It's too dark for this now. Let's go back." I stop moving. I don't know which direction to go in. "Ash?" I close my eyes. "Say something."

"I love you."

"I—"

"No, don't say it yet. I want to look into your eyes when you say it for the first time."

"But I can't find you."

"Follow my voice."

"Then don't stop talking."

"I love you, I love you, I love you, I . . . love . . . you . . . I . . ." His voice seems to fade, slowly, like a photograph that's been in the sunlight too long. Maybe it's because he's moving farther away from me, or maybe it's just that I can't hear its brightness anymore. I chase his voice, but I don't know what direction he's going in. My ears pop. Everything sounds fuzzy. I feel unstable. Close my eyes to steady myself. Lights fill my eyelids. Pseudohallucinations that look like millions of stars, millions of years old, twinkling and twinkling and moving closer to me.

He's by my side again. "Kam," he says. "There's something I want to share with you, but you have to promise not to judge me."

JUNIOR YEAR

My heart stops when we cross the threshold into the park. Memories of Ash flood my mind. I'm here with the GSA, but I'm also there, with Ash and his parents. All the Joshua trees look different. They also all look alike. My eyes circle the desert, searching for some clue of where we went that night we wandered off.

"Kam, I'm sorry," Bodie whispers. "Can we just talk this out before we get there?"

I can't answer. I'm trying to control the overwhelming fear and sadness of being back here.

"If at any point it's too much, we can go home." Bodie almost puts an arm around me, but reconsiders when I pull away. "You don't have to prove anything."

I'm not here to prove anything. I'm here to find him.

"I'm sorry I didn't tell you Louis said he loves me." Bodie sighs. "Are you still mad at me?"

I'm too afraid to say yes. I can't break down right now. Mr. Byrne and Ms. Robin will think I'm not ready to go back to the desert. They'll make me turn back. "I don't want to talk about this anymore here," I say. "We can get into it when we're home."

Ms. Robin pulls the RV into a parking spot in our campground. We quickly settle in before we're met by our tour guide for the day, a grizzly bear of a man who leads us through the park and talks us through its history. We learn the park is home to the largest Marine Corps base in the whole country. We pass by Cap Rock, the spot where Gram Parson's body was doused with gasoline and burned, and of course I think of Ash gleefully telling me that story. Tourists swarm that rock, taking selfies with it behind them. I hate that they're turning a man's macabre death into a photo op. It feels like it's Ash's disappearance they're turning into some tourist destination, some fleeting Instagram post.

Throughout the day, I feel like my consciousness is fading in and out. I miss half of what's happening. Lost in what I can remember, desperate to summon what I've blocked out. I catch bits of conversation here and there.

Ms. Robin says, "We shouldn't pledge allegiance to a country when a country by definition divides both nature and humanity. We should pledge allegiance to our Earth."

Bodie says, "Wait, there's a simulated Middle Eastern war zone in the desert? That's . . . gross."

They all yell out, "WE CONTAIN MULTITUDES!"

Their words, and my yearning, disappear into the desert.

When the tour ends, we choose a hiking trail. The names amuse everyone. Dream Sequence, Bambi Meets Godzilla, Poodles Are People Too, Middle Age Crisis. The group picks a trail called Eureka in honor of one of our favorite drag queens.

Bodie sees two campers in the distance walking a dog on a leash. He grabs my arm. "You doing okay?" he asks. "You haven't said a word all day."

"Yeah." I blink too fast, trying to pull myself back to this moment. To stop my mind from floating.

"Scooby-Doo?" he asks, pointing to the leashed dog.

I nod, because if I don't play along, he'll ask more questions.

He counts down, "One, two, three."

He says Iggy Pop and I say Christina Ricci. Neither of us laughs.

Olivia, who sticks close to Bodie, says, "What was that about?"

I wait for Bodie to explain our strange little game to her, but he just says, "No reason, it's silly." Part of me is grateful he chose to keep the game our secret. Another part of me stings from him calling it silly, like it's me he's calling silly even though he invented the game. Maybe I am, though. Silly for coming back here, searching for answers in a place that's one big question.

* * *

That evening, we roast marshmallows at a designated fire-pit. I film as Byrne plays his guitar and teaches us the lyrics to some of his favorite folk songs. We all become obsessed with one about seeing seventeen pink sugar elephants. The lyrics are absurd and funny, but also mystical and sad. "*So we just sat,*" we all sing. "*That early autumn morning. Sun not yet risen and magic everywhere.*" Our voices seem to travel across the land like clouds, adding to the magic. The energy is so giddy that Tucker tells Byrne to play the song again, and then Olivia begs him to sing it a third time, Fiona a fourth, Bodie a fifth. We sing it seventeen times in honor of the "17 Pink Sugar Elephants" that give the song its title.

When we've sung the final boisterous rendition and I stop recording, Olivia announces, "Okay, I think it's time for the grown-ups to go to bed."

"Excuse me?" Ms. Robin asks with a raised eyebrow. "Aren't we having a queer old time?"

"Look, you guys might be queer and fun, but you're still grown-ups. There's some things we can't do with you around."

"Like?" Byrne asks.

"Like . . ." Olivia cues Bodie with a nod. Together, they squeal, "Never Have I Ever!"

"Yeah, that's definitely our cue," Ms. Robin says.

"Lord knows I don't want to know what these kids have or haven't done," Byrne adds.

Ms. Robin stands up first. "You kids better play with cider and if you need us, we'll be—"

"Byeeeee!" Fiona yells out, and everyone laughs.

Mr. Byrne and Ms. Robin hesitate before finally leaving us alone. I wonder if it's the raucous game they're concerned about. Or is it me?

It's probably me.

When they finally disappear into the RV, Olivia and Bodie team up to give everyone a glass of cider. Bodie holds the plastic cups. Olivia pours. Bodie hands everyone a full cup. "Everyone knows the way the game works, right?"

Lincoln, the shyest of the group, lets out a quiet, "Um, not really."

"You've never played Never Have I Ever?" Bodie asks in shock. "Ever?"

Lincoln shrugs. There's a hint of embarrassment on his face, which makes me want to defend him. "It's not a big deal, Bodie."

Bodie flinches. "I didn't say it was a *big deal*. I just asked a question."

If I had the energy for a confrontation, I would tell Bodie that sometimes he asks questions in a way that makes it clear there's only one right answer.

Olivia gets between me and Bodie. "Okay, here are the rules. We go around a circle and we all say 'Never have I ever . . . ,' then we say something we either have or haven't done. And everyone who's done it drinks."

Olivia sits back down so we're in a circle again. Bodie jumps in. "So like, if I said, 'Never have I ever played Never Have I Ever,' we would all drink except for Lincoln."

I roll my eyes. "You're really obsessed with that," I say.

Bodie ignores me. "Does everyone get it?"

Lincoln leans forward. "Not really. I'm really confused, because the thing is, I've never played this game. You guys know that, right?" We all laugh and it immediately lightens the mood.

I take a deep breath. Release a long exhale. I don't know why I can't let go of my anger at Bodie.

"I'll go first," Fiona announces. "I have a fun one." She raises her cup up high. "Never have I ever wished I was cis and straight."

At first, no one drinks. And then, as we all eye each other suspiciously, we all drink.

"I mean, I don't wish for that anymore," Tucker says. "But like, have I *ever* wished that? Sure."

"Same," Olivia says. "Like, these days, being cis and straight seems like a fucking curse. But when I first came out to my parents and I saw my mom doing everything she could to hide her despair . . ."

Bodie puts a hand on Olivia's shoulder. Gives her a moment to compose herself. "Your mom loves you. We all love you."

Olivia shakes off her sadness. "No, I know that."

Bodie raises his glass. "That wasn't exactly a fun one. Here's a fun one. Never have I ever had a crush on a teacher."

"Bodie, ew!" Olivia squeals.

"Don't yuck my yum," Fiona says as she drinks. "It's just

a crush, not a crime. And I happen to think Ms. Carolina is hot."

"Ms. Carolina?" Olivia asks, aghast. "The chemistry teacher who constantly talks about how she's wasting her PhD teaching high school?"

"In fairness, what she's really wasting is her Ph-double-Ds," Fiona quips. Even I laugh at that. It feels like we're drunk, even though there's no alcohol in our cider.

"Okay, okay, it's the newbie's turn," Lincoln declares. "Never have I ever been caught hooking up by my parents."

At first, no one drinks. But then Olivia wags her finger at Bodie in mock consternation. "Nobody lies during this sacred game, especially in this sacred desert."

Bodie blushes. "We weren't *hooking up*. We were just *kissing*." My throat stiffens. I know what a big deal kissing is to Bodie. It's intimacy. It's what he usually pushes away.

Olivia cackles as she says, "You said Louis was sucking your face like a vacuum cleaner when your dad walked in!"

"Fine, I'll drink." Bodie takes a small sip of cider, his gaze glued to me. We have a whole conversation with just our eyes as Tucker says he'll go next. Bodie's eyes tell me he's sorry for not telling me about this incident, which we should've laughed about by now. If we were still us, he would've entertained me with impressions of his dad walking in on them. My eyes tell Bodie I'm shocked, disappointed, pissed off at how much he's hiding from me.

"Never have I ever had . . ." Tucker hesitates, then he starts again. "I don't like that one. Okay, wait, here's one. Never have I ever considered not going to college."

"College?" Olivia echoes. "These are supposed to be about embarrassing episodes in our lives, not our educational plans."

Fiona ignores Olivia and drinks. "I don't know that I'll *never* go to college," she says. "But I'm definitely doing the Peace Corps like my parents did after high school. Then I'll decide."

Bodie and I both hesitate, then drink at the same time. "I don't know if this counts, but Kam and I are taking a gap year together," he says.

"Yeah, maybe," I mutter.

"What do you mean maybe?" he shoots back. "We're doing it."

"You haven't even told your dad." I'm aware of everyone's eyes on us.

"People, this game is supposed to be fun!" Olivia squeals. "I'm going next. Never have I ever crapped my pants."

Everyone bursts out laughing. "Do sharts count?" Lincoln asks. We all laugh even harder at that.

"Of course they count," Bodie says. "Crap is crap."

Lincoln shrugs and drinks. He casts a judgmental eye on each one of us. "I refuse to believe none of you have ever sharted, but whatever."

"Okay, my turn," Danny says. "Never have I ever had an STI."

Bodie laughs and shakes his head. "You guys really go dark."

Only Fiona drinks. "I got chlamydia once." She doesn't seem at all self-conscious. "It really wasn't such a big deal, minus the burning pee and the humiliation of having to tell my mom about it."

"Never have I ever been so happy to be asexual!" Tucker yells as he takes a giant slug from his cup.

"You say that every time we talk about sex!" Fiona squeals.

"Okay, okay, I have another one." With her eyes on Bodie, Olivia says, "Never have I ever truly been in love."

Bodie looks at her, and then at me. I know exactly what's happening. She's daring him to tell us all he's in love with Louis.

I drink, of course.

No one else does.

And then Bodie drinks too, his eyes locked on me. I feel my heart sink into my stomach. A wave of sadness seems to crash inside me. So he *is* in love with Louis. That's why he's pulling away from me. There isn't room in his heart for me anymore. I feel too upset to be happy for him. Abandoned by my best friend in the same desert that took my boyfriend from me.

"Play them the video!" Olivia demands giddily.

"Nobody wants to see that," Bodie says, blushing.

Olivia looks at the group. "Trust me, you want to see it. That video is, like, hashtag couple goals."

"Show it to us immediately," Fiona pleads.

"Fine, whatever." Bodie takes out his phone and pulls up a video of Louis, in nothing but a bathing suit on a beach. The rising sun glows on his toned body as he tells Bodie he loves him.

"Doesn't his body make you sick?" Olivia asks.

"It looks fake," Lincoln comments dryly. "Like, that body was created by AI."

Bodie basks in the attention. On the screen, Louis says, "Now that I've said it on camera, maybe I won't be afraid to say it in person."

Olivia and Fiona let out a prolonged "Awwww" when the video ends that makes me cringe. Maybe I'm annoyed that they're cooing over Bodie and Louis like they're the *Heartstopper* boys or something. Or maybe what's really bothering me is that when Ash and I were together, no one oohed or "awwwwed" over us, ever. I guess we weren't cute enough to be this excited about.

I push myself up a little too forcefully. Bodie turns to me. "You okay?" he asks.

"Yeah, of course I'm okay," I blurt out. "Why wouldn't I be?" Realizing how petty I sound, I try to justify my mood. "It's just that I thought we all agreed to put the phones away in the desert."

"Seriously?" There's a sneer in his voice. "You're the one filming everything!"

"Because Ms. Robin asked me to," I argue, realizing how right he is.

"Whatever, I'll put the phone away if that's what's upsetting you," he offers.

"Do what you want," I huff.

Everyone exchanges concerned glances like I'm not still standing right in front of them.

"You want to go talk somewhere?" Bodie asks.

I feel my veins pulsing with rage. I can't hold it in anymore. "That's the last thing I want."

"Oh, wow. Okay, then." Something in Bodie's tone makes me feel even more isolated than I already was, like I'm the one behaving irrationally.

"Don't look at me like I'm the one acting strange when you're the one who's been keeping all the secrets from me." I can hear my voice rising.

"Kam . . ." His eyes plead with me to stop.

"You didn't tell me he said he loves you," I continue. "You never told me you love him."

"I haven't said it back," he argues.

"You drank during the game, when Olivia asked if you'd been in love," I spit out. "And the thing is, I'm happy for you!" I can hear how unhappy I sound. "But you should've told me first. I'm your best friend." I throw a quick glance at Olivia. "No offense, Olivia."

Olivia smiles. "None taken."

"I'm sorry, okay." Bodie's voice is curt. It feels like a forced apology.

"No, you're not," I snap. "You're just saying that because you don't want everyone to think you're not fucking perfect.

265

And you're not, by the way."

"I know I'm not—"

I cut him off. "And you know what your biggest flaw is? Trying to be perfect all the time. Wanting to be right all the time. Liked all the time. Maybe if you were willing to risk not being liked at every moment of every day by every person, you would've just told me you love Louis and you would've told your dad you don't want to follow in his footsteps and be a lawyer. But no, you tell people what you think they want to hear because—"

"Holy shit, you're jealous." He stands up to face me.

"What?" My jaw clenches. "I am so not jealous of your basic boyfriend and his cheesy half-naked dance routines."

"Wow. Fuck you too, Kam." His eyes are filled with hurt and rage.

"I'm going to bed," I say. "Sorry if I ruined your night, everyone."

"Kam, you didn't ruin anything," Olivia says. "We know how hard this must be for you."

"Thanks," I croak. I can't say any more. I'm too afraid I'll break down.

As I walk away from them, I can hear them all telling Bodie not to take it personally. I'm just reacting to being back in the desert. It's not about him.

Just before I reach the RV, I hear Danny's voice behind me.

"Kam?" he asks.

I turn around. "Hey," I say quietly. "You didn't need to come after me. I'll be okay."

"I know I didn't need to," he says. "I wanted to. You know we're friends, right?"

I don't look at him when I say, "Yeah, of course."

He puts a hand on my shoulder and gives me a squeeze. I feel a bit of my tension melt away. "It's just that sometimes it feels like there's no room for another friend in your life."

"Because of Bodie?" I ask.

He nods. "Can I ask you something?"

"Yeah, anything," I say.

"Have you and Bodie ever . . . I mean, you know . . ." He stops himself from saying more.

This was not the question I was expecting. "You mean, like, have we ever . . ." I can't say it either.

"Yeah, like . . . dated or hooked up?"

I laugh to shake off my discomfort. "No, definitely not."

"Okay. I was just curious."

Neither of us moves for a few long breaths. The stillness of the desert air feels like it freezes us too.

Finally, I ask, "Wait, why did you ask that?"

He shrugs. "I don't know, I guess it's natural to wonder, because you're so close. Everyone talks about it."

"Everyone talks about what?" I ask.

"Just how close you are." He struggles with his words, like he wishes he could take them back. "Sorry, I shouldn't have asked. I just wanted to say I'm here for you. If you need a friend right now."

In the distance, I can see the others in a circle. I have no idea what they're talking about. Hopefully anything but this. "I've been such an asshole today," I say. "I'm really sorry. I guess it's a lot, being out here again. Will you tell everyone else how sorry I am?"

Danny offers me his hand and I take it. He grips me firmly, steadying me. "Is it okay if I hug you?" he asks softly.

"Yeah." He pulls me in. I collapse into his arms. He holds me until my tears dry in the parched air.

I can't sleep. The desert noises keep me up. So do the memories that haunt me, and the ones I wish I could summon. Old memories of losing Ash in the desert. And new ones of fighting with Bodie in the same desert. I suddenly feel so stupid for coming back here. Of course it was a mistake. What was I thinking?

"Bodie," I whisper to my sleeping friend at midnight. I want to beg for his forgiveness. Tell him how sorry I am for lashing out at him. "Bodie, are you asleep?" He doesn't answer. No one even shifts at the sound of my voice. They're all fast asleep.

I crawl out of my sleeping bag. Tiptoe toward the little kitchenette and open the refrigerator for some water. The light of the fridge invades the space, but still, no one wakes up. The cold air from the fridge makes me realize I'm freezing. I put my hands in my pockets to warm them, and my right hand hits something hard.

The tincture from the apothecary. I forgot all about it. I pull it out and open the bottle. Rub some oil onto my wrists, then onto my neck. I take a deep inhale, letting the perfume fill my body, willing it to help me remember. But it doesn't. It just makes me feel dizzier.

I wiggle back into my sleeping bag as quietly as I can. I clutch my hands together. Rest them near my head on the pillow. The new scent on my wrists makes me woozy. What did she say was in the tincture?

Frankincense . . . patchouli . . . and also . . .

I must fall asleep before I remember the rest because I'm dreaming of Ash. I hear his voice from the night we disappeared into the desert.

Come on.

"Ash?" I hear myself whisper. I sit myself up. "Am I dreaming?" I ask myself.

His voice seems to be coming from outside. *Let's find a rock we can climb to get closer to the stars.*

I see my shoes, lined up next to everyone else's by the door. I stand up. Put my shoes on and step outside into the glacial winter night.

Closer to the stars, he says.

I want his voice to lead me through the desert, into every crevice of rock, past every tree, until it finds him. "Closer to the stars," I echo back, looking up at all the stars and constellations, perfectly clear in the desert sky. "Okay, don't leave me, Ash. I'm coming."

He says nothing.

"Ash, where did you go?" Fog escapes my mouth with every word, every breath. "Ash?"

I close my eyes and see nothing. I rub them open. I still

see nothing. There's no one in sight. Certainly not Ash. I look back at our RV. Feel an urge to crawl back into my sleeping bag, hold on to Bodie tight.

Then his voice is in the distance again.

Follow my voice.

I walk into the night. I hear a howl. Some kind of animal, maybe. Or maybe it's him, howling for me. I study every star, every tree, every bush, for some clue. Did Ash walk this trail that night? Or that one? Or this one? But I find no answers, just more questions.

Follow my voice, he says again.

I want to turn around. To be safe. But I've gone too far, walked too long. I have no idea for how long. Time slows down here, or speeds up, or both. I have no idea how to get back. My heart races. My fingers tremble. My body feels like it's both burning hot and freezing cold. I want to scream for Bodie, but instead I hear myself scream for Ash.

"Ash! Ash!" My throat feels scorched. How did I get here? How long was I walking? I'm still walking. No, running. Toward his laughter. He's happy. "I hear you. I'm coming!"

I chase the sound of his laughter to a rock covered in graffiti. I've seen it before. I've been to this rock before. My body feels like it's sinking into another time, in this exact place. "We were here," I say. "That night. We were here, Ash."

I fall from the shock of memory. My knees hit the dirt. I put my hands on the earth to steady myself. I look up, my body in a state of supplication, my eyes searching the heavens. In the sky, a shooting star races across the universe.

I turn around and see Ash. He's here. In front of me. Running. I hear my voice, but I'm not saying anything. I'm remembering . . . Not imagining. I'm recalling. Or summoning. "Ash, stop!" I begged. "It's too much now. We won't be able to find our way back." I wait for him to say something, but there's just the deafening desert silence punctuated by gusts of wind, bits of birdsong. "Ash?"

I turn right, in the direction of the arrow. I run and run and run until I hear him again.

Look at that one. That's not a Joshua tree. That's Martha Fuckin' Graham.

I close my eyes tight, desperate to stay in the memory. Scared it'll all disappear on me again if I make one wrong move.

"That *is* Martha Fuckin' Graham," I said. And that one. I pointed to another Joshua tree, its branches stretching out into the sky. "That one is Bob Fuckin' Fosse."

They're all dancers. It's all a performance. He danced. He swayed through the desert like he was floating above it all. *Nature is an immersive experience.*

"Don't bring that whole immersive experience thing up again, please. I wish you and Bodie would just get along."

I don't want to talk about Bodie. All you talk about is fucking Bodie.

I open my eyes, shocked by his tone. He was angry that night. Erratic. Different.

271

"I'm sorry," I said. "I won't bring him up again." I feel a chill go down my spine as my eyes land on a tree. On a rock. I've seen them before.

Kam, there's something I want to share with you, but you have to promise not to judge me.

"What is it?" I asked. He's in front of me. Just like he was that night.

It will bring us closer than we've ever been.

"I can't imagine feeling any closer to you."

You'll see. It'll break down all your barriers.

"Do I have barriers?" I asked.

His laughter has an edge. *You don't think you have barriers?! You haven't even told me you love me yet.*

"But you said you felt it."

What was I supposed to say? That I wish you loved me as much as you love your best friend.

"I don't— That's not— I mean, that's a different kind of love."

Is it? It's so obvious he's in love with you.

"Bodie? What? No, he's not."

And sometimes I think maybe you're also—

"I thought we weren't going to talk about him," I said. "I thought we were going to feel more connected than ever."

Right. I know. I'm just scared. You have to promise not to judge me.

"Yes, I swear, I promise."

He pulled something out of his pocket. A plastic baggie

with different pills inside. *Sometimes when I come out to the desert, I take—*

"Ash, what the hell? What are those?"

It's just oxy. And Molly. If you take them together, it's like the most amazing—

"Take them together?!"

I know what I'm doing.

"No, you don't."

If you loved me, you would share this experience with me.

"What? That's not true."

Maybe you're just scared. Is that it? Scared to truly live? To take risks?

"I am scared," I said. "For you. Please. Give those to me. Please."

You're trying to change me. This is who I am.

"No, it's not. I know you. The real you. This isn't you."

Yes, it is. I'm trying to share myself with you, and you're pushing me away.

"Ash, give those to me. You don't need those. You have me."

I knew you'd judge me. You're just like my parents and my sister. Boring. Fucking conventional, that's what you are. You're a bore.

"Your family loves you. And they're so not boring."

They think I have a problem. They don't get it. The world is the problem. We all live like fucking zombies. Disconnected from anything that matters. I just want to feel connected to the universe.

"I can do that for you. I can love you so hard that you'll feel connected—"

But you don't really love me, you're just saying it now to stop me!

"Ash, I'm begging you *because* I love you. Look at my face. Don't do this."

You're just like them. You love a version of me, but not all of me.

"That's not true."

Don't tell me what's true for me.

"Maybe you're right. Maybe I do love some other version of you. Because this version . . . You never told me you did this. You weren't honest about yourself."

And you? Have you shared all of you with me?

I feel tears fall down my cheeks, then and now. "No," I whispered. "No. I've hidden the worst parts of me too. The parts I'm ashamed of. But maybe we can start over. If you'll just promise me you'll throw those pills out and stop. For me. Stop for me."

You don't hide from him.

"From who? Is this about Bodie again?"

No, it's about you. I can't make you happy. Maybe he can. I'm no good for you. I'm no good for anyone. I'm sorry. I really am.

He ran and ran, and I stayed put, begging him to come back. "ASH?" I screamed. "ASH?" I howled his name over and over until I passed out, exhausted.

* * *

I open my eyes. I'm not there in the past anymore. I'm here in the present, haunted by the memory. I close my eyes, willing him back to my side. But he's gone. I remember it all, but I can't summon him again.

"Where is he? Ash!" I beg, tears now flowing from my eyes. Cold tears in the icy air.

A loud voice yells out, "HE'S HERE. HE'S HERE. THANK GOD." Is that Bodie's voice?

I rub my eyes. The sunlight feels blinding. Two search and rescue dogs being led by a park ranger make their way to me. The dogs bark loudly. They lick my cheeks.

"HE'S HERE." Bodie sounds frantic. And relieved.

"He's here," I echo in a dry hush.

"KAM, THANK GOD!" Bodie runs toward me. "HE'S HERE, EVERYONE, THE DOGS FOUND HIM!" One by one I see my friends and teachers rush to our side as the park ranger mumbles something into a walkie-talkie.

"He's here." My mouth is so dry that my words crackle like an old radio trying to be heard.

"You're not making sense," Bodie says. "Are you okay?"

"I remembered," I blurt out. "Ash. He's here. Or . . . nearby."

"Where?" Bodie doesn't look for Ash, though. His eyes are on me.

"I don't know." I look around. The rangers rush toward me. I yell at them. "You need to look for him. He's nearby somewhere."

Bodie cups my cold face in his warm hands. "I'm so sorry I hid so much from you. I love you, Kam. You know that, right?"

I want to tell Bodie everything I remembered. But one of the rangers asks Bodie to move. The ranger kneels down by my side and opens his medical kit. He shines a light in my eyes. In my mouth. Takes my vitals. "You need to find him," I beg the ranger.

"We need to get you to a hospital," the ranger says. "You need fluids." The ranger calls for an ambulance on his walkie-talkie.

"I can drink some water," I croak out. "Ash—"

"You need an IV now," the ranger says.

"I'm fine." But when I sit up, it's obvious I'm not fine. My breath is shallow. My head dizzy. There's concern on everyone's faces. I've put them through hell. "I'm so sorry," I mutter, barely audible. My eyes flutter. They plead for forgiveness from my friends, from Mr. Byrne and Ms. Robin, then they land on Bodie, begging him to forgive me for being such an asshole, for disappearing, for worrying him.

"There was graffiti on a rock, somewhere around here . . . I can draw the graffiti . . . You can retrace our steps from there." I massage my throat. The pain makes it hard to talk.

The park ranger near me puts his hand on mine. "Your teachers told us who you are. We'll look for Ash. But first, we need to take care of you."

In the distance, the sound of an ambulance heading our

way. I look in Bodie's eyes. I'm so afraid to tell him the whole truth. Scared he'll blame Ash for trying to give me drugs. Or worse, blame me for saying no and making Ash run away. I don't need the judgment. All I need right now is for them to find him.

The ambulance arrives. Two rangers lift me up off the dirt. I feel weightless in their arms. Like I'm floating. My eyes haven't adjusted to the light yet. Or maybe they're just seeing differently now. Nothing looks the way it looked yesterday. The desert opens itself up to me in a new way. I close my eyes.

When I open my eyes again, I'm in a hospital room, hooked up to an IV. Bodie is by my side.

"Where's everyone else?" I ask.

"In the cafeteria," he says. "Your mom's on her way."

"Oh." I feel a pit inside me, thinking of how mad she'll be. "Is she angry?"

He shakes his head. "I think she's relieved. Like I am."

"I'm sorry I acted like a jealous asshole," I say. "I know you love Louis—"

He cuts me off. "I never said I loved Louis. You just assumed that part."

"Don't you, though?" I ask.

"I don't know." Bodie shakes his head. "The other day, I told him we were planning on taking a gap year together, and he said he could take a gap year and join us." He sighs. "I should be happy about that, but it was like something was holding me back."

I can't help but think of what Ash said about me and Bodie. "Ash—"

"Don't worry." He squeezes my hand. "They're going to look for him. I think they're going to want to talk to you more first." He pauses, scared to ask. "What did you remember?"

I hesitate, but I don't need more secrets. "He was an addict," I say quietly. I can't believe how liberating it feels to speak these words. I wish I had spoken the same words to Ash about my dad.

"What?" Bodie asks.

I look into his shocked eyes. "He took pills that night. He . . . he offered some to me." I take a deep, steadying breath. "I had blocked it all out."

Bodie doesn't judge me. Or doubt me. "I'm so sorry, Kam. He must have been in so much pain."

I look at Bodie, surprised at his enormous capacity for empathy. "Yeah," I say. "I think he was."

I close my eyes. There are things I know now. But there are also things I'll never know. I'll never know exactly what happened to Ash that night after he ran away from me. Maybe he took the drugs. Or maybe he was bitten by a snake. Could've been both. There are so many things that could have happened.

But I know that when he looked at those trees he loved so much, he felt what I feel now. Forgiven.

There's so much more I want to say to Bodie, but my mom barges in before I can. She hugs us both. Sits next to Bodie. "It's okay." She keeps her agitated eyes on me. Stops short of crying. "You're okay." I nod, letting her and Bodie comfort me.

Through the small hospital window, I see a mountain. I can almost see Ash's spirit above it. I breathe in the desert's forgiveness. I let it forgive me for blocking out the memories that could have helped us find his body sooner. For not seeing that Ash was hurting when there were so many signs.

I forgive myself for surviving.

PART 3

EVERYWHERE

JUNIOR YEAR

"We have time for one more share before newcomer time," Mr. Byrne says. We're in a small room at the recovery center. Twelve teens, all touched by addiction, sitting on folding chairs in a circle.

I raise my hand. "I'd like to share." Mr. Byrne gives me a nod. I start slow. "So . . . they found Ash's remains." I look around.

My mind travels back to the Greenes asking me to come over so they could tell me the DNA results confirmed Ash was finally found, thanks to what I had remembered. They told me they'll be planning a celebration of life for him, on his birthday this summer. I thought they'd hate me for not saving him. But they all thanked me instead, for helping to find him. Mrs. Greene even asked if I would make a video compilation for the celebration.

"I guess the thing I keep coming back to . . ." I swallow

hard. I feel uncertain of how to say this, but the eyes of my fellow Alateen members keep me going. "It's just how Ash and my dad were both addicts, and I never connected it. Even though I was coming to meetings. Even though they were so similar in some ways." My fellow Alateens offer me their silent support. "The erratic behavior. The way they seemed to glow when they were on. It's so fucked up. That I found a guy who reminded me of my dad, and didn't even realize it, you know. It's like I used Ash's intensity to escape my dad's."

Everyone nods. A timer dings.

"One minute, I hear that." I take a deep breath. "Ash and I met because we both wrote the same song down on a piece of paper. 'God Knows I Tried.'" I can almost hear Lana singing in my head, keeping me connected to him. "And the thing is, he did try, and I tried too. Maybe all we can do is keep trying."

Tears flow down my cheeks. I let the sadness pass through me, knowing there will be more sadness to come. More joy too. More music. More mystery. More life and more death.

I wipe the tears away. "Thanks for letting me share, everyone."

They clap as I sit. "It's time for newcomer shares," Byrne says. But his eyes aren't on the newcomers. They're on me. He looks proud.

Byrne and I head out of the recovery center together after the meeting. "You need a ride home?" he asks.

"No, Bodie's picking me up. I'm surprised he's late. He never is."

"Okay. Nice share today." Byrne unlocks his car. It beeps twice from across the block. I get on my phone as I wait for Bodie. I scroll through old photos and videos, first of Ash. But it feels like I've been studying those for two years now. I scroll further, to videos of my dad doing funny voices, dancing in the kitchen. And then further, to videos of Bodie. Sometimes of us together, the camera strategically placed to capture us both. Bodie teaching me how to make tahdiq. Bodie and me attempting to dress up as our moms for Halloween before thinking better of it. Bodie shaving for the first time, cutting his chin in the process. Bodie spinning a globe, placing his finger randomly on a country to decide what cuisine we'll order. Bodie studying. Baking. Smiling. Living.

Bodie's arrival is preceded by the sound of his blaring pop music through the open windows of his dad's car. Bodie rounds the corner and honks three times quickly, followed by two slower honks. Our secret knock, adapted to a car horn. I smile as he double parks and yells through the open window, "Sorry I'm late!"

I get in and turn the music down. "Were you fighting with your dad again?"

He turns the music completely off and throws me a somber look. When we returned from the desert, I wasn't the only one who went through a major shift. Bodie, who spent a few terrifying hours thinking I might have disappeared in that desert, decided that life's too short to be wasted on anything but our greatest passions. He finally told his dad about the gap year, and wanting to go to culinary school instead of law school. It didn't go as well as it could have, but it didn't go as badly either.

"No, actually." He stops at a red light and turns to me. "I was with Louis. He came over with gifts from his trip to Ojai with his family. He made me my own bath salts."

"That's very sweet," I say, trying hard to sound like I mean it.

"I broke up with him," he announces when the light turns green and his foot hits the accelerator.

"That's a very severe reaction to bath salts." Realizing he's not in the mood for a joke, I turn serious. "No, really, what happened? Are you okay?"

"Yeah, I'm okay." He lets out a sad laugh, shaking his head. "He said we should start planning our gap year now that my dad knows about it. And suddenly I realized I didn't want that. I finally told him I loved him, but I didn't think I was in love with him."

"Oh, wow, that sounds . . . awful." I put a hand on his knee and squeeze. "Did he take it badly?"

"It was pretty bad. He was so upset. I feel terrible. I mean, if I can't love someone like Louis . . ." Bodie stops. "He said—" Then he pauses again.

"What?" I ask.

"Nothing." He looks over at me with desperation in his eyes, broken open in a way he's never been before.

"I'm sorry," I say as a gust of crisp air passes through the open windows. I think about what Ash said about Bodie that horrible night in the desert.

"It's okay, really." His voice isn't okay. It's raw. So are his eyes, which are red from crying.

"He accused me of already being with someone else." He bites his lip.

"That's absurd," I say. "You would never do that." I think to myself that I would never do that either. Maybe that's why I didn't tell Bodie what Ash said about us. I couldn't do that while he was with Louis.

He smiles, but there's still a sadness in his eyes. "Anyway, it's over. I'm single again. You're single again. And we're going on our gap year after high school. Everything the way it used to be."

Is it, though? I ask myself. Everything feels so different.

He parks the car in the driveway of a canyon home on Mulholland. The roads leading to the house are winding and jagged, but the house itself is breathtaking. Maybe the road to beauty is always winding and jagged.

"BOYS, YOU'RE LATE!" his mom shouts from behind the front door.

We head inside to help our moms set the house up. They order us to move a couch. Hang some borrowed art. Lay out appetizers picked up from a Persian restaurant and a tray of cookies baked by Bodie. We put out bottles of sparkling water and place a sign-up sheet by the door. We make everything look as perfect as we can, but we can't conceal the house's little imperfections. The cracks in the ceiling.

The stains in the kitchen marble. The scratches in the wood floors. Maybe the imperfections are the house's great assets, proof that love existed in this space.

The doorbell rings as we're fluffing pillows. "I thought the listing said the open house starts at one," I say.

"I think it might be for you," my mom says to me. She shares a look with Bodie's mom.

"Who is it?" I ask.

"It's your father." I can read the concern on her face.

I look to Bodie. "Did you know about this too?"

"I swear I didn't." One look in his eyes and I know he's telling the truth.

My mom approaches me slowly. "I didn't want to tell you before he arrived because . . ." She's nervous. "I just couldn't be sure he would show up." She nods. "But if he's here now, it means he's gone to at least three meetings. Those were my terms." I'm surprised by the way my mom is discussing his addiction without judgment.

"Right. Okay." I feel my body tense up.

The bell rings again. "Go answer it," she says. "He's been desperate to see you."

He looks different when I open the door. Softer in places where he used to be hard. Like he's been cracked open and then put back together. "Hi," he says.

"Hi," I echo.

He looks at me for a few long breaths, saying nothing. I feel self-conscious, wondering what changes he's noticing in me.

"Three meetings," I finally say to my dad, breaking the silence. "Mom said you went to three already. That's good."

"Is it?" he asks.

"It's a start," I say. "Do you have a sponsor?"

He shakes his head. "I did try. I made an appointment to meet a sponsor, and he canceled last minute for a toothpaste commercial audition. I told him I'd find someone more reliable. But I haven't. Yet."

"That's so LA." I laugh. "And so you."

He glances toward my mom, who huddles with Azam and Bodie. The two moms quickly evade my dad's gaze, but Bodie doesn't look away. He keeps his eyes on me, ready to swoop in if I need help.

"Not seeing you for so long . . . It's why I'm going to these meetings."

"But you can't go for me," I tell him. "You have to go for *you*." This feels weird, like I'm the parent and he's the child.

He almost puts a hand on my cheek, but he pulls away. "Can we talk somewhere?"

My mom approaches us, her heels clicking against the hardwood floors. The familiar sound of her authoritative gait makes me feel safe again. Grounds me. She doesn't hug my dad. But she does greet him politely. Then she suggests we talk by the pool, since potential buyers will be arriving soon.

My dad and I head out to the home's infinity pool. The edge of the water seems to lead to nowhere. It falls into the canyon like magic. Ahead of it is a glorious view of the city. All the homes and billboards and buildings and life.

Part of me wants to hurt him the way he hurt me. "How have you been?" he asks.

I don't answer. I let the anger pass.

"This is the kind of house I wanted to give you and your mom," my dad says.

"Dad . . . You don't . . . You didn't do anything wrong by not becoming some asshole millionaire."

"I know." His smile is even more crooked than it used to be. "The problem is I just became an asshole instead."

We stare out at the view. When we finally look at each other, I burst out laughing.

"What's so funny?" he asks.

"Nothing. Everything." I shake my head. "I don't know, just you, acknowledging you were an asshole."

"I'm still an asshole; I can't change that fast." Now he laughs too. It feels like so long since I've seen this laugh. I realize it's probably the first time he's laughed sober in many years.

"It's kind of hard imagining you in a meeting," I confess. "I'd love to see the look on your face when people start talking about their Higher Power."

He turns to see if my mother is watching us through the window. Of course she is.

"Not that I don't think you'll find your Higher Power," I say.

He raises a thick eyebrow. "I will not be finding God."

"Right, no, I know that—"

"Have you?" he asks. "Found God in your meetings?"

"No!" I say too quickly. "I mean, not like . . . a religious God. But I guess maybe I've found . . . some kind of faith. That helps me make sense of the randomness of the world, you know. The loss."

He nods. "I'm sorry about Ash. Your mother told me they found his remains." After a strained breath, he adds, "Your mother and I always wanted to protect you from our grief. We lost so many people in Iran."

"I know," I say softly. I also know how hard it is for him to say those words. To open up. And I don't want to push him too far.

He chuckles to himself before saying, "Someone in my meeting this morning called their Higher Power an HP."

"I've heard that before."

"It sounds like God is a printer," he jokes, and I laugh.

"Dad?" I wait for him to look at me. "Are you coming back home?"

He shakes his head. "Your mother and I aren't getting back together. I won't be moving back in with you two when you—"

"When we what?" I ask.

"Nothing," he says. "I just want you to know it's my fault. Please don't blame your mother. Somewhere along the line, I stopped being her best friend, and your wife has to be your best friend for it to work." He quickly blurts out, "Or husband."

This tiny acknowledgment of my sexuality feels huge to me. "I'm sorry, Dad," I murmur.

I've never seen him more vulnerable than this moment when he quietly accepts my sympathy. "When you were born, I imagined you would be my best friend," he says. "I wasn't prepared for who you would be. I don't understand so much about you. I don't think I'll ever be your best friend."

"I already have one of those," I say.

He nods. "Someone in one of my meetings said our true parent is our Higher Power."

I offer him a wry smile. "Maybe. Or maybe you're my true parent."

"I won't pretend that I can change in a day," he says.

"Good, because I won't pretend I'll forgive you in a day."

He bends his head down humbly. His phone dings. He pulls it out and reads an email. "I should go. I have an interview at a temp agency. Words I never thought I'd speak again." He pulls his head high, like he's trying to keep his self-worth from sinking down that infinity pool and disappearing into the canyon.

He puts a hand on my cheek. His fingers are coarse. But his palm is soft. I close my eyes and imagine the heart line of his palm growing. A tear falls down my face, onto his fingers, absorbed into his skin.

"I'll see you soon," he says, but what I hear is, *I see you now.* Maybe he does finally see me. Or maybe it'll take a little more time. He'll see me soon.

I linger by the pool when he leaves. My mom comes outside and guides my head onto her shoulder. The intimacy of it shocks me. She rarely touches me unless it's the obligatory Iranian hello and goodbye kisses. "Are you okay?" she asks.

I cry on her beautiful blazer. "Dad said you're not getting back together."

She shakes her head. "I'm sorry."

I bring my head up so I can look at her. "It's not your fault."

"Sometimes I can't help but ask why I can handle life's hardships better than your father. Why I get to be here, in this country, when my father and my grandfather both lost their lives in our country. Why I've survived when so many of our people haven't." I tremble in her grip as she lets her sentence evaporate into mist. She never talks about her past. It scares me to hear her almost acknowledge it.

"Mom . . . ," I whisper.

"It's useless to ask yourself why," she continues. "Some people survive and others don't. Never feel bad about surviving. Do you hear me?"

"I do." I know she's talking about the people she lost, the ones in her life who didn't survive. But she's also talking about Ash. This is her way of telling me not to move on, but to move forward.

"Did your father tell you we're listing the house?" she asks.

I shake my head. "He didn't. But it's okay. I mean, maybe it's time for a new start. In a place where there are no memories."

She runs her fingers through my hair. "The memories follow you. I left Iran before you were born, and I can still smell the country if I close my eyes."

"What does it smell like?" I ask.

She closes her eyes and inhales. "Like home," she says quietly. She opens her eyes and looks at me. "We never know where life will take us, but I do know that wherever we end up, our past always travels by our side."

The first potential buyers to arrive are a gay couple with a teacup Pomeranian in one of their arms. They apologize for bringing the dog, but explain he's a puppy and they didn't want to leave him home alone. When the one holding the dog puts him down for a second to write his name and number on the sign-up sheet, the dog rushes to Bodie's mom and pisses right next to her.

"Evah!" she screams, trying to dodge the stream of piss but catching a small splatter on her right heel. "Boro, sag!" she yells. *Go, dog!*

Bodie and I can't stop laughing.

"Oh my God, we're so sorry." One half of the gay couple grabs some napkins and leans down to clean Azam's heel.

She kicks him away. "I can do it myself," she says.

The other dog owner picks the dog up and holds him up in front of Azam. "Say you're sorry, Madonna." He grabs the Pomeranian's paw and waves it in the air. "He's sorry," he assures us all.

Azam's face scrunches in confusion. "What kind of name is Madonna for a boy dog?"

My mom smiles. Inches forward. "Imagine what a good story this will be if you two buy the house. You can tell all your friends that your dog urinated on one of the real estate agents."

I turn to Bodie covertly. "My mom will turn anything into a sales tactic."

Bodie turns to me. "And my mom has officially dabbled in canine water sports with a dog named after the queen of pop."

We both laugh as Azam angrily clicks her heels before heading to the bathroom. My mom hands the men more napkins to clean the floor with.

As the dog pitter-patters toward us, Bodie holds him up. "I think we can both agree this dog looks nothing like Madge." A smile on his face, he asks, "You want to stop off at the dog park for more rounds of Scooby-Doo?"

I shake my head. "I think I need to go work on my William Blake paper, which is over two months late."

"It's nice to see you focused on schoolwork again."

Bodie doesn't turn any music on when we get in the car, which is new for him. Bodie rarely sits in silence. He stops at a red light. Olivia sends him a text that reads *MUST WATCH IMMEDIATELY* but he doesn't look at his phone.

"My dad's been to three meetings," I say, looking out the

window at the bare jacaranda trees, waiting for spring to bloom again.

"That's great, right?" He throws a quick glance my way, trying to read my expression. He briefly loses control of the car. It swerves into the neighboring lane. The driver next to us honks and gives him the middle finger.

"Whoa, are you okay?" I ask.

"You tell me. Can't you read my mind?"

"Are you regretting breaking up with Louis?" I ask. "He was kind of perfect."

He turns onto my street recklessly and parks the car in front of my house. "Maybe I don't want perfect. Maybe I want—"

"Me," I hear myself mutter.

"Wait, what?" he asks.

"Sorry, nothing." My stomach is clenched. It's not the right time. He just broke up with Louis. What am I doing?

Bodie eyes me curiously before saying, "I'll see you later, okay?"

"Yeah. Right. Of course," I stammer nervously. I open the car door and get out. I look at Bodie driving off. I wonder what he's thinking. He's never been a mystery to me before. Now he feels like one big question. I feel so stupid for suggesting he wants me. I close my eyes to steady myself. Adrenaline races through my body. Every part of me seems to tremble. And then, my eyes still closed, I suddenly feel like I can see more clearly than I ever have before. What I see is that whether Bodie wants me or not, *I* want *him*. I feel like an idiot for not realizing it before. For not knowing my own heart.

Images fly into my mind. Memories I've long cherished, being seen through a new lens. A new perspective. Double vision. Bodie, letting me fall asleep in his arms when Ash ghosted me. Bodie, asking me if I thought there's someone better for him out there than Louis. Bodie, drinking when Olivia asked if he'd ever been in love. I thought that meant he was in love with Louis, but he wasn't. There's only one other person it could be. I see it all now. The love I was too scared to accept.

Ash was right. Bodie loves me. That's why he never wanted to date other guys.

And I think I love him too.

The whole world is upside down. The ground doesn't feel steady beneath my feet anymore. Everything feels tangled up in itself as memories swirl. Bodie, always circling me. Making me laugh. Inventing silly games for us to play. Holding me when I grieved. Listening when I vented about my family. The true constant of my life is him. He's been my sun, the warmth I orbit around, the thing that makes me feel safe.

My whole body feels lit from within. There's a growing flame inside me. A new understanding. Bodie was never jealous of me for having a boyfriend. He was jealous of Ash. And he didn't tell me how he feels because he was scared. Too afraid to potentially ruin our friendship.

I have to find him.

I take a deep breath and run in the direction of his house. Byrne's voice is in my head, telling me that the biggest burden of all is love. That's what Bodie is. My burden. And I couldn't see it. But Ash could. Ash cracked my heart open and taught me how to love. I have so much love in me right now that I feel like I'm going to burst from it.

I see Bodie at a stop sign and run faster. He lets another car cross the intersection, then accelerates.

"BODIE!" I yell out. He doesn't slow down. I speed up, my skinny legs doing everything they can to catch up to him. "BODIE."

I manage to reach him. He rolls his window down, confused. "Kam, is everything okay?" he asks as he pulls over. "What happened?"

"Get out of the car," I demand.

"Did something happen?" he asks as he exits the car and faces me. "Are your parents okay?"

"Something did happen." I start talking faster. "That night, those last moments with Ash— There's something else he said. . . ."

"Kam, what?" His eyes are heavy with concern. "Something you didn't tell the police?"

"It's not something for the police," I exclaim. "It's about us. Me and you. He saw that you loved me. And that I love you too. And he was right. He saw what we couldn't see or weren't brave enough to say."

His face registers shock, then confusion, then sadness. There's resignation in his voice as he utters, "See, all this time, you really couldn't read my mind like you thought you could."

"So, Ash was right. You do love me?" I ask, suddenly nervous.

"It doesn't matter," he says. "You're not ready, Kam." He looks straight at me. "They haven't even had Ash's celebration of life yet. You're still grieving."

"But that's him," I say. "And this is us."

"And I just broke up with Louis," he continues. "It's too soon."

"Who says?" I ask, unwilling to back off. "Who makes up these rules?"

"People with more experience than us!" he exclaims. "We can't fuck up our friendship. That'll just ruin everything."

"But . . ." I feel desperate. This wasn't what I envisioned happening.

"We're still best friends, okay?" He almost touches me, but stops himself. "That's the most important thing. Our friendship."

"Right, yeah. Best friends," I say sadly, watching as he gets back into his dad's car. "I'll see you soon, then?" I say it like a question. One I've never had to ask before.

Bodie doesn't show up for school the next day. I text him. No response. I call him. Straight to voice mail. By that evening, I still haven't heard from him. I call his home line. His dad answers. "Kamran jan," he says. "Farbod is already asleep, I think. He has a cold."

"Oh, sorry. Um, tell him I called?"

"Of course," he says. He hesitates. I wonder if I should hang up, but then he says, "Kamran, perhaps you can talk some sense into Farbod about this gap year business. If you two take a gap year, you'll be one year behind all your peers. Your careers might never recover."

I take a deep breath. "Mr. Omidi, I think you know as well as I do that once Bodie makes up his mind about something, it's very hard to stop him."

"Unfortunately, that's a quality we share." His voice is hard. "I'll tell him you called."

The next day, Bodie's not in school again. I wonder if he's really sick. Or if he's just avoiding the awkwardness of seeing me. In our afternoon GSA meeting, Olivia gets a text from him that makes her laugh. He's obviously feeling good enough to text her as he keeps freezing me out. It feels like I'm being replaced. A horrible emptiness eats away at me, pulling me down a spiral of anxiety and sadness. I have to crawl back up to the light, reignite the fire inside me.

After the GSA meeting, I ask Ms. Robin if she has a moment. The two of us huddle in a corner while everyone else leaves school for the day. "What's up?" she asks.

"It's just . . . I was wondering if you could help me edit some videos together."

"Is it your submission video for my senior filmmaking class next year?" she asks. "Because I'll be disappointed if you don't apply."

"No, it's not—I mean, I do want to sign up next year. But right now, I need to make a movie, and the thing is, I have hours of videos but I don't know how to edit or add graphics or music or—"

"Are you asking for my help?" she asks.

"I am, yeah," I say.

"Then meet me in the art room after school tomorrow." She smiles. "I knew there was a budding filmmaker hiding in there."

"Oh, I don't know about that. This is just a personal project." I feel myself blush.

Ms. Robin puts her hands on my shoulders. "Kam, all works of art are personal projects. That's what makes them so precious."

Bodie doesn't show up to school the next day either, but he does answer my lunchtime call.

"Where have you been?" I ask. "Are you okay?"

"It's just a cold," he says vaguely. It sounds like he's lying. "I tested. It's not COVID."

"So you're not just avoiding me after—"

He cuts me off before I can bring up our last conversation. "Why would I be avoiding you?" he asks, daring me to go there again.

"No reason. Things just feel . . . different."

"You want to come over and study?" he asks, to prove he's not avoiding me.

"I thought you were sick," I say.

"It's just a cold. I'm almost better. Anyway, you don't have to come."

I consider bailing on Ms. Robin, but I don't want her not to give me another chance. "I would, but I'm going to work with Ms. Robin on a . . . project."

"A project?" he asks. Then he realizes. "Oh, right. You're making that video for Ash's memorial." He sighs. "I'll see you tomorrow if I'm feeling better."

"Okay," I say. "Bodie?"

"Yeah?"

"I miss you," I say.

"Miss you too," he says quickly. Then he hangs up. His voice is in my head as I walk toward the art room.

Ms. Robin sits at the back on her computer, with an open smile. "Ready to make movie magic?" she asks.

Five hours later, when school is completely empty, we're done with the edit. I take a deep breath, filled with hope and possibility for the first time in months. I've never felt so clear about who I am or what I want.

Bodie doesn't show up to school again the next day. Just as classes are about to begin, I get a ding on my phone. It's a text from my friend Emily asking how I'm holding up. I sent her my number when I closed down my account on the grief forum. I quickly text her back that I'm doing okay as class begins.

"Phones away!" Mr. Silver says curtly. "Now let's lay out our goals for today. First up, we're going to have a pop quiz."

The class groans. I can't focus. I push my chair back to stand up. It makes a loud screech as it slides on the floor.

"Mr. Khorramian," Mr. Silver says, annoyed.

"I'm sorry, I need to go to the bathroom." I approach his desk and grab the bathroom pass.

He stares me down. "Class began less than a minute ago. And we're about to have a—"

"I know. I'll be quick, sorry."

"Six minutes or detention!" he yells as I rush out into the hallway. "Can't you kids use the bathroom *before* class starts?"

I don't go to the bathroom, though. I run down the hallway toward the front door. Push the heavy entrance doors open and feel the cool air hit my face. I run toward Bodie's house, my legs gaining speed as I go.

I bang on the door when I get there. Bodie answers in sweatpants and a tank top. "Kam, what are you—"

"Are your parents home?" I ask.

"No, they're both at work," he says. He doesn't look sick at all. Confused, sure. But not sick.

I push past him into the house.

"Kam, what's going on?" he asks.

"Just shut up. I have to show you something." I go to the Omidi living room and turn the television on. I connect it to my phone.

"Is this—Kam, I'm sorry, but I really don't want to see the video you made for Ash's celebration of life right now."

"Just shut up," I demand gently.

"No, I won't shut up!" He walks in front of me. Faces me. "I told you this isn't the right time."

"That's just another one of your deal-breakers!" I take his hands in mine. He pulls away. "Don't you get that this is what you do?" I ask. "You search for a reason to say it's not the right time or the right person or—"

"You are the right person," he says, cutting me off.

"I am?" I ask.

He nods. Then shakes his head. "But the timing . . ."

I hold his hands again. This time, he doesn't pull away. "Bodie, there's never going to be a perfect moment for anything. Instead of . . . I don't know, looking for what's wrong . . . Maybe we can look for what's right. Like us. *We're* right together. We always have been."

"Don't you think I know that?" He lets go of my grip and turns away from me. He can't even look at me as he says, "Don't you get that the whole reason I can't be with you yet even though I really do fucking love you—"

"You really do fucking love me?" I ask with a smile.

"It's because you're still not over him!" He turns to face me again. "I don't want to fuck things up by being with you when you're still haunted by him. It's too much. I couldn't compete with him when he was alive, let alone now that he's—"

"Just stop, please." I start the video. The sound of our younger voices comes from the speakers. Eleven-year-old us, dancing in our fathers' oversized suits.

"What is this?" he asks.

"Shh," I say. On the television is thirteen-year-old us, baking a cake, flinging vanilla batter at each other.

"This is what you worked on with Ms. Robin?" he asks.

I nod. Shift my gaze back to the screen, which jumps from one memory to another. A history of our friendship beams out from the television in quick cuts. The depth of our connection, the wealth of our memories, plays out before us. The two of us dressed as salt and pepper shakers for Halloween. Dancing like our dads at a Nowruz party. Playing cards with our moms. Baking. Swimming. Sleeping in the back of his dad's car. Crying, but from laughter. In the movie's final frames, the screen splits and splits and splits again, until different iterations of us share the screen. Different ages. Same souls. Over these images, three words appear on screen. *I love you.*

I look in his eyes when the movie ends. "I am ready, Bodie. I've grieved for two years. I'm ready to live again. And I don't have a life without you. I mean, you are my life."

His eyes well up with tears. "You're my life too," he echoes as he moves closer to me and brings his lips close to mine. I can feel the heat of his body, the warmth of his breath. I've felt it all before, but never like this. Never with this electricity between us. "Kam . . ."

"Stop talking," I say.

"I'm good at talking," he says. "I'm not good—"

I press my lips against his.

He moves his tongue into my mouth, and at the same time we both burst out laughing.

"That was so weird," he says.

"Incredibly strange," I agree, smiling at him. "But not bad."

"No, not bad." He smiles. "I wanted to tell you how I felt so many times. But I was always so scared of fucking up our friendship. It just . . ." He laughs at himself. "I guess I'm a broken record, because it never felt like the right time."

"It rarely feels like the right time to change everything about your life," I say.

He nods in agreement.

I speak deliberately, choosing my words carefully. "But I think the right time to make a big change is when you're sure about what you want."

"So you're sure?" he asks.

"I am." I love the way my whole body feels like it's coming back to life. I feel like I'm in a new skin. A stronger one. Now I see my own resilience. "I'm sure I love you. And I'm also sure that I want to go to film school."

"After our gap year?" he asks.

I shake my head. "The gap year was always your dream."

"But you're a part of that dream."

"Wherever you go, you know I'll be waiting for you. And besides, we're still juniors. We have time to figure all that out." I run a hand through his thick, beautiful hair. "Let's just promise we'll both support each other's dreams, even if those dreams mean we have to be physically apart sometimes."

"I promise," he says. He pulls me closer. Sings in my ear. *"It's you, it's you, it's all for you."*

I put a finger on his lips to stop him. "You don't have to sing Lana to me. She was me and Ash's thing."

"Then what's our thing?" he asks.

I think for a moment, then I say, "Everything is our thing. We've shared our whole lives. The whole world is our thing."

"I love you," he whispers.

"And I love you." I close my eyes, basking in the sound of those words on my lips. I realize it's not just him I love. It's this new version of me who goes after what he wants. Who doesn't live in doubt or fear. I'm done hiding.

From outside comes the sound of a car pulling into the driveway. Music blares from the car's speakers. The Beatles, "Here, There and Everywhere." Bodie's mom sings along loudly as she parks the car. Then, abruptly, the music stops.

"I can't deal with seeing my mom right now," he says.

"How do you think our moms will react when we tell them we're . . ."

"Oh God, they'll start planning a grand Persian wedding tomorrow." He laughs. "And our dads will probably be totally confused."

"Back door escape?" I ask.

He nods. We throw our shoes on as fast as we can and run out the back door before his mom comes in. We run toward my house. When we reach it, we're breathless and giddy, like little kids hiding a secret. I sit near the giant ficus that's become part of our home.

"Can we try again?" I ask.

"Try what?" he wonders aloud.

"You know . . ."

He runs a finger along the shape of my lip. "You have the best lips."

"This is so weird," I say. "Will it ever not be weird?"

"I don't know," he says. "The only way to know—"

"Is to try," I say.

"What are you most scared of?" he asks.

"Your deal-breakers!" I blurt out.

"Fair enough." He laughs. "But I already know you so well, and nothing's broken the deal yet. You might not be perfect, but to me you are."

We sit side by side and watch the light change. I lean my head on Bodie's shoulder.

"Okay, I'm coming in for our second first kiss," Bodie announces.

His soft lips touch mine. I inhale his breath, and he accepts mine. The sweet taste of him lingers on my lips when I gently pull away. "That was better," I say, grinning. "But I think our third first kiss will be the best one yet."

He laughs. Licks my neck slowly, sensually. I feel goose bumps.

"I can't believe you tried to push me away," I tell him. "It's a good thing I wouldn't take no for an answer."

"Okay, that is not the story we'll be telling." He keeps kissing my neck as he talks. "Maybe you said it first, but I *felt* it first. That has to count for something."

"You're infuriating," I say lightly.

"It's my signature quality," he says proudly. "Should I bottle it? Infuriation, the new fragrance from Bodie Omidi."

I breathe in his scent. "No, I'm the only one who gets to smell you." I pull his face up from my neck. Guide his lips to mine for our third first kiss. I know already that there will be a fourth first kiss, and a fifth, and a sixth. This will be a part of our story. A lifetime of first kisses.

"Ready?" Bodie asks.

I look into Bodie's eyes, and I can see our future in them. Well, not our entire future. If the last three years have taught me anything, it's that the future is hard to predict. But I can see the love.

I take his hand, and we walk inside together.

AUTHOR'S NOTE

This novel is inspired in part by my first boyfriend. When I met Damon in November of 2000, after weeping through his brilliant musical *Bare: A Pop Opera*, I was twenty-four years old and still in the closet to my family. If you've read *Like a Love Story*, you know the level of fear and shame Reza deals with as a teenager. I was still there into my midtwenties—ashamed, afraid, convinced that being myself would destroy my family and my life. Damon changed all that. Our magical first date was at a Brazilian restaurant on election night 2000, a night that changed history. During our almost-two-years together, Damon gifted me a kind of attention that I had never been shown before. Many of the details in this book—the mixtape, the introduction to nature, the printer paper that reads *I love you* countless times—come from our time together. Damon threatened to break up with me if I didn't come out to my parents. I firmly believe no one should be forced to come out. I certainly don't condone ultimatums. I also can't know what my life would have been like had I not received this one. Would I have remained in the closet forever? Perhaps not, but certainly much longer. Would I have become an author? I don't know. Damon was the one who berated me into believing I had something unique to say as an artist. Would I have the loving family I am now blessed with? I can't know. He set me on a new path. A more honest and therefore more daring one.

The desert was important to Damon. Like Ash, he would disappear into its beautiful barrenness, sometimes for days, sending me into panic. He was a brilliant musician and a seeker. He told me he was in the desert seeking inspiration, composing, hearing melodies. I was young. Naive. I believed and forgave everything. I never wondered if he struggled with addiction or mental illness. There is so much I didn't understand until much later. After we broke up, we remained close and I started to see that for all his light, he had a frightening dark side. I couldn't fathom how dark until after his death in 2013, an event that changed my life as much as meeting him had. It is certainly not a coincidence that I self-published my first novel the year after he died, a novel about being in the closet as a gay Iranian. Losing him was a reminder of the person he showed me I could be. A person who didn't wait for others to grant me permission to live boldly. And, of course, his death was and is a reminder that life is often far too short and should be lived with passion and purpose.

I've long contemplated writing about him because he's

fascinating. He deserves to be written about, as do all those impacted by him in positive and negative ways. But fiction is how I make sense of life's mysteries, and this story is a wholly fictionalized version of the questions he inspires in me. Like, how did I end up being stronger than him when I felt so much weaker? And how did he gift me so much light when so much of the rest of his life was lived in darkness? He made me a much kinder, more honest person, and yet he hurt countless people in his own life in devastating ways—myself included, eventually.

The specifics of his story are sadly not as unique as I once thought. Since losing Damon, I've lost many more queer friends, colleagues, and acquaintances to addiction and suicide. There is still, I believe, an epidemic of shame in our community. Overcoming shame is so difficult. It requires patience, self-care, the support of friends, family, community. I dedicate this book to my friend Jennifer Elia because her many decades of friendship have made me feel supported through all the ups and downs of my own struggles. But my own journey out of shame (which still lingers, of course) required a lot of therapy too, and, eventually, Al-Anon meetings to better understand the role of addiction in my life and to help me turn the things I can't control over to a Higher Power. This spiritual practice has been so necessary for me as a queer person who often felt, as my and Kam's beloved Lana once sang, that *me and God, we don't get along*. Turns out God and I get along just fine. God loves you too. Forgives you. And will never shame you.

There's no shame in true spirituality. Only forgiveness—of others and of ourselves.

If you're dealing with addiction in your life or in the lives of your loved ones, there are so many resources out there. AA and its sister programs, Al-Anon, Alateen. Therapy. Countless organizations and helplines you can call, from SAMHSA to the Trevor Project and onward.

If you'd like to help, please consider making a donation to Awakening Recovery, a nonprofit recovery community that my beautiful husband, Jonathon Aubry, helped open and sits on the board of. What a miracle that the once-closeted young man writing these words has the husband and children he once thought of as impossible fantasies. What a miracle that so many who struggle with addiction lead lives of sober abundance thanks to communities like these. God grant us the serenity to accept the things we cannot change, the courage to change the things we can, and the wisdom to know the difference.

ACKNOWLEDGMENTS

Writing a novel is an emotional endurance test. First and foremost, I'm grateful to my husband, Jonathon Aubry, our children, Evie and Rumi, and our little boy, Disco, for filling our home and my heart with love, laughter, and adventure. I would be incapable of writing or living with fearless vulnerability were it not for them.

I'm a better writer and a better person because of family and friendship. To my dearest friends, I thank you all. To my parents, brother, aunts, uncles, cousins, and especially to our family's next generation, I love you all. I'm eternally grateful to come from such a vibrant family, and to have married into such a beautiful family. A special shout-out to Mandy Vahabzadeh for taking my author photo and for exposing me to the arts in my most formative years.

John Cusick is a dream agent because he's as generous as he is incisive. I'm so lucky to have him and his Folio colleagues by my side.

Before meeting Alessandra Balzer, I wrote what I

thought others wanted. Thanks to her, I write from the heart. That's a gift I'll always be grateful for.

Megan Ilnitzki is a champion of authors, and I'm so grateful to have a new editor who believes in the work and in doing the work with kindness, passion, and honesty.

I'm thankful for Mitchell Waters, without whom I wouldn't be an author, and for Brant and Toochis Rose for their belief in me as a screenwriter.

Big thanks to everyone at HarperCollins who worked on this book, including but not limited to: Erin DeSalvatore, Audrey Diestelkamp, Kathy Faber, Caitlin Johnson, Kerry Moynagh, Mimi Rankin, Patty Rosati, John Sellers, Heather Tamarkin, and Jen Wygand. The cover for this novel brilliantly captures the vastness I felt while writing it. Thank you to artist Katherine Lam, and to designers Julia Feingold and Alison Donalty for creating visual magic.

Robbie Couch, Lilliam Rivera, Eliot Schrefer, and Courtney Summers are superstars. That they took the time to read this book and lend it their support means the world to me. Go read their books. Then go read more books. There's nuance and learning waiting for you in their pages.

Thank you, Lana Del Rey, for reminding our careening world to slow down and live poetically. Thank you, Jessica Pratt and Happy Rhodes, for being the other voices in my headphones as I wrote this book.

Thank you to Al-Anon and to my sponsor for the guidance (and patience—I might be stuck on step four forever). Thank you, Julia Cameron, for writing *The Artist's Way*. It changed my life.

To the young adult and middle grade authors standing by their work as many of us are being attacked and threatened, thank you for your bravery and camaraderie. To all educators supporting queer students, you are heroes and I appreciate you. Without educators who supported me long before I was ready to come out to my family, I'm not sure who or where I'd be.

To the book banners, thank you too. You almost destroyed my will, but in the end, you simply reminded me of why the work matters. As my favorite writer, James Baldwin, once said (and as my favorite artist, Madonna, loves to quote), "Artists are here to disturb the peace." That's exactly what our community of writers is doing. Baldwin also said, "Art has to be a kind of confession . . . if you can examine and face your life, you can discover the terms with which you are connected to other lives, and they can discover them, too—the terms with which they are connected to other people."

My books are my confession, and all I want is for them to create connections between humans who are under the illusion that we are a divided people when we are, and always have been, pure oneness. So, finally, a thank you to the readers all over the world (olá fofos Brasileiros) who have shared their own confessions with me. You've helped me understand the most important lesson of all: that we are never, were never, and will never be alone.

Abdi Nazemian. Los Angeles. May, 2024.